A Legacy of Love and Murder

By

Brenda Whiteside

A Wild Horse Peaks Sequel

This is a work of fiction. Names, characters, places, and incidents are either the product of the author's imagination or are used fictitiously, and any resemblance to actual persons living or dead, business establishments, events, or locales, is entirely coincidental.

A Legacy of Love and Murder

Second edition, originally published as book 3 in The Love and Murder Series

COPYRIGHT © 2023 by Brenda Whiteside

All rights reserved. No part of this book may be used or reproduced in any manner whatsoever without the written permission of the author except in the case of brief quotations embodied in critical articles or reviews.

Contact Information: brenda@brendawhiteside.com

Cover Art by Alison Henderson

A Wild Horse Peaks Sequel

Published in the United States

ISBN: 9798373273664

Acknowledgements

Republishing the second edition of a book is never an easy task. Thanks to my family for encouraging me. Thanks to two successful authors, Jannine Gallant and Alison Henderson, for priceless advice.

Dedication

This book is dedicated to the real-life Harte, my good and loved friend who lives in Austria, within sight of the Alps. He allowed me to use his proper name, exchanged countless emails with me, and corrected my German.

A note from the author…

Although I've lived in other places, my heart resides in the west. Born and raised in Arizona, I have a love for the rural and small-town atmosphere from the southern desert to the northern high country. Although most will conjure cactus and desert when they think of Arizona, there are snowy ski slopes and beautiful prairies too. This is the country of the Wild Horse Peaks novels. I hope I not only offer you entertaining stories but also show you a side of Arizona you didn't realize existed.

To receive special offers, news about my latest books, and to be eligible for quarterly and year-end gifts that only members of BNG receive, join Brenda's Newsletter Group. You'll find the link on my website at www.brendawhiteside.com.

CHAPTER ONE

"Oh, Mom, there it is." August Myer craned her neck to catch the first clear view of the walled castle atop the hill. "A real Austrian castle and it's all—ow!"

Her head clunked the side window, and she braced her hands against the dashboard. Her mother had swerved the rental car to the edge of the narrow, mountain road then stomped on the brakes. The seatbelt cut into August's shoulder and held her like a vice as the white BMW ground to a stop off the pavement.

"Mom, what the hell?"

The scream of a siren blotted out her mother's obscenity. She caught a glimpse of a dark-haired man whose face telegraphed an apology as he whizzed past. The silver Porsche 911 with a portable flasher on top barely missed nicking their front end when he zipped around them.

Her mother slumped forward, head on the steering wheel and chest heaving. "Where did that crazy idiot come from?"

August rubbed her shoulder where the seatbelt held her in a death grip, then straightened the red scarf draped around her neck. She glanced out the rear window and the settling dust. "That last corner was totally blind. You'd think a cop would know how to drive on mountain roads." She patted her mother's shoulder. "Are you okay?"

She sat back slowly. "Yeah. He might've thought to put his siren on *before* climbing up my butt." She flattened her palm on her chest as if checking her heartbeat. "How about you?"

"A bump on the head and severe seatbelt burn on my neck, but hey, driving with you is always a treat."

"I appreciate the guilt trip." Her mom snickered. "He probably could've gotten past us without my panic maneuver. But he appeared so suddenly in my rearview mirror. Sorry, kiddo."

"No need to excuse him." Not inclined to let the cop off the hook, she widened her eyes and exclaimed, "Mad Austrian arm of the law!"

Mom chuckled, then stared out the windshield. "There's nothing ahead except the castle and estate, and that's the end of the road. Wonder what's going on?"

August followed her gaze to the castle nestled in the foothills of the Alps. The walled fortress covered the top of a small peak. Higher mountains loomed above the estate with patches of snow on their tops.

The silver Porsche had disappeared, eaten up by heavy forest obscuring all but the last quarter mile of the road leading into the castle entrance. As she admired the ancient fortress, the car reappeared in front of the gate and stopped. An iron grate lifted and disappeared into the wall above. When two mammoth doors swung inward like something from a movie about medieval Europe, she shivered with anticipation of entering another world.

The Porsche inched forward then sped inside the walled estate where flashing lights topped two emergency vehicles.

"That answers your question. Apparently, there's an emergency at Castle Luschin."

The giant-sized doors closed slowly, but not before August saw the courtyard, or what the castle occupants might call the bailey. A circular drive surrounded a deep green lawn. Thickly flowered shrubs on each side of a walkway led to steps that in turn led to highly polished, double wooden doors. Stone benches were scattered on the green. Uniformed men, maybe police, stood on each side of the entrance.

"I doubt that's our welcoming party," she quipped. This didn't look like a normal day at the home of her great-grandfather. She'd not met the man or ever visited his castle estate, but emergency vehicles didn't bode well for their first visit.

Her mom frowned. "I hope it has nothing to do with Herr Luschin."

August gazed at the vanishing scene before them as the gates closed. Her stomach fluttered like the first time her parents took her to Disneyland. She remembered exactly how her ten-year-old self felt standing before the pink make-your-dreams-come-true castle. Thirteen years later, this fairytale fortress, although not pink, loomed larger than Cinderella's castle. The stonewall surrounding the estate glistened white under a nearly clear Austrian sky, while the green, multi-tiered roof matched the lush Norway pines and beech trees covering the foothills. Behind and above the castle, the peaks of the Alps rose and poked at a lone, white puff of cloud. She caught her breath at the beauty.

"And I thought the peaks of Timberline were breathtaking." Mom echoed her thoughts.

"Falling in love with Timberline's handsome sheriff might've colored your vision."

"Oh, August." She flipped hair from her shoulders to her back.

"Really, Mom. You're like a schoolgirl lately. Sometimes I think you're younger than I am." Her chest welled with joy for her mother whose face glowed with happiness about her newfound life. This trip was the opportunity to meet her grandfather and help her discover more about her roots. Their roots.

August slapped the dashboard. "What are you waiting for? Get this heap started so we can claim our inheritance."

She checked all the mirrors twice before pulling out onto the road leading to Castle Luschin. "Attitude, August. I don't think we'll be too welcome if we try to storm the fortress."

Mom was wound tight. She hadn't used *attitude, August* since her high school years. "They know we're coming, and I'm joking. This is fun, Mom. Admit you're as excited as I am."

"Oh, I'm excited, kiddo. And by the way, *my* inheritance."

"Ha. Right. Going to get picky about that little age clause, are you?"

"I am. I have a year before you're twenty-five and nearly five years with your brother before I have to worry about my kids knocking me off to grab the castle estate." Her words teased, but she frowned and stared ahead.

"What's wrong, Mom?"

"I'm just a bit concerned about what's going on at the castle."

"A tourist probably had a heart attack making the trek up."

Her mother bit at her lip, worriedly, and concentrated on the winding road. Having never met her grandfather before, she was no doubt nervous.

August fidgeted, a bit wound up, too. An estate this size and this old had to hold a plethora of art. The reasons for this mother-daughter trip had three purposes, and the order of importance was different for both of them.

Her mother's attention was fully focused on the short distance to the castle entrance. Only months before, she'd learned about her birth parents, who were killed in an airplane crash that had left the infant Lacy the lone survivor. Her search led to a father which led to a bloodline deed to this castle estate.

Discovering more about their lineage was important to August also, but not as important as it was to her mother. The hoped-for bounty of art that lay within the walls of the centuries-old castle was a fascinating draw and an added enticement to make this journey. Collecting art for her Tucson, Arizona gallery was her passion. Of course, she'd like to learn more about her ancestry and meet her great-grandfather, who, amazingly, was still alive. But the art in a castle and inheritance to boot? Her palms sweated as she imagined the artists of ages past, perhaps painting a portrait of her ancestors or sculpting a piece for the garden.

The third reason was only a blip on August's radar but a driving force for her mom. Mom thought an adventurous trip was what August needed to get past the *trauma* of her recent divorce. She'd given up trying to make her believe that as long as her bastard husband didn't fight her for the gallery, then all was right in the world. And in return, Evan wouldn't get his reputation destroyed for knowingly selling forgeries. She could get past the lost love part; she would never have gotten over losing the gallery. Her father had left her the money in his will to purchase it, and she wouldn't lose it no matter what.

The castle loomed larger. The green-roofed spires of the corner towers poked above the wall surrounding the estate. She tapped her toes against the floorboard, anxious to be walking the grounds of the ancient fortress.

The car slowed then stopped as the mammoth wooden doors towered before them.

August rolled down her window, stuck her head out, and peered upward. The square openings, only big enough for a head or maybe guns to poke out, in the turrets on each side of the closed entry appeared empty, understandably so. Not too many conquering armies tried to breach the wall in this century. She glanced in either direction. If a wall walk existed at the top, no one strolled along it today.

"Now what?" She brought her head back in. The cool air followed her, and she lifted a corduroy jacket off the backseat. July in Tucson was triple digits, but she guessed today's Austria temperature around seventy.

Her mother pushed the heel of her hand against the horn. After a moment's blast, they both craned their necks to look out the front windshield. The outer grate of iron was recessed into the stone archway above, but the doors, made from foot-wide slats of wood and crosshatched with black iron bolted into the wood at intervals, remained tightly shut.

"Do it again." August opened the car door to stand on the gravel drive. When the horn silenced, she stooped and looked into the car. "Maybe the hullabaloo inside has everyone occupied."

"I would think your great-grandfather would be looking for us. You told him the time we thought we'd arrive, right?"

"Yeah, but—"

At a noise behind her, she straightened. A common-sized door within the castle wall had opened, and a uniformed policeman stepped out. She had no love for policemen after the few run-ins she'd had in high school, but if all Austrian cops looked like this guy, she might set aside her prejudice. His navy beret was cocked to one side, navy jacket hugged a well-formed chest, and the pants with their oversized pockets low on the legs couldn't disguise his muscular thighs. This wasn't the typical uniform of an American policeman; although, one hand rested on the gun riding on his hip. He was probably near her age of twenty-four.

As he approached the car, he pushed his jacket sleeves up to his elbows, exposing a golden layer of down catching the sun. "*Wie kann ich euch helfen.*"

"Yes...whatever that means," she muttered, then held her tongue when the side of his mouth ticked up. "Er, we don't speak German." From his bemused face, he must've understood a bit of English.

Her mom got out, rounded the front of the car, and met him by the front bumper. "Do you speak English?"

He tipped his head in response, but his bright, blue eyes never left her. "Yes, I do. Americans?"

"Yes, we are. My name is August Myer, and this is my mother, Lacy Dahl. I mean Meadowlark. Lacy Meadowlark." She hadn't gotten accustomed to her mother's new married name.

Mom snickered.

"*Guten Tag.* Excuse me. Nice to meet you. I am *Polizist* Kurt Gruber."

His accent gave her a flutter low in her abdomen. "So, what's going on inside?"

"Police business."

Her mother stepped closer, but seemed content, if not amused, to let her handle the situation. Was it so obvious she found the policeman attractive?

"We need to go inside." August reached for a more formal and authoritative attitude. "If you could have someone open the doors, we'll drive in. I don't think we should leave our car outside."

"I'm sorry, Ms. Myer, Ms. Meadowlark. Today is not a day to be the tourist." When he smiled, there was something about his face that struck her as dangerous. A glint in his eyes? Or was it the way his mouth…

"But we aren't," her mother broke into the conversation. "We have an appointment with Herr Lenhard Luschin. He's expecting us."

"I—"

"Perhaps I can help." Porsche Man stepped through the open doorway and strode next to Policeman Kurt. "I am Chief Inspector Tobias Wolf."

The beret tipped toward the new man on the scene who apparently had more authority than Golden Boy. The Inspector muttered some unintelligible information that she wouldn't have been able to understand even if he'd spoken loudly. Yet, without understanding German, the younger man's dismissal was obvious. He nodded at his superior, stepped back, nodded at them, and spun on his heel. A last glance over his shoulder, and the door closed behind him.

The Inspector regarded them. "Can I be of assistance?"

"I hope so." Her mother's voice sounded strong but strained. "I'm Lacy Meadowlark and this is my daughter, August Myer. We have an appointment with Herr Luschin."

"Nice to meet you." The inspector tipped his head to each of them. "The castle is closed today. I am sorry, Ms. Meadowlark, Ms. Myer."

Disappointment at seeing cute, and maybe dangerous, Kurt disappear was replaced by agitation at the appearance of the man who'd only moments before run them off the road. "*You* should be sorry," she snapped. "You ran us off the road."

"And I'm sorry for that, too." He raised a brow. "You were saying you had an *appointment* with Herr Luschin?"

When his brown eyes regarded her, August thought of warm, toasted almonds and was immediately annoyed with herself. She set her shoulders to address his half-hearted regret. "Which we almost didn't make after getting run off the road and nearly killed." Mom deserved more than a cursory apology. He'd scared the hell out of her. "You're lucky my mother has quick reflexes."

"I'm very happy that she does." He offered a reserved, yet attractive smile. "My apologies, Ms. Meadowlark. Monday isn't a normal day for Castle Luschin to accept tourists. I didn't expect to encounter anyone on the road so close to the castle, but my carelessness is inexcusable."

Although heavily accented, his English was good. At least fifteen years August's senior, he had a kind of James Bond quality about him, exuding a seductive confidence with her every move she couldn't ignore, in spite of her irritation. He wore a well-tailored, light gray suit that didn't hide the ruggedness of his physique. A scrape on the knuckle of one hand and an emerald ring on the other reflected virility and sophistication. His square jaw and tanned face certainly didn't belong under florescent lighting. The Alps as a background suited his cool and craggy aura. She studied his chestnut hair, longish compared to the golden policeman Kurt when, with a half-smile, his attention came back as if to gain acceptance of his apology.

His toasted almond gaze caught her admiring his profile. She swallowed deeply to regain her composure. "Yes, we have an appointment." She hadn't listened so much to the words he'd said as to his deep, smooth voice with the exotic accent. "Can you please tell the gatekeeper, or whoever controls the entry, to let us drive in? Or shall we just leave our car here and enter through there?" She stepped toward the door.

He made the slightest movement, and although she could've easily stepped past him, the air of authority he radiated stopped her abruptly.

"I'm afraid Herr Luschin will not be able to see you."

She bristled. "Why not?"

Her mom's forehead creased. "Has something happened to Lenhard, Inspector Wolf?"

He hesitated a fraction of a second, his stern authority wavering. "Yes, I'm afraid so."

An anxious tightness wrapped around August's middle. "What?"

"I don't think the family would want me to discuss such matters."

"We *are* his family." Mom's voice cracked as she touched the inspector's forearm.

Inspector Wolf blinked. "What do you mean?"

"I'm his granddaughter. His only son, Hartmut, was my father."

August took her mother's hand, and the tightly gripped response made her chest flutter. Her mom had traveled so far to meet her only blood relative. If she couldn't know her father, she keenly wanted to meet her grandfather.

The inspector appeared lost for words. He glanced back and forth between them, rubbed his jaw from chin to ear, and frowned. "Can you prove this?"

"Of course."

Her mother's birth certificate, a letter from her grandfather, and the deed to the Castle Luschin Estate were proof.

"Please, Inspector, what's happened?" her mother implored.

"I'm sorry." He glanced at both of them before speaking. A sighed deeply. "Herr Luschin is dead."

****

Tobias waited as the white BMW maneuvered around the myriad of emergency and police vehicles. When Ms. Meadowlark had proclaimed her relationship to Herr Luschin moments before, he'd realized why her unusual green eyes seemed so familiar. The late Herr Luschin's eyes were the same light green.

Funny. He hadn't noticed August Myer's eyes. Her heart-shaped lips and feisty attitude had drawn his attention to the point of distraction from the conversation. Lovely, high cheekbones added to her haughtiness—haughtiness that bordered on caustic. The quiet classiness the older woman embodied was more typically attractive. And yet, he felt no physical attraction to Ms. Meadowlark. He couldn't say the same for her daughter.

The women parked. Outside the car, they spoke to each other a moment, and the daughter patted her mother's back as they walked around the drive and toward him. He buried his hands in the pockets of his slacks and admired lovely calves below the short jean skirt of the younger woman.

"I agree." Albert Feld, his partner, appeared at his elbow. "Fine legs on the young woman. Although, I find the curve of her mother's ass more to my liking."

"I hadn't noticed."

"And I'm the King of England." Albert chuckled, disturbing the buttons trying to hold his too tight jacket around his thick belly. His partner was only months from retirement and had already relaxed in several ways. "Ah, yes, nice indeed." He sighed. "I doubt I could keep up with even the mother."

"Iris will be happy to hear that." He followed his partner's appraisal of the women, admiring in silence.

With the mention of his wife's name, Albert drew a hand over his face and smiled at Tobias. "Keeping up with Iris isn't always easy."

He laughed. "Too much information, Inspector."

"Are we dealing with stray tourists?"

"Stray relatives. Apparently, Herr Luschin had heirs in America."

Bushy, gray brows rose. "The plot thickens."

"You want to go in and take some staff statements?" He cocked a thumb toward the castle behind them. "I'll handle Frau Luschin and the nephew once I've settled what to do with the new relatives."

"I can do that." His partner scratched the top of his balding head and ran a hand along the thicker gray hair over his ears. "Be careful with the young American woman. She looks like a handful." He retreated before Tobias could come up with a retort.

His gaze fell on August. She definitely had a different look about her. Brown hair barely touched her shoulders where the spiky, burnished gold ends matched the gold loops in her ears. Three loops on one ear and two on the other. Small-breasted, her nipples peaked beneath her clinging blouse…

He cleared his throat. He had a job to do.

"This way, ladies," he called from the main entrance.

Ms. Meadowlark's shoulders sagged noticeably. She'd seemed quite shaken with the news of her grandfather's death. The daughter slowed, admiring the intricate slate and marble pattern inlaid in the four steps leading up to the wide landing.

He might have gotten on the wrong side of the daughter, assuming there was a right side, but her tenderness and worry for her mother as she quickly caught up touched him. When the women's gazes lifted to the door as he opened it, Ms. Myer gawked at the intricate wood and metal artwork of the highly polished surface, slowing them further. He wanted to urge them along, but he understood their fascination. He'd grown up with this castle practically in his backyard, so he tended to overlook the centuries-old beauty. His family estate was just as old and regal, although not quite so large.

He tapped his fingers against the polished copper handle. "Ms. Meadowlark? Ms. Myer?"

The older woman nudged her daughter, and they hurried forward, passing him to enter the Great Hall, the public entrance. Police and medical personnel would be ushered in and out of the family's private entrance several yards away. Alone in the Great Hall, he would be able to quietly question them and discuss the news of Herr Luschin's death.

"Let us sit over here, shall we?"

Tobias led them past the first pillar to the second one farther from the door and in front of the mammoth fireplace. He gestured for them to sit on the circular bench surrounding the second pillar.

"Where is everyone?" Ms. Myer asked. Her gaze wandered overhead to the colorfully painted, domed ceiling.

"This is a public area. The family quarters are in another area of the castle. Please, sit. We'll talk."

"Isn't that where we should be?" The daughter persisted while she remained standing.

Her impatience could wear his patience thin.

Ms. Meadowlark sat and tugged on her daughter's hand to join her. "What happened, Inspector Wolf?"

Once both women were seated, he made an effort to gentle his voice. "Herr Luschin's wife found him dead in their bedchambers this morning."

"How awful." Ms. Meadowlark's grip grew tighter on the daughter's hand. "How did he die?"

"Mom, he was eighty-six, pretty old." She patted her mother's hand. "Did he have a heart attack or something? He sounded fine only a few hours ago."

He took a pad and pen from his jacket pocket. "Exactly what time did you speak to him?"

"It sounds as if you're questioning us." Ms. Myer narrowed her eyes at him. "How did he die?"

There was no point in avoiding her questions. Her personality and steadfastness would only cause him anxiety if he chose to ignore her inquisitiveness. He'd get his own questions answered sooner or later. "At this point, it appears to be suicide."

"Appears?" Ms. Meadowlark's eyes grew round. "How did he…?"

"An apparent overdose of his prescription medication." He kept his voice level and noncommittal. He'd been fond of the old lord, but his years of police work made setting aside his own feelings a matter of habit.

"And you think he did it on purpose?" Ms. Myer frowned in disbelief.

"It could have been an accident. These deaths are always investigated before a ruling is made." He offered his standard by the book answer, ignoring the niggling doubts rising in his gut.

"Maybe he had a stroke or something." The brash young woman encircled her mother's shoulders with her free arm. "He sounded excited to see us today, not suicidal."

"That's true, Inspector," Ms. Meadowlark added. "I'd spoken to him a couple of times before we left the States." Her voice cracked, and she swallowed deeply. "Learning of our existence shocked him, but it was a joyful shock. He said having a granddaughter and great-grandchildren made his life complete."

The little bud of doubt Tobias had about Herr Luschin's death transitioned to full bloom. "Can you tell me about the proof you have regarding your relationship, and how you came to make the trip now, Ms. Meadowlark?" He addressed the mother, ignoring the sultry mouth of her daughter.

"When both of my adoptive parents died, I decided to find out what I could about my birth parents." She slipped a hand into the bag on her shoulder and drew out a manila envelope. "This is my birth certificate."

Tobias carefully read the document that proved her to be the daughter of Herr Luschin's son, Hartmut. He looked into her green eyes and was again reminded of the elder man.

"Hartmut traveled to the States in the sixties, met my mother, Kaya Mochta, and I was conceived," Ms. Meadowlark explained. "It seems my father was estranged from his family. But after my birth, they decided to reunite with the Luschins in Austria. Unfortunately, the small plane taking them from Timberline, Arizona to catch a plane for Austria crashed. I was the only survivor." When he handed her back the birth certificate, she gazed at the document with misty eyes. "I learned about my mother only months ago, and there are no living blood relatives on her side. I'd hoped to come here and meet my grandfather." She cleared her throat. "And find out what I could about my father."

She pulled another envelope from the oversized khaki bag. "This is a deed to the estate. Only a few items, some pictures, some art and this deed, were left to me from my birth parents. I don't read German, but I've had it authenticated. I'm sure you'll see the estate is a bloodline inheritance. My father was an only child, and I'm his only daughter. I realize Herr Luschin has remarried recently, but the estate wouldn't be part of whatever he might leave to her. I have a letter from Lenhard, too, mostly a personal acknowledgement of his joy at discovering us and inviting us to come."

He read the antiquated document, which had been encased in plastic. Apparently, Ms. Lacy Meadowlark now stood to inherit the entire Luschin estate. Fabian Bauer, Lenhard's great-nephew and the presumed sole and indirect heir, would be surprised. It appeared Herr Luschin hadn't mentioned Fabian to the women.

"So, this is why you are here? To survey your inheritance?" The timing was uncanny. When exactly had they arrived in Austria?

"I'd hoped to meet—"

"I don't like your tone," the daughter interrupted with plenty tone of her own. "Mom just told you why we're here. What are you implying?" Her beauty flared with her temper.

"I'm not implying anything, Ms. Myer. As I said, we investigate every angle of a death."

"Well, investigate in another direction, Inspector, because the only thing my mother wanted was to meet her grandfather, and learn more about the father she never knew."

Why the hell did he feel any attraction to this woman? She was, without a doubt, a passionate person, but too young and too quick to temper. He handed the document back, and stared into her glittering eyes.

"Calm down, August." Ms. Meadowlark shook her head, blinking slowly as if fatigued.

"I'm sorry if I've offended you," he said, and dipped his chin for emphasis. Her protectiveness was admirable, but the young woman would have to find a way to deal with his questioning. And there would be more questions.

"You seem to be sorry a great deal, don't you?"

Had he thought her feisty earlier? Fiery was more like it. He wasn't scoring any points with her so far. *Doubt she would want to go to the gasthaus and have a beer later.* Attractiveness aside, she'd not be good company anyway. Best to keep a professional distance and full attention on the questionable suicide. He shifted his attention to the mother who'd clamped her hand on her daughter's arm.

"The fact you spoke to him this morning, and a couple of hours later he's dead, could be important. You might be the last person he spoke with outside of the castle." He'd like to get closer to Herr Luschin's state of mind. The daughter's opinion that he wasn't suicidal coincided with his.

"*I* spoke to him this morning," Ms. Myer corrected.

"Yes, I'm referring to both of you, actually."

"Did he leave a...note?" Ms. Meadowlark's eyes glistened with sadness.

"No." And the fact he hadn't added to his suspicions.

She clasped her hands then nervously played with her rings. How unfortunate she wouldn't get to know a most agreeable man to have as a grandfather. He'd offer his heartfelt condolences, but her daughter would probably bite his hand.

"Are you two traveling alone? You said grandchildren. Are your other children in Austria, also?"

"Not in Austria. I have a son at school in Paris. My daughter and

I are traveling together."

"I see. Well, I'd like to hear more about what you and Herr Luschin discussed over the last few weeks, Ms. Meadowlark. And how he sounded the last time you spoke. Could you help me understand what led up to this sad day?"

Her lovely face softened. "Please, call me Lacy, and yes, I'd love to help."

"Thank you, Lacy." The daughter's mouth remained tightly closed. *Amusing.* "This bench is hard and cold. May I offer you comfortable chairs and some coffee?"

"Yes, that would be nice."

"Let me see…" He pivoted and scanned the wall on either side of the fireplace. "This room is intended for receiving guests at large functions, but…" He searched his childhood memory of the layout. "The large door behind the dais goes to the kitchen. There's a sort of den…" He regarded the two smaller doors, one on each side of the fireplace. One led to a display of seventeenth century clothing, the other to a small room reserved for special, visiting tourists to relax.

He chose a door, turned the ornate glass handle, and found the small, richly furnished den he'd expected. "Here we are." He held his hand out in invitation.

Lacy passed by him then the daughter.

The younger woman paused for a split second, tipped her head to bridge the gap between their heights, and looked him in the eye. In her flat sandals, he guessed she stood at least five six. Her tightly closed mouth relaxed, and one brow twitched upward.

"Ms. Myer?"

"You may as well call me August. Looks like we'll be spending a bit of time together."

The pause was long enough to see the deep brown of her eyes with a curious green rim and to feel the warmth of the hot-blooded American woman whose body brushed his as she passed.

CHAPTER TWO

August sat on the Biedermeier chair and held her breath for a moment in awe of plopping her butt on such a treasure. She brushed her hand over the pink floral pattern mixed with green stripes then ran her fingertips over the walnut veneer along the arms that curled into the legs. Her gaze flitted around the elegant room while her mother perched on the edge of the matching sofa.

"Would either of you like something?" Wolf stood between them next to what she guessed was a tilt-top tea table, not particularly old, probably 1800s. "Tea? Coffee?"

Magic words to her ears. She hadn't had time for a second cup before they left the hotel that morning. "Coffee. Please, with—"

"Espresso?"

Oh, hell yes. She practically swooned at the suggestion and relaxed back against the brocade. "Wonderful!"

He crooked a smile, one hand in his jacket pocket and a dip to his chin, striking an aristocratic pose. "Double espresso with steamed milk?"

Would his accent ever stop delighting her?

"Are you a good judge of a person's coffee tastes or is this part of your inspector skills?" It was suddenly harder to be irritated with Inspector Tobias Wolf. She wondered if his friends called him Toby, but quickly shunned that idea. The name didn't fit a man who dressed in designer suits and exuded so much masculinity.

"Lucky guess." The way he raised one brow when amused was damned attractive. "And for you, Lacy?"

"I'd love a tea."

"White?" Wolf asked.

From breakfast this morning, August had learned this meant with cream.

"Please."

"I'll return shortly." He walked around the sofa to the wall, touched what appeared to be a candleholder attached above his head, and a panel slid open.

Momentarily speechless, August watched as he stepped out of the room. When the panel began to close behind him, she bolted, but the opening had disappeared before she got there. Her fingertips toyed with the rim of the candleholder.

"You shouldn't, August. Wait until the inspector comes back, and I'm sure he'll show you."

Reluctantly, she let her hand fall to her side. "I suppose." She strolled around the room. "Wouldn't Penny get a kick out of this castle?" She thought of her newest friend back in Timberline, a hotel clerk, whose taste ran to all things gothic and medieval. "Secret passageways would be right up her alley."

"I can imagine." Her mom laughed. "You two sure hit it off at my wedding."

"The Black Fairy, as you call her, is a classy, smart chick. Her Goth style fits her." And was the reason for the nickname. She stopped in front of a cabinet, and when two wine glasses from the Renaissance era sparkled, her mind raced and her pulse thumped. "Mom, have you taken a look at some of these things?"

"I'm not sure I know exactly what I'm looking at. This room is plush...comfortable. And I can see it's decorated in exquisite taste." Her voice didn't match the enthusiasm that had August's pulse kicked up. "What do you think of Inspector Wolf?"

"You mean do I find him attractive?" She darted a glance at her mother.

"No, I meant do you think he'll be of help." The worried lines around her mom's mouth smoothed slightly. "Although, he is very handsome."

"Mom." She couldn't be playing matchmaker at a time like this, could she?

"What? I didn't mean from my point of view. But I can see you think so."

"Hardly." August avoided her mom's eyes and concentrated on the glass-fronted cabinet before her. "He's too old."

"Old?" Her mother laughed the word.

"Whatever." She waved a hand in dismissal of the Wolf subject. "Look around, Mom. This room is luscious."

She smiled. "I know I'm seeing antiques."

"Antiques?" The word didn't live up to some of the art treasures surrounding them. "Look at this collection of cristallo wine glasses and goblets. During the Renaissance, everyone copied the Venetian glass but these—these are *original*." August tipped her nose close to the glass of the intricately carved, maple curio cabinet and practically salivated. The lock on the cabinet discouraged any notion of getting a closer look. "Most look to be from the 1700s but this one…" She glanced back and pointed at the second shelf. "This goblet has to be from the late 1500s."

"You are a plethora of knowledge, my daughter. Good to see your education stuck with you."

Sighing, she straightened and smiled. "Do you know what you're sitting on, Mom?"

"My butt?"

"Yes, another antique, but I was referring to the Biedermeier sofa." She barely got the words out of her mouth before her attention locked on a painting on the wall. "This looks like a Weissenkircher, but I didn't know he did anything this small. The ceiling paintings in the Great Hall are his." She strode to within a foot of the twelve-inch square oil painting. "If I'm correct, then it could be priceless considering the size." She glanced around the art-rich room. The place put her on art overload. "Perfect for this room."

"And for your gallery?"

"Seems a shame to hang it anywhere other than here." The room was a piece of art all by itself. "But the landscape by Karl Aigen in the Great Hall? Now *that* I'd love to have at the gallery. I can't wait to take a tour of this place. Can you imagine…?"

One glance at her mom, whose unfocused gaze looked in the opposite direction, told August she'd lost her.

How insensitive of me. Art would be the last thing on her mind.

She'd let her passion override concern for what her mother must be feeling—a real link to her past had been jerked from her yet again.

"I'm sorry." August stepped to the sofa, sank beside her, and threw an arm around her slumped shoulders. "I'd rather Grandfather Luschin was here to give us a tour."

"I don't understand why he'd say he was looking forward to our visit and then commit suicide the morning we were supposed to arrive." Her mother frowned and shook her head. "And if it was an accident? He didn't seem the least bit senile in conversation."

"He seemed so…so…excited and alert." She patted her mom's back and eased her against the sofa to relax.

"It doesn't make any sense, does it, August?"

"Here is your coffee and tea, ladies."

She started at the inspector's voice. Wolf had silently entered the room through a different panel in the wall behind them.

August's curiosity rose over the existence of hidden tunnels as her pulse increased with the reappearance of the inspector. "Secret passageways?"

"Not all are secret. Shortcuts you might say. This one leads to the *Vorratskammer*, the buttery, so the servants could make a quick jaunt into this room to attend to the lord of the castle. Handy as a shortcut now to bring beverages to special guests." He set a tray with cups on the table in front of them.

"Buttery?" She grabbed her espresso. A whiff of the strong coffee overtook her. "Oh jeez, this is wonderful."

"Yes, the place you get beverages from, in castle terms. Of course, they did not serve espresso in medieval times." He sat in the chair across from them, pad in hand.

Mom clasped her hands around the tea as if she needed the warmth, and gazed pensively into the cup.

"Did you know my great-grandfather?" August asked between sips of her coffee. Wolf might want to interview them, but she had questions, too.

Her mom's chin lifted and regarded the inspector.

"He was a friend of my grandfather, who died ten years ago. I did not know Herr Luschin *well*, but we had shared some common interests and on occasion attended the same functions." His attention went to Lacy as he opened his mouth to continue.

August didn't give him a chance. "So, he wasn't a recluse?"

His brows lifted. "Not in the least."

"What do you know about his wife? When I Googled him, I saw an article about their marriage."

"Yes, he and Eike have been married five years. She's quite a bit younger."

August clicked her nails against her coffee mug. *Yes, yes. Tell me something I don't know.* She flashed Wolf a quick smile. "She was forty-five when they married. And if he was vibrant enough to marry a younger woman, and seemed happy when we spoke to him, then what reason could he possibly have to off himself?" Her mother tensed beside her, but she forged ahead. "Did he have bouts of depression? Is he bankrupt, and this castle is just a ruse? Did he—"

"I'm beginning to wonder who the inspector is in this room." He leaned back into his chair, casually crossing his ankle over the other knee, and glared into her face with the slightest smile on his lips.

He stared at her so deeply, she stammered on a comeback.

"I knew him well enough to question his suicide." He addressed her mother and spoke softly. "Because you are family, albeit unknown, I wanted to hear your reactions."

August tensed. What he wasn't saying struck her. "Do you think he was murdered?"

"August, please." Mom frowned while opening her eyes wide, a displeased expression that always wilted her. "Where did that come from?"

After what her mother went through only months before, August realized her question was harsh and thoughtless. But damn, Wolf seemed to lead her down that path.

"I'm sorry, Mom."

"Do you doubt it was accidental?" her mom asked Wolf.

He tapped his pen on the pad. "I'm finding it curious for all the reasons you've stated."

"What was his wife's reaction?" August glanced at her mother, whose attention was thankfully again on Wolf and not her, awaiting his answer. She drained her last drop of coffee, sorry to see it gone so soon.

He appeared to be weighing his words. Or was he at odds with her asking another question?

"Frau Luschin is every bit the grieving widow."

The timbre of his voice exposed his opinion.

"You don't like her," August stated.

His eyes narrowed for a moment, but he recovered quickly. She inwardly smiled.

"Did Herr Luschin mention planning any events for you; perhaps formally introducing you to the family?"

Her mother lifted a strand of hair and ran it over her chin like a paintbrush, thinking. August was touched by the familiar gesture. Mom had regained her composure.

"Not anything in particular that I remember. But you know, Inspector, I'm surprised he didn't mention Frau Luschin to us." She looked to her for confirmation.

"Never mentioned her," August agreed. "He mainly talked about having family in the house again and asked me about my life. Are there any other family members, besides his wife?"

"There is a grand-nephew, Fabian Bauer, and as far as I know, the only blood relative, excluding you two. He's the son of Herr Luschin's late niece, Irmgard."

"And where is he?" Mom asked.

"He happens to be here, visiting from Vienna." Wolf's expressions gave nothing away, but his suspicions bled through with his simple statement.

She darted a glance at her mother who didn't seem to be picking up on the inspector's subtle gives. She itched to pepper him with more questions, convinced he was investigating more than an apparent suicide. Perhaps there would be an opportunity without Mom around. She didn't want to upset her.

"Can we meet him?" Her mom's bright smile accompanied an uplifted tone.

"I have not had a chance to speak to him yet. But I would assume he would be eager to meet you. I will express your desire."

"I'd like to meet Frau Luschin and...if possible...see my grandfather." Her mom sat her cup on the tray and met the inspector's gaze with the strength August was accustomed to seeing her exhibit. The news had shaken her, but she always rebounded.

"I'm sorry. The medical examiner is still with the lord, and then he will be moved to the facility."

Mom's shoulders sagged with a sigh.

"For now, the room is closed."

August's ears pricked. "Closed? Do you consider it a crime scene?"

"The sequence of events that led to Herr Luschin's passing are still under investigation. This is normal procedure."

Her neck heated. Wolf was a study in control, but his lack of disclosure had her imagination ramped. "Surely, my mom—"

"If you want to follow the ambulance when he is moved...but I think it might be best to wait for the funeral."

Autopsy.

August decided not to pursue in deference to her mother's feelings.

"No." Mom patted her hand. "We don't want to go wherever it is you're taking him. We, of course, will stay for the funeral."

Wolf nodded. "I hoped you would remain in country for a few days, at least until the investigation is complete."

Her mother was silent, but August could practically hear her thought process, which was most likely the same as her own. What to do about the estate? Technically, it belonged to them now, but what was the next step? August gave her mother a we'll-talk-later nod.

The inspector regarded them with a serious slant to his expression. "You are the closest of kin, and there are arrangements to be made." Inspector Wolf apparently guessed what they were thinking.

Mom chose to interpret it vaguely. "I'm sure his wife will have all the arrangements under control, but if you'd like us to be of some assistance during the investigation, we'll be happy to stay a few days."

August scooted to the edge of the sofa. "About the investigation." She tilted her head, tried to ignore his James Bond assuredness, but found herself gazing into his eyes. "You have to have more than just, 'Gee the guy seemed too happy and healthy to do this.' Why the suspicion?"

"Call it intuition, call it gut reaction. Or call it sadness over a grand old lord ending his life this way." He abruptly stood, bringing the meeting to an end.

His sudden movement jarred her. She swore he fought a smile as his jaw tensed and relaxed. The man was too damned polished and too...much of a cop. She had to shut off whatever it was about him that intrigued her.

"Where are you staying?" he asked.

"We're at the Hotel Karnten in St. Veit. Lenhard had invited us to stay here, but we'd already book the room and have it until tomorrow." Her mother stood. "We thought we should keep the room one more night in case our meeting didn't go well, or we'd misunderstood the invitation. It now appears we were correct to be cautious."

She couldn't help the deflated mood disappointment brought. Staying in the castle would've been so much fun. But now, with Great-grandfather Lenhard's death, the castle would be in mourning, the atmosphere, at the very least, subdued. Mom's sorrow might be worsened with more time spent inside the castle. She sighed and rose. "We can come back tomorrow, Mom."

Her lips pinched together in thought then curved into a smile. "Oh, August, you know you'd love to spend the night in a castle."

She restrained a ripple of enthusiasm. "But considering—"

"I do think we should meet Lenhard's wife before we rule out staying here for a few days." She addressed August, but nodded to Inspector Wolf.

"Hmm." The inspector rubbed his jaw. "I'm not sure staying here is a good idea." He opened his mouth to add something, but instead shrugged.

"Why?" Her stomach fluttered. He wasn't telling them everything.

"The nephew is here. And, as I said, Frau Luschin is quite distraught..."

Right. He hadn't gotten any more sincerity in his voice this time around when he mentioned the woman married to her Great-grandfather. She couldn't wait to meet Frau Eike Luschin. There had to be something about her that rubbed the inspector wrong.

"I'd love to meet our cousin." Her mom smiled. "We certainly don't want to impose, but we *are* family, and at home invitations aren't needed for family in times like this."

She understood the veiled meaning, and from the crook of his brow, so did Wolf. They were here on the bequest of her great-grandfather, the sole owner of the estate. With him dead, her mother owned the estate. The invitation was no longer Mrs. Luschin's to make.

"Does she know we're here?" her mom asked.

"I'm afraid I whisked you away before anyone found out."

"Then would you take us to her, or at least ask if we could see her?"

"Of course, Lacy." He checked his watch. "If you would not mind waiting?" A corner of his mouth ticked up as he glanced at August. "I will have some more white tea, espresso, and *Vanillekipferln*—cookies—brought in."

As antagonistic as she found him, he had a knack for reading her wants. His half-smile ruffled her, and not in an entirely bad way.

****

Tobias strolled along the route back to the buttery. The sconces threw yellow light over the stone walls in a circular pattern, dimmer halfway between each one. The thought of August's bright eyes, excited with the possibility of secret passageways, brought a smile to his face. Too bad the hallways were now lit with electric lights. The young woman would've loved to make her way through an inner castle passage with candles burning as in centuries past.

He hoped they wouldn't find Eike to their liking. He didn't want them staying in the castle, not until the details of Herr Luschin's death were fleshed out, especially if Fabian Bauer, the supposed heir until now, intended to stay on. He couldn't imagine the brash, young August bonding with the icy Eike Luschin. The young woman's honest, in-your-face style would contrast sharply with the veiled personality of the Frau.

Suspicion, that's all he had, and there was no way to force the women to stay in town instead of in the castle. Without any evidence, there would be nothing to dispute suicide or determine accidental overdose. Openly sharing his concerns with Lacy and August would be highly unprofessional. And to what end if his conjecture was nothing more than that?

But he couldn't shake his gut reaction. It seemed too coincidental Bauer should be visiting his uncle at the time of his death. Tobias would need to find out just how often the nephew visited and why.

The passageway forked, a lighted path toward the buttery one way and dark the other. He followed the light.

As far as Bauer knew, he owned the estate of Herr Luschin. Except now a granddaughter and great-granddaughter stood in his way. Tobias's gut tightened. The fact Lacy appeared intelligent and observant lessened his concern a notch. They were close, mother and daughter, and would certainly have each other's back. August had picked up on his skepticism, and woe to anyone whom she needed to defend against for her mother.

Ahead of him, a light flickered and burned out.

And then again, his suspicions may prove nothing more than that. He didn't know Bauer, nor had he spoken to him yet, but the comfort the nephew had offered the grieving widow when Tobias first saw them appeared too intimate. The familiarity they displayed for each other slipped the boundary of nephew and step-aunt. Hell, they were the same age, he'd guess. Considering Bauer lived in Vienna, you wouldn't think they'd know each other all that well. An affair didn't have anything to do with the nephew inheriting the estate; given the bloodline inheritance, it would've been his alone anyway. As far as he knew, the wife had no legal rights. But a nephew doing that to the elder gentleman, an affair with his wife, rubbed him more than wrong.

Tobias stepped into the buttery, updated from its original medieval purpose to now resemble a small kitchen. He made his request for Lacy and August, hoping the refreshments would arrive as ordered considering the state of the butler. She nodded, sniffed, and dabbed her eyes. Every member of the staff had acted in the same manner.

"You were fond of Herr Luschin?"

"*J-ja, Inspektor.*" Her round frame trembled.

"Have you given a statement yet?"

Sniff. "Yes."

"Did you notice anything different about Herr Luschin lately? Maybe keeping to himself, not talking much?"

"No, no." She shook her head, her pudgy face jiggling with her emphatic opinion.

"Did he appear sad or more quiet than normal?"

"He had been in a very good mood of late."

"Happy, huh?"

"Yes." She sobbed. "Yes."

He patted the poor woman on the back and reminded her of the beverages to take to the den.

She dabbed at her eyes with her apron, set her shoulders, and waved him off with a thick hand.

"You'll notice a light has burned out along the passage way."

"*Danka.*"

He left the buttery and entered the bottlery. Although the two rooms had changed from their medieval versions, the bottlery was still used for much the same purpose. But no one presided over the racks of wine, now left for the butler to keep stocked.

Outside the main kitchen, the next room, he met his partner leaving. "How is it proceeding, Albert?"

"Nothing earth shaking, but the same story more or less. A good employer, fond of the old lord, and shocked at his death. No one has any insights."

"Questionable suicide."

His partner thought on that a moment. "Questionable..." He tucked a notebook in his pocket. "If I dare speculate at this point." His shoes clicked on the stone as he walked away.

When Tobias entered the kitchen, three staff members huddled in a corner, commiserating, and startled with his entrance.

"I'm just on my way upstairs. No worry."

They each nodded; the female of the three had red-rimmed eyes from crying.

Albert would've questioned them thoroughly, so he didn't pause. He continued on, his mission to speak to the Frau and the nephew. He'd gotten only a preliminary statement from Eike in a state of shock and nothing from Bauer.

Once out of the kitchen, he entered a short hall with a circular staircase at one end. Cool air funneled through the round, winding, upward passage. The ancient stone steps, smoothly indented from centuries of use, led to the solar suite of rooms with the Lord and Lady's chambers, as well as the sitting room. He assumed Eike and Fabian would be in the sitting room with the doctor, castle manager, and whoever else they'd called to assist them.

He knocked on the door.

Bauer greeted him. "*Hallo, Inspektor Wolf.* Am I correct?"

"Yes. And you are Fabian Bauer?"

He nodded. "Please come in."

Tobias glanced around, stunned again at the modern version of the ancient sitting room. He'd been in the private area a few times prior to Herr Luschin's marriage. Then, the furnishings harkened back to the sixteenth century when the Luschin family came into possession of the estate and surrounding land. It had taken Frau Eike Luschin less than a month to wipe out over three hundred years of elaborate Renaissance ambiance in the private solar. After visiting Herr Luschin's chambers earlier, he was glad to see she hadn't been entirely successful.

He was also surprised to find Bauer alone

"Have a seat. I'm having a snifter of brandy. Can I get you something?" The man didn't wait for an answer as he strolled to the sleek, glass and walnut liquor cabinet.

The guy already had a strike against him. To call Remy Martin

X.O. "a brandy" could get him shot in some circles.

Tobias chose the leather chair against a wall and with the best overall view of the room. "No, thank you. Little early in the day for me."

He scrutinized Bauer. Summer-weight, wool slacks bloused around thin legs ending in highly polished, loafer-type shoes. The pale-yellow polo shirt did nothing for his pasty-white complexion.

"Well, I'm having one for Uncle Lenhard. I am sure he would appreciate it."

"Hmmm…I bet he would."

Bauer gulped half his snifter.

Tobias cringed at the lack of reverence for the fine sipping cognac. "Was Herr Luschin a cognac enthusiast?"

The nephew held his glass in front of his face, swirled the amber liquid, and shrugged. "I really couldn't say." He leveled his gaze at Tobias. "But Uncle Lenhard would appreciate a toast on his behalf." Hefting the bottle again, he splashed more of the fine beverage into his glass. "Actually, I think my uncle preferred ale." He sauntered to the matching divan facing Tobias and sat, one leg crossed over the other.

"Where is Frau Luschin?"

"She's in the Bower with the doctor. He thought it best if she retired to her private chamber and take something to calm her nerves. She is upset, you might say." He ran a hand through his hair. "As we all are." Judging from his tone of voice, he spoke the truth.

"I'd like to use this opportunity to take your statement, Herr Bauer." He'd been delayed in taking the statements of the nephew and wife when Lacy and August arrived. If Eike didn't appear by the time he'd finished with Bauer, he'd ask the American women to wait at their hotel until he sent for them.

The nephew remained silent, his hand tight around his glass.

He took a pen and pad from his suit coat. "When did you arrive, sir?"

"Day before yesterday. For dinner and, well, the weekend." He drummed his fingers on the divan arm and stared into his cognac.

"Do you visit often?"

"Why do you ask?" His reddish brows furrowed over blue-gray eyes.

The nephew sounded a bit defensive, and Tobias wanted to play off that. "I'm wondering how well you knew Herr Luschin."

"He was my uncle, Inspector. I've known him all my life."

"Ah, you were close."

"I wouldn't say that." Bauer pinched thin lips together for a moment. "Not like we're neighbors and visit regularly. But I do, uh, did know him. Family." He lifted his glass as if toasting. "A fine man."

"Could you tell me what happened this morning?"

"There isn't much I can tell you, Inspector. Eike found my uncle while I was still in my bedchamber. She screamed out. I ran to her assistance, but my uncle had passed by then." He stared into the amber liquid as if fascinated by the contents. "I'm sorry to see the old gent gone."

"You are the supposed heir to the Luschin estate, correct?"

Bauer narrowed his eyes, took another drink, and huffed. "I'm not exactly destitute, Inspector Wolf. And my uncle was quite old. I doubt he would have lived much longer anyway."

Defensive.

"You live in Vienna, correct?"

"I'm sure you know I do." Bauer glanced around the room as if on edge.

Tobias had already given his office some facts to check, but asking the mundane questions usually loosened the tongue.

"What do you do there?"

"I own a car dealership, and I do quite well." Now he made eye contact.

Tobias read the snobbery of his comment. "You said you have no relatives, but are you married? Divorced? Children?"

"No, no, and no. I am the last of my line."

He held the next question a beat. Bauer should have no trouble digesting the implications of his response and tone.

The man's right eye twitched as he ran a finger inside the collar of his polo shirt.

"You said you arrived here day before yesterday. Saturday?"

"No." He frowned in thought. "I've lost a day somewhere. I arrived Friday evening."

"And you had planned on staying, until when?"

"More than likely, I would have left today." He gulped more cognac.

Tobias leaned forward, rubbed a finger on his chin. "What would you say about Herr Luschin's state of mind?"

"I'm not a psychologist, Inspector."

"Give me your best guess."

He shrugged narrow shoulders. "My uncle was not as jovial. More quiet than normal. I actually saw him only at Saturday lunch for any amount of time. He was in bed on Friday night when I arrived, and Sunday morning he went shooting clay birds, which he loves to destroy."

"So, he was active, not physically debilitated in any way for a man his age?"

"I didn't accompany him."

"And later in the day yesterday, Sunday?"

"I-I don't know." Again, the eye twitched.

The mention of the day before Eike found the lord dead brought obvious discomfort to Bauer. Tobias's gut wrenched a notch tighter. "No?" A little push…

"We didn't dine together. I believe he went into St. Veit to lunch with friends, but Eike might know for sure. And last night, I stayed in my bedchambers. No appetite."

"Do you know where Herr Luschin was last night?"

"No, this estate is quite large."

"And what are your plans now?"

"Now?" He finished his drink. "Out of respect for my uncle, I will stay and help Eike, of course, through the funeral and beyond if she needs me." He rose and walked to the liquor cabinet. "I am all she has now."

CHAPTER THREE

"Do you think Herr Luschin—"

Tobias's question for Bauer was interrupted by Eike's appearance, her tall frame floating beneath her lavender robe. No matter. He'd gleaned all he could at this point from the lord's nephew.

"*Au, Tobias.*" She smiled weakly from across the room. "I wondered where you had gotten off to."

"I thought it best to give you some time before we spoke again."

"How kind of you." She wavered when she stepped toward him.

Tobias jumped to his feet, but the doctor, close on her heels, took her elbow and guided her to the divan. She sank beside Bauer. Her short, blonde hair was brushed back from her face and accentuated her long, slender nose. The robe did little to disguise her rounded curves, a bit plump for Tobias's taste, but nonetheless sexually presented.

"Oh, please, Franz. I'm just a bit light-headed from whatever you gave me." She made a shooing motion toward the doctor whose mouth turned down in a maligned expression.

"Eike, dear, Franz has been nothing but helpful." Bauer threw an apologetic smile at the physician.

"I'll leave now anyway. There are sleeping pills on her bedside table if she needs them. One should be sufficient. She took a gentle relaxer for now." The doctor stepped closer to Eike. "Stay away from alcohol, Frau Luschin. It doesn't mix that well with what I gave you and is a depressant."

She lifted her chin and smiled lightly. "Thank you, dear. I'll take that under consideration."

Shaking his head, the doctor made his departure.

"Franz?" Eike called softly.

He glanced back.

"Thank you. Really."

With a smile, he left the room.

"Fabian, be a dear and get me some of that wonderful cognac before you finish the bottle."

"Did you not hear—?"

"He said it didn't mix *that* well." A pout settled on her full lips. "He offered a loophole."

Tobias didn't miss the way she touched his knee in a most un-aunt-like gesture. Bauer cast a glance at him and rose quickly from the divan.

"Now, what would *you* like from me, Tobias Wolf?" she asked.

"I'll need some time with you, Eike, to take an official statement. But first, you have some visitors who would like to meet you." Technically, he should take the statements first, but this surprise might be beneficial for his investigation. His gut told him all was not as it seemed, and a shakeup could bring some evidence to the surface.

Her eyes opened widely. "Wh-who?"

"Relatives. The granddaughter and great-granddaughter of Herr Luschin. He was expecting them today. Did you not know?"

A loud clunk sounded at the liquor cabinet. Tobias looked over in time to see the nephew catch the bottle of Remy Martin before it hit the floor.

"A granddaughter?" Eike's hands grasped the divan on each side of her as if to stay grounded, and in spite of makeup, her color paled. "Is she an imposter? His son died decades ago."

"Yes, in a plane crash, but his daughter survived, was adopted, and recently learned who she really is. She wants very much to speak to you and meet her cousin."

"I-I'm speechless, Tobias. Lenhard…" She played with her wedding band. "I had no idea."

Bauer, stone-faced and apparently under control, handed Eike her cognac.

She stared at her nephew's profile as he lowered onto the couch. Frowning, she sipped, settled her shoulders against the couch, and raised a brow at Bauer. "Fabian, did you know you had relatives?"

"No, but then, Uncle Lenhard didn't exactly confide in me."

Eike held the cognac close to her face, breathed the vapors then lowered the snifter. "How do you know they aren't treasure hunters who somehow heard of Lenhard's death?"

"I doubt the news has had time to travel beyond the castle wall. And they're Americans, arrived in Austria late last night. The granddaughter, Lacy Meadowlark, has proof of her relationship. They knew nothing of Herr Luschin's apparent suicide."

Bauer's eyes narrowed at Tobias.

Eike shook her head, tears welling in hers. "He never mentioned them. Not a word."

"What do you mean *apparent*, Inspector?" Her step-nephew leaned forward, a note of irritation in his voice.

"The investigation has to be completed before a conclusion is reached." He studied the man's body language. Was this the concerned nephew, or was something else behind the man's knee-jerk reaction?

"Fabian, please." Eike brushed Bauer's forearm with a well-manicured hand. "Where are these women, Tobias?"

"Waiting in the den off the Great Hall."

"Well, fetch them. We mustn't keep the granddaughter and great-granddaughter of Herr Lenhard Luschin waiting."

****

"I'm going to take another look at the Great Hall." August rose from the settee.

"Too much espresso to sit still, huh?" her mother asked.

"Maybe." She laughed and opened the door. "Want to come?"

"I think I'll stay here and call Chance." She checked her watch, and commented more to herself than to August. "Eight hours difference. He should be finished with dinner and sitting by his phone waiting."

"Ah, love, the second time around." With happy flutters in her chest for her mother, she stepped into the Great Hall, leaving the door open behind her.

Stopping in the middle of the room, she pivoted to get a feel for the entire space. The beauty, the history surrounding her, and the size of the room filled her with awe. The frescoed ceiling, rounded between arches that formed between each pillar, drew her gaze upward. The area where each arch came together, painted in gold and browns in an intricate pattern of squares, circles and triangles, made her giddy; the only way she could describe her reaction to the room—a beautiful work of art, and in *her* family.

Between the arches, each space had a different scene depicting ordinary folk and events of the times. They were all painted by Weissenkircher, and she guessed they dated from the early 1700s. One of a town market scene fascinated her.

Three painted scenes across the ceiling and five lengthwise, each painting the size of a typical room in a house. The Great Hall equaled the size of fifteen rooms in a normal American house. Her gaze drifted downward. She stared at the gaping mouth of the fireplace that was topped with another fresco. Although sad she couldn't stand here with the great-grandfather who linked her to this remarkable architecture, the overwhelming knowledge of what this place now meant to her mother, and to her, dwarfed those feelings of…what? Loss? No. Perhaps Mom felt the loss. For herself, disappointment left her slightly melancholy. Yet, she couldn't lie. Even the melancholy paled in comparison to the excitement of inheriting a castle and the treasures within.

Tempering the bubbling exuberance while in her mother's presence was probably best.

She scanned the walls on either side of the long room. Only three oils hung on the inner wall where the door to the den was, but they were each at least five feet tall. One was definitely by Karl Aigen, but the other artists weren't immediately recognizable. Later, she'd have to study them closer. The other long wall, an outer one on her right, allowed light to flood the room from three floor-to-ceiling windows and at least a dozen small windows spaced high near the ceiling. The stone carving over each of the three large windows depicted men on horseback in various poses. The ceiling drew her gaze upward again.

"Truly beautiful, no?"

She whirled to face *Polizist* Kurt Gruber. "Yes, it is."

The space between them closed as his heavy-looking, black boots moved surprisingly quiet on the stone floor. "Are you now playing the tourist?"

His beret seemed at a cockier tilt than before, so unpoliceman-like, and so cute. The thick-soled boots added another couple of inches to his six-foot frame. He was obviously fit, although lean compared to Wolf.

She twitched. The need to make comparisons between the two men perplexed her.

"Sort of. My mother's in the den. We're waiting for Inspector Wolf, and I thought I'd use the time to look around. This is a magnificent room."

"It is lovely, but not as...as..." His blue eyes squinted as if he could see the words in English if he tried hard enough.

"Grand? Beautiful?"

"Yes, to both."

He gestured with a hand, smiling in a slightly embarrassed way. *Could he be any cuter?*

"Not as grand or beautiful as some other castles in Austria, but lovely, and with great history."

"Do all castles have Great Halls?"

"Yes, of course."

"Why of course?"

"A very useful area." He gestured with a sweeping motion as if he was serious tour guide. "As you can see, it is a large space. A visitor would enter into the Great Hall, first, in centuries past as it is today." He scanned the hall as he spoke. "Now, only tourists use this room, but in the past, it was for dining and a place to receive guests. At night, if castle guests or soldiers needed lodging, they would sleep here on the floor."

She imagined lords and ladies milling with soldiers in the large room. Socializing in the Grand Hall would be one thing. Sleeping on the hard stone floor would be quite another.

"Is the raised area with the long table at that end of the hall for the lord and his family to eat?"

"Exactly. The door to the right leads to the kitchen."

"How do you know so much about castles?"

He shrugged. "I am Austrian." His full smile teased—with dimples. "Will you do more traveling when you leave Castle Luschin? More castle sightseeing?"

"No, I don't think so. We're here only to see this castle." With a brief glance toward the door of the den, she wondered if Wolf was back yet.

"And will you be here long? I hope."

He fingered the thick belt slung around his hips that holstered his gun. His full smile brought out his dimples again. Flirting came easier than English.

A ripple of pleasure teased her abdomen.

"A few days at least." She'd not had a man take an interest in her for a few years, but his meaning couldn't be mistaken. Now that her divorce was final, maybe her mom had the right idea about mixing a little play in with her work.

"Perhaps we can, can...*ach*, my English!" His cheeks pinked with frustration.

"Maybe we could have a drink together in town?" That was a first—helping a man ask her out.

"Yes, wonderful idea. Tonight?"

She laughed. Somehow his bad English gave her the lead in this plan. "I—"

"August?" her mother called from inside the den.

"Wolf must be back. I have to go."

His cheeks tightened with a suppressed smile, probably finding her irreverence of calling the inspector by only his last name humorous.

"Will you be around the castle for a while?" she asked.

"No, everyone is leaving. I came in here in hopes of seeing you before I left."

"How nice." And she meant it. She'd never normally consider being sought out by a policeman a good thing. Must be the beret.

"Where will I be able to reach you?" he asked.

"We're most likely staying here, and if not, we'll be at the Hotel Karnten in St. Veit. I have no idea about tonight. We have—"

"August?" Mom stood in the open doorway. "Sorry to interrupt, but we need to go."

His eyes narrowed in a split-second reaction to the interruption, then quickly relaxed. "An idea." Kurt pulled a matchbook and pen from his pocket and scribbled some numbers. "Here. My phone number." He stepped back and nodded. "I hope to hear from you." Another step back and another nod in the direction of her mother. "Ms. Meadowlark."

August gave him a wink as he smiled, did an about face on his heel, and left. A brief glance at the matchbook pleased her, and she palmed the phone number.

Wolf appeared behind her mother and watched the retreating golden policeman leave. She didn't know how to read the inspector's expression, or more precisely, lack of one. His square jaw with the nicely formed chin—was there a hint of a clef?—didn't so much as flinch. Maybe policemen weren't supposed to socialize with anyone while on the job. His dark eyes, rimmed in thick lashes, held a hint of…interest? Maybe. She probably read far too much into his gorgeous but passive face.

****

When August reentered the den, Tobias locked gazes with her, and her lips curved into a crooked smile, the imperfection of it sexy. At least she was finally smiling. The mother and daughter exchanged a look, no doubt a silent communication only they knew the meaning of, although, he'd bet it had something to do with Gruber.

"Do you mind going the back way, through the passage, to the family quarters?" he asked. "Otherwise, we would go outside and up the private stair—"

"Of course not." August hooked her arm around Lacy's. "Would we, Mom?" Her expected agreement lit her face. In spite of the bad news the women had received, August's enthusiasm for the castle bled through.

Lacy patted her daughter's hand. "Lead the way, Inspector Wolf."

As he ushered them along the tunnel, into the buttery, bottlery, and finally the kitchen, he told them what history he knew of this part of the castle. Built in the eleventh century, the Luschin family bought the estate in the sixteenth century, a century before his family built a neighboring castle.

"Herr Luschin opened the estate to tourists when Hartmut was a boy. A restaurant was added to the grounds, but I believe it closed when his son went to America. Tourism is now limited to weekends."

They stepped from the kitchen to a short hall, which led to the landing and the stairs.

August touched the common wall. Her eyes glazed over as if the certain coolness on her fingertips from the ages old stone sent her mind wandering. "We're actually behind the Great Hall, aren't we?"

"Yes." Her sense of direction was true.

"Kurt explained some of the layout of the castle to me and the uses for the Great Hall."

Young Gruber knew how to catch the attention of the pretty American.

"This way."

At the top of the stairs, he tapped lightly on the family quarters' door, and this time was greeted by one of the men he'd seen in the kitchen on his first trip to the private rooms.

"*Inspektor Wolf.*" The short, stout man bowed slightly at the waist. "Frau Luschin is expecting you. Please come in." His formal demeanor cracked a bit when he caught sight of the pretty American women.

"Thank you."

Tobias held out his hand for the women to precede him. Lacy's scent wafted over him, but as pleasant as it was, August's enticed him so much more. Where Lacy smelled sweet and exotic like roses with a Middle East bent, August's totally indiscernible scent piqued his interest.

Inside, the walnut table had been readied for lunch. Eike had changed into a straight black skirt, although not too straight on her curvy hips, and a dark gray, tailored blouse. She dabbed at her eyes with a pink hanky, rose from the couch, and swept across the dove gray carpeting with an outstretched hand. Bauer rose, but stood in place, no welcoming gestures or smile.

"Frau Eike Luschin, may I introduce Lacy Meadowlark, Herr Luschin's granddaughter and his great-granddaughter, August Myer?"

"Welcome. Welcome to Castle Luschin." She clasped each woman's hand. "I am surprised and happy to meet you." Releasing August's hand, she again dabbed at her eye. "This is most extraordinary. On such a sad day to meet you." For a moment, she seemed lost for words, her lips trembling as she dropped the mother's hand and placed hers to her chest.

Lacy spoke first. "Frau Luschin, we are so pleased to meet you. I'm so very sorry for your loss and do hope our presence doesn't bring you further discomfort."

"Of course not. This is most touching to meet my dear husband's granddaughter." She took Lacy's hand in hers again. "And great-granddaughter." August's fingers filled her other hand. She sniffed then blinked. "Oh but, you have a relative." Without looking back at Bauer, she beckoned him. "Fabian?" She released them and tented her fingers as if praying.

Bauer stepped beside her, his gray eyes glancing between the women.

"Herr Bauer, these are your cousins." Tobias made the unneeded introduction while he scrutinized the man closely.

The cordiality extended by Eike didn't exude from cousin Fabian. His pasty face remained slack.

"Ms. Meadowlark." He bowed slightly, stiff with formality. "Ms. Myer. Extraordinary indeed. How nice to meet you." His voice held no welcome.

Lacy's hand grazed his arm. "Please, call me Lacy and my daughter, August. We're so very happy to meet you."

"Of course. Fabian to you then."

August smiled, but her eyes were far more active than her expression gave away. She'd perused the room when they'd first entered, obvious disappointment showing on her face at the modern décor. Now, she gave the same studious appraisal of her step-great-grandmother and newfound cousin.

"Please, come in and be seated. Lunch will be served shortly." Eike gestured to the two facing divans. "Herr Bloch," she addressed the man who'd answered the door. "Would you check on lunch, and let the kitchen know we will be ready shortly?"

With a nod, he left the room.

As the family approached the divans, it was as if the two sides were facing off, and with the glint in August's eye, Tobias could tell which side would enjoy this encounter more.

****

August chose the divan facing into the room and nudged her mother to join her. Their cousin, Fabian, took a corner of the matching furniture facing them, with Eike floating into the middle of the same. The woman tugged the bottom of her tight black skirt, but her attractive knees remained exposed.

If only her own knees and calves looked that good twenty years from now. Great-grandpa had good taste in women if looks alone were the gauge. She glanced down at her own legs, exposed several inches above her knees and looked up in time to catch Wolf's quick assessment. A tingle of pleasure caught her off guard.

As he chose an armchair at the end and between them, she diverted her gaze to Fabian. She glanced from her mother to her cousin, searching for a family resemblance, but there was none. Her mother's skin tone and facial structure came from her Hopi heritage. Only the startling shade of green eyes from her father, Hartmut, gave some hint of her Austrian heritage. Fabian's eyes were a dull blue-gray and his skin tone pale. His nose was straight, sort of regal, but his face was flat otherwise. His lack of warmth toward them wasn't endearing him as family.

Eike, on the other hand, was at once likeable even in her dramatics. With that thought, August chastised herself. Dramatics might be unkind considering she was dealing with the loss of her husband. Earlier, Wolf had hedged questions about the wife who was so much younger than her husband. He might find Eike's age and physical attributes distasteful for a man in his eighties like Great-grandfather.

"So, Fabian, how are we related?" She might as well get the conversation going. Why he was at the castle at this time, conveniently when Lenhard supposedly committed suicide, seemed suspicious. At least, that's the vibration she picked up on from Wolf earlier. After meeting the unlikeable Fabian, she wouldn't have trouble agreeing.

He touched an empty drink glass on the table beside him, seemed lost for a moment, but considered her. "My late mother was Lenhard's niece."

"Do you have brothers or sisters?"

Wolf hadn't known of any other relatives, but Fabian might.

"No, I'm an only child. In fact, I am, or was, the only one left in the family." His feet shuffled, and he picked up his empty glass. "Anyone care for a drink?"

He made to scoot from the divan, but Eike's silky voice stopped him.

"We'll have wine with lunch. You can wait, dar…Fabian."

August choked back a giggle. If it was appropriate to call your step-nephew darling, Eike wouldn't have caught herself. She had to hand it to her, the woman showed no sign of a misstep, but smiled sweetly as she corrected herself and smoothly transitioned into conversation.

"Lacy, I'm sorry Lenhard chose to keep you a secret. I can only think his erratic moods of late to blame for not letting me know of your visit." The pink hanky came to her eye as she sniffed.

"He'd been troubled lately?" Her mother's concern clouded her face.

"He'd always been an extremely private person, even with me. The pains of growing older had greatly bothered him." She tilted her chin down. "I feel so to blame. The differences in our age…perhaps I was thoughtless expecting him to keep up with me. I don't know what else to think. Committing suicide?" When she raised her face, her eyes were watery, giving an iridescent glow to her blue irises. "It is such an unexpected shock."

It wouldn't be a shock if it was expected. She slipped a glance at Wolf. He'd been fond of Lenhard and didn't approve of the younger wife, but he kept his face neutral after her admission.

"You can't blame yourself, Eike." Fabian's droll expression changed, softened, his concern for his uncle's wife evident.

What is there between these two?

"Of course you can't," her mother agreed.

"Lenhard was, after all, approaching ninety." Fabian tapped the divan arm. "The incidence of suicide in the elderly is quite high."

"Is that so?" Wolf broke his silence.

"Why yes, it is. I read about it just the other day in the newspaper." Her cousin's chin lifted in a defensive stance.

"Still, I wish I'd been there for him." The pink hanky was flourished again, the initials EL stitched in white on one corner. "He had not wanted to take our early morning walk today, so I went without him."

August glanced at her mother, who still looked concerned. During the conversation with her great-grandfather this morning, he hadn't sounded like a distressed man. As if she'd read her mind, Mom's gaze met hers.

"I'm sorry we didn't read his mood either when we spoke this morning." Her mom scooted slightly forward. "If we'd known, well, maybe we could've contacted you."

"How sweet, Lacy. But how would you know? Fabian and I should have been more in tune to his state of mind."

"He wasn't as social as usual when I arrived. I'm sorry I didn't...do something." The nephew's words were stiff.

She studied her cousin. He didn't look all that stressed over the death of his only relative. Or so he would've assumed his only relative. A fortune and the wife were thought to be his prizes, she suspected, and now, what did the nephew think of his future? Disgust welled up in her chest. She darted a glance at her mother, afraid her thoughts were being read. Her mom had that knack and wouldn't approve of her typical rush to judgment. And just as typical, Mom gave everyone the benefit of assuming truth in their words and smiled with empathy at her new cousin.

Herr Bloch entered the room. "Frau Luschin, lunch is ready."

"Thank you. Please bring it in."

The short, stout man wheeled two carts to the table. Eike stood, signaling everyone else to rise. "Fabian, dear, would you please bring the wine?"

He pulled a bottle of red from a wine rack and a bottle of white from a wine refrigerator next to the liquor cabinet. Eike took the head of the table with Fabian at the other end. She directed Wolf to one side and Mom and her to the other. August took the seat closest to Eike to better watch her cousin from afar without being too obvious. He had trouble disguising his body language, which exposed his less than hospitable feelings toward his newfound relatives.

Once seated, Eike glanced around the table. "*Guten Appétit.*"

As Fabian uncorked the bottles, he asked, "Red or white?"

"Nothing, thank you," Wolf answered.

Her mother chose red, as always. August glanced at the covered dishes on the cart. Herr Bloch smiled and lifted the cover on one of the cart dishes. She recognized *Wienerschnitzel,* veal. "White, please."

"I can't tell you how special it is to have you here on this sad day." Eike dabbed her nose with the hanky and squared her shoulders. "Lenhard…" A sigh.

Apparently, mealtime was not disturbed by the suicide of a husband. Then again, overriding grief, with the comfortable rituals of the wealthy class of Austrians, might explain eating such an elaborate meal within hours of the death of the castle lord. Too bad much of the food would be wasted. Everyone took no more than a polite amount of salad and potatoes onto their plates. Luckily, the coffee had deadened her appetite, and she could follow suit.

Eike waved off food altogether. "Lenhard's favorite meal was midday." Her bottom lip trembled.

"I know this is a very difficult time for you, and we don't want to impose." Mom needlessly wiped her mouth with the napkin. "I hope we can be of assistance to you and not a hindrance."

"That is wonderful of you to offer." Eike signaled for the *Wienerschnitzel* to be added to the table.

"Would tomorrow be too soon to come back and see more of the estate?" She didn't glance at her mother whom she expected would object to her directness. When Mom didn't speak up, she decided her mother might agree with getting all the cards on the table.

The nephew's fork clinked his plate. "Eike has many things to do considering—"

"Fabian, don't do not be rude." She frowned, but smoothed her brow when her glare left him." I know you were expecting to learn more about your grandfather, were you not, Lacy?"

"And my father, Hartmut."

"Of course you were, dear. This is a very sad day for you as well. You must *stay* with us. I will be happy to make Lenhard's personal possessions available to you so you can find answers about your father."

"Oh, Eike. How very generous of you." Mom held her napkin to her mouth as if overcome with emotion, but August could see a smile behind the cloth, too. "We'll go back to St. Veit after lunch and come back tomorrow." Her voice was strong, and if Eike heard the tone correctly, she'd know Mom considered the invitation a formality only.

Cousin Fabian's face looked particularly rigid except for a twitch on the outer corner of his right eye.

Her attention drifted to Wolf who had been quiet. He'd set his fork aside, his forehead had the slightest wrinkle, and he met her gaze through thick, brown lashes. He appeared concerned, yet his eyes were too engaging to get a logical read.

"Would anyone care for dessert?" Eike asked.

She wrenched her gaze from the inspector. Around the table heads shook. She would've liked to at least taste what she assumed would be something she'd not had before, but everyone seemed anxious to end the first meeting.

"It was a lovely meal, Eike, but I'm afraid my appetite…"

"Understood, Lacy. I find difficulty also." She twisted the pink hanky between her fingers.

Her mother stood, signaling Wolf and Fabian to rise. "I think we should leave and let you rest."

"Yes, I suppose I should." Step-grandmother pushed her chair from the table, rising as if it took great effort. "It's been a great surprise to meet you both. I'm so sorry the circumstances…" She swooned and leaned on the table.

All three men jumped to her aid, Fabian at one elbow, Wolf at the other, while the bulk of Herr Bloch slowed him to stand behind her chair.

"Eike?" Fabian leaned close to her face.

"I'm fine, fine." Yet she leaned into her nephew. "Perhaps the doctor's advice to not mix the sedative with alcohol was more than a suggestion." She smiled weakly. "Yes, I'll rest. Lacy, August, tomorrow."

CHAPTER FOUR

Tobias escorted Herr Luschin's granddaughter and great-granddaughter to their rental car, walking respectfully behind. Lacy looked pale after the meeting with Eike and Bauer. August, although solemn, appeared to be concerned for her mother yet otherwise not affected.

An ambulance pulled out from the family's private entrance at the far side of the castle. The women stopped, watching it leave through the gate. Herr Luschin's body on the way to autopsy.

When they reached the car, Lacy addressed him. "Thank you for your help today, Inspector."

"I am sorry for your loss, Lacy. Not being able to meet Herr Luschin..." He wasn't sure where he was going with the words that flowed without thought. *Thoughtless.*

"I'm fine, Inspector. I've had more than a few disappointments in my life, but there's always something good to come from them. I regret not having the opportunity to meet my grandfather, to speak to him, ask him questions, but..." She let her words trail away yet managed a smile.

August patted her back.

"He was a fine gentleman." He opened her car door. "I hope you have a relaxing evening at the Hotel Karnten. You should have dinner in the hotel restaurant. It is the best St. Veit has to offer."

Hopefully, they would find the hotel to their liking and change their minds about staying in Castle Luschin. After interviewing Bauer, he was no less concerned about their safety. The nephew appeared to be a drunken twit, but until a final ruling on Herr Luschin's cause of death had been reached, his possible involvement could not be overlooked.

"Would you like to join us for dinner, Inspector?" Lacy's cheeks pinked.

He gazed on August, who also showed a bit of color in her cheeks, perhaps brought on by her mother's invitation. Keeping his distance might be the professional thing to do, but they all had to eat. One more quick glance at the lovely August—how could he refuse?

"Very nice of you to ask. I'd love to join you for dinner."

****

"There's something hinky about the relationship between Fabian and Eike." August pulled tan slacks from a hanger in the armoire in their hotel room. "Did you pick up on it?" From the shelf, she chose a thin, purple sweater to layer over her red T shirt. Summer nights in St. Veit were cooler than Tucson, Arizona.

"They're both under a great deal of stress. I'm not sure what I'm reading about them." Her mother had donned cream-colored slacks, a long-sleeved, yellow shirt, and draped a deeper yellow cardigan on the bed.

She held the purple sweater out, considering if it would be too light for evening hours. "Wolf got all touchy when I asked about her. Maybe the young wife wasn't so good to Lenhard. And Fabian is the reason why."

Her comment was met with a wrinkled brow. "All touchy?"

"Yeah, he kind of clammed up." She pulled the sweater over her head, added her red scarf around her neck, then facing the mirror, scrunched her hair back in place. "Something's going on there."

"I think you're paying more attention to the inspector than I am."

She ignored her mother's smirk. There was something more than the investigation of her great-grandfather's death bubbling below Wolf's surface. What she picked up on, she wasn't sure. Yet. "He's not telling us everything."

"He wouldn't, August." She ran a brush through her hair. "He has suspicions about Lenhard's death, and he's investigating. More than likely, he's not too sure about us either."

"Ugh. You have more patience with cop-stuff than I do." She plopped onto the foot of the bed. "I just get the feeling he's got something else going on."

The smirk on her mother's face this time was more obvious. "And I'd say you're seeing the man and not the cop."

He was certainly easy on the eyes and ears. "Hardly." She scooped her cell from the side pocket of her purse. "In fact, I'm rather attracted to another cop." From the inside of her purse, she lifted the matchbook Kurt gave her at the castle and flipped it open. She read his phone number, then winked at her mom. "I'm meeting Kurt for a drink later."

Her mother's eyes widened.

She punched in the numbers and listened as the rings ended in a voicemail recording she couldn't understand. "Hmmm." Her thumb depressed the end call button. "I think a text might be better with the language problem." After sending the brief message, she smiled at her mom. "We should be done with dinner by nine, so I'm meeting Kurt in the bar downstairs."

Her mother laughed. "Unbelievable."

"What? You're so concerned about how the divorce hit me. I thought you wanted me to get back on the horse."

"Yes, August. But a cop? I never thought I'd see the day."

Now, she laughed. *How true.* "Well, my *wild* high school days are many years behind me. An arrest or two for smoking pot shouldn't get in my way now."

"Agreed. It's just your general attitude toward police has been less than favorable. I seem to remember an incident that had nothing to do with illegal substances—"

"Mom, please." She raised her hands in protest. "I take a swing at one cop in my life, and you'll never forget it."

The ring of the room phone interrupted their banter. Her heart skipped a beat, and although farther from the phone, she volunteered to answer.

"Hello, August," Wolf's voice greeted her. "I am downstairs in the restaurant. I have a table and will wait for you and Lacy." The accent and smooth delivery pleased her more than she wanted.

"We'll be down shortly, Inspector." Even with effort, she couldn't keep out the softer, girlish tone reserved for men of interest. Her mom heard it, too, judging by the smile and averted gaze. She replaced the phone on the table.

"What possessed you to invite Wolf to have dinner with us?" August kept her voice matter-of-fact as she pulled a hand mirror from her purse and freshened her eyeliner and lipstick. The idea of spending more time with this Austrian James Bond appealed to her even if she wouldn't admit it out loud.

"I want to hear more about Lenhard's life." Her mother scooped her sweater from the bed. "Inspector Wolf was an acquaintance. He might've heard something about Hartmut from Lenhard, too."

"Actually, maybe a social setting will loosen the inspector's tongue. I want to know more about our dear cousin, Fabian. If he did have anything to do with Lenhard's death, he's not the greenest leaf on the family tree. All he had to do was wait, and not very long. How much longer could Lenhard have lived anyway? Fabian would've had the estate soon, or so he thought, considering great-grandfather's age."

"I'm guessing, from our conversations and the fact Lenhard married a second time and younger, that Grandfather was pretty spry for his age." Mom lifted her sweater from the bed. "He might have lived another ten to fifteen years."

"Maybe Fabian couldn't wait that long." She tucked the mirror and makeup into her purse.

"This is really unsavory speculation." Her mother's tone hit a low note.

"Sorry." She stood and gave her mom a hug. "But I'm afraid until the *Polizei* have completed their investigation, the possibilities are gruesome."

"You're absolutely right, kiddo. But I don't have to like it."

The frown on her mom's face bothered her. "Besides, Mom, we're probably way over speculating on this. Let's not worry, okay?"

Her phone buzzed with a text message. Pulling it from the side pocket of her purse, she read and smiled. "Brief and to the point. Kurt says yes." She slung her purse over a shoulder, and walked toward the door. "What did you think of the modernization of the castle's family quarters? Disgusting, huh?"

"I didn't particularly like the look." Mom opened the door to the hallway.

"It'll be interesting to see what Lenhard's private chambers are like."

"I wonder where Grandfather kept things that relate to my father—photos or mementos. Eike did offer to let us look through them." A tone of hope mixed with sadness came through in her voice.

She hugged her shoulders for a moment as the door closed behind them. "I'm sure we'll learn so much about your father soon. Now, let's go find out if Wolf has any more to tell us."

August led the way down to the first floor. At the base of the stairs, the restaurant was on the right side of the landing and the bar to the left. She glanced briefly into the bar, the modern design catching her attention. The butterscotch-colored chairs were only half-occupied. The area behind the bar glittered with hot pink lighting above and the same color as the chairs on the lower half. She angled toward the restaurant, and they stopped at the podium where a tall, thin man with heavy-framed glasses greeted them.

"Can I help you?" the host asked in English.

"Inspector Wolf is waiting for us," August replied.

"This way, please."

"He chose English without asking," she whispered to her mother. "I guess we don't look Austrian."

They skirted the main dining area filled with tables covered in white cloths and walls of deep rust, and followed him out to the patio. There, against the backdrop of stars twinkling above potted pines and evergreens, Wolf reclined at a table. He'd changed from his light gray suit into tan slacks and a brown sports coat. His tanned face and neck were striking against the cobalt blue shirt. She swallowed deeply to relieve the catch between her throat and chest.

****

Tobias smiled and rose from his seat. "I hope you are okay with dining outside. It's quite nice out this evening, and the fresh air will do us all good after this unhappy day."

"A wonderful idea, Inspector Wolf," Lacy answered for them.

The host pulled a chair out for Lacy to his left.

Tobias reached for the chair to his right, but August seated herself across from him. He hoped her choice was to give herself a better view of him, rather than making an unnecessary, independent gesture.

The recessed lighting of the honey-colored patio walls bathed the young woman in a glow that set the spiky ends of her hair on fire. The soft breeze carried a honey scent across the table, and he had an "aha that's the scent" moment, unless the power of suggestion fooled his nose. His stare resulted in a smile as she toyed with the red scarf around her neck, then glanced around.

"Your hotel choice is excellent." He nodded at the two women. "Herr and Frau Siegel, the owners, are friends whom I have known for years. They believe in quality of service. Not only do they maintain a first class establishment, but this restaurant is a top culinary choice."

"Did you write the brochure?" August snickered.

He chuckled with her. "I do sound rather biased."

"Our room is quite nice," Lacy said. "You're not overstating it. I suppose we should reserve judgment on the food until we've eaten. But you've set the bar pretty high."

"The bar? Yes, it is well stocked."

Both women laughed.

Although he enjoyed the ring of their laughter, he was perplexed by the cause. "I take it I misunderstood your meaning."

Before the laughter died, Heidi Siegel, in a crisp white blouse and pencil thin, black skirt, stopped at their table and greeted him in German. "Tobias, how nice to see you."

"Heidi." He rose and embraced his friend.

"Two women tonight?" She whispered in his ear. "About time you did something besides work."

He squeezed her arm and shook his head when he released her, happy that August and Lacy didn't speak German. "I just mentioned you to my dinner guests." He spoke in English.

Heidi blinked then chuckled. "Ah. Then telling tales, are you?"

"Truth and compliments. Heidi, these are visitors from the States. Lacy Meadowlark and August Meyer."

She extended a hand to Lacy then August. "How nice. What brings you to our small city?"

August darted a glance at her mother and answered for them. "Castle Luschin. Lenhard Luschin is my mother's grandfather, my great-grandfather." She grimaced. "I suppose I should say was."

"I am so sorry. I heard about the misfortune only a few moments ago." She glanced at him. "Are you handling…"

"Yes, Heidi."

"Well, then, in good hands." She patted his arm and tipped her head to the women. "Let me start you with some drinks. Cognac, Tobias?"

She knew his choice. A good friend, but also a good hostess. "Yes, thank you."

"And for you, ladies?"

"I'll have wine with dinner so nothing now, thank you," Lacy answered.

"I'll have what Wol...the inspector is having, please." August's eyes grew round for an instant, her crooked smile uncontained.

Apparently, she preferred to call him by his last name only, when not in his company. Perfectly fine. He found it appealing—familiarity he might enjoy.

"I'll bring you water, Ms. Meadowlark, and *Liptauer*—a cheese appetizer—with your drinks."

"Thank you, Heidi. Is Thomas in tonight?" Although he saw her husband at the monthly meetings of *Der Neue Widerstand,* The New Resistance, he hadn't been able to spend much time with his friend in a long while. Tobias's off-duty schedule had become increasingly busy.

"He'll be in later." She patted his hand. "I'll get your drinks."

"She's very nice." August opened her menu as Heidi left. "And she reminds me a little of Eike with the very blonde, short-cropped hair and her height."

"The resemblance ends there."

She glanced up from the menu, eyes wide.

He couldn't help the annoyance that had crept into his voice at the mention of Eike. "Their personalities are *quite* different."

"But physically? Correct me if I'm wrong, but Aryan comes to mind."

August was either very intuitive or visually driven. "They could, perhaps, have similar lineage. It's part of our history." He pushed the menu aside. The Aryan subject always fascinated Americans. "Are you familiar with our history?"

She shook her head. "Only superficial stuff I might have retained from school. I could probably give you more art history facts of Austria than any other kind."

"Then I guess you were impressed with the Great Hall. As I understand it, the Luschin family possesses some extraordinary works of art."

"Oh, I'm impressed all right."

Her eyes sparkled, and even in the dim light, her cheeks were visibly pinked with enthusiasm. She launched into a description of what she'd seen in the den as well as the Great Hall and her words were punctuated with animation. He recognized a few of the names, but was more enthralled by the passion she exuded than the brief art lesson. He'd never found the mention of the sixteenth and seventeenth centuries quite so sensual.

Heidi arrived at the table with a tray of drinks and the appetizer. "Do you know what you'd like, or shall I come back?"

Lacy studied the menu, but gave up with Heidi's question. "I have no idea. I don't normally ask someone else to choose my food, but I may have to defer to you, Inspector Wolf."

"August?"

The headstrong young woman surprised him and pushed her menu in his direction. "I like surprises. The responsibility's on your shoulders."

"Good. Please bring us *Lammkeulen mit Erbsen und Kartoffeln*, Heidi, and a bottle of *Gruener Veltliner*." To the two American women he added, "This is a pork chop dish and a local white wine I'm sure you'll enjoy."

"Excellent." His friend gathered the menus and left the patio.

"I did a bit of research on the estate and the Luschin family, Inspector," Lacy said. "I discovered they'd lost it for a brief time when it fell into the hands of the Nazis in World War II." She sipped her water. "What little I learned is fascinating." Her thumb made circles on the side of her glass. "I'd hoped to get a firsthand history lesson." Startling green eyes saddened for a moment.

There was nothing he could say. He doubted whether Fabian or Eike would be much help to her. "There are few left who can give us their account."

"You said your grandfather and Lenhard were friends. Does your family live in a castle?" August asked.

"We do have a smaller estate east of Castle Luschin." A wave of nostalgia he'd not felt in a long time came with the mention of his childhood home. He hadn't stepped foot on the estate in several years. "There are many castles in Austria. For over five hundred years, this was the center of the Holy Roman Empire. The Hapsburg and Badenburg dynasties of Austria held power over much of Europe."

"And did the Nazis take over your castle during the war, too?" August leaned forward.

"We...no, actually, that was not the case with our land." And not a subject he cared to discuss with anyone. "What do you think of the *Liptauer*?"

"Wonderful." Lacy swallowed. "And I've never had such tasty pumpernickel. I think I could have this for dinner. Is there goat's milk cheese in the spread?"

Tobias shrugged. "It's a blend, so could be."

"*I've* found my new favorite drink." August lifted her Remy Martin cognac.

"Then perhaps we've found our first common ground." He raised his glass to her and then sipped. Her eyes audaciously smiled back.

"Have you learned anything more about my grandfather's death, Inspector?"

Lacy's question drew him away from the silent exchange he sensed with her daughter.

"Nothing definitive, but it is early. Tomorrow, we'll be able to review all the interviews and facts gathered from today."

"What do you think of Fabian?" August toyed with the rim of her snifter.

"In what reference?"

"In regards to my great-grandfather and the estate that now isn't his." Her eyes shone brighter than the dim lighting. "If anyone is to come under suspicion, he's sitting in the perfect seat, don't you think?"

"Hmm." Discussing his opinions openly with these women wouldn't be professional. Yet, because they were in the middle of this case, they were the perfect ones to bounce off ideas. They were just enough removed and just enough involved. Still, not typical protocol…

"Come on, Inspector Wolf, surely you have some idea of his involvement, or at least some suspicion."

The inquisitive daughter would prove to be a challenge, and one he would enjoy.

"I'm quite an opinionated man, August, but I'm not at liberty to discuss my opinions about an open investigation."

Heidi and a waiter stopped at their table, trays of food on their arms. A welcomed interruption. "Would you care for another cognac or shall I open the wine?" she asked as the young man dispersed the plates.

"August?" he asked.

"No more for me, thank you."

"We'll move on to the wine, Heidi."

Uncorked and ready for pouring, she offered him the first taste. "Splendid," he judged.

She poured each a half-glass, the young man withdrew from the table, and Heidi smiled. "Let me know if you require anything else, *bitte.*"

August picked up the interrupted conversation immediately upon Heidi's absence. "Then let's hear your opinions as a man, Tobias Wolf." Her lips parted slightly and his name rolled off her tongue like a verbal aphrodisiac.

He shifted in his seat and looked away from her for a moment. When he glanced back, her eyes blinked slowly with insatiate curiosity. The evening had not mellowed her inquisitive nature.

He cleared his throat and met her gaze straight on. "Unfortunately, I'm in my inspector role even as we dine, and my opinions must be kept to myself."

She set her fork down, canted forward as if to say more, but Lacy interjected. "Then perhaps you can give us some history. I found it fascinating that the Luschin family lost the estate during the war, but were able to regain it. Lenhard must have been a young boy at the time."

The verbal dance, more of a tango, with August ended. She leaned back in her chair, her head tilted at an angle, and her crooked smile hinted there would be more to come.

"Yes, he was. My grandfather was a young teen. The Nazis marched into Austria in 1938 and began expropriating property. Castle Luschin was targeted for the center of SS activities in the area. The Luschin family didn't sympathize with the Nazis and were forced out in early 1941." And for that, he held a high respect for the family. He expanded his chest with a deep breath to loosen the tightness brought on by speaking of the history.

"Out of the country?" Lacy frowned as if concerned.

"No, only from their home. They remained in the area until the occupation ended."

"Thank goodness it ended by 1945. Those four years must have been very hard on the family. What a horrible time for Austria, and all of Europe, and hopefully not to be experienced again."

"Only if we keep vigilant, Lacy." *Always vigilant.*

"What do you mean?" August tipped her head and frowned. "There can't possibly be Nazi sentiments anymore. Austria seems such a *mellow* country."

"Ah, well, we are a quiet people for the most part, tied closely to our land and our traditions and not prone to radical politics of domination. But there are stirrings."

He sipped his wine and stared into the young woman's face. What beautiful, high cheekbones she possessed. She leaned forward with interest. Her naiveté concerning Austria was youthful, yet charming.

"The roots of the Nazi movement were never killed, August, only stunted for a while."

"Really?"

The door to the patio opened, and two men dressed in traditional *Burschenshaften* strolled to the far side and took seats at a table. His stomach muscles tightened with their appearance. Although they had removed the customary red sashes that slung from shoulder to waist and the brimless, gold and black caps, the white coats with gold ropes across the opening of their jackets and the black trim at the neck and cuffs could not be mistaken.

"The men who just took seats to your left?" He didn't glance in their direction, not giving the men cause to think he took any notice of them.

Her glance produced a smile. "You mean the marching band members?"

"Marching band?"

"Yeah, the uniforms look like something a college marching band would wear." She shrugged. "Kind of geeky."

"Geeky?"

She laughed. "Sorry, lapsing back into my school days. You know, silly, unattractive."

"Ah, well, not so innocuous...or geeky." He took a sip of wine to smooth his distaste. "The *Burschenshaften* have a two-hundred-year history of loyalty to the German state. Hess and Himmler were *Burschenshaften*. Those two probably just came from a meeting. Until recently, the members were more secretive about their organization, and you wouldn't have seen them blatantly appearing in public in uniform."

"And what changed that?" Lacy asked.

"The state of world affairs. And a faction of our government is in support of fascism." His shoulders drooped with the weight of his knowledge while his gut churned with a desire to wipe the proponents of the growing cancer from the face of the earth. "Sadly, there are pockets all over the world in support of radical authoritarian nationalism."

The tone of Wolf's voice brought gooseflesh to August's scalp.

"Are all Austrians aware of what's happening?"

"Not enough of them. But we're working on that."

"As an inspector, that's part of your job?"

"I'm speaking as a citizen." One eyebrow rose. "As a man."

The gooseflesh now skittered down her neck and arms in a more pleasurable way. The by-the-book inspector, although urbane, was interesting. Wolf, the man, had an undercurrent of passion.

She just might like to get to know the man.

She set her fork on her plate. "So, this is what you do when you aren't working?"

"I'm a student of World War II. It was a very complicated time period and still has ramifications in today's world. And I'm sorry to ramble on so. How was your pork chop?"

"You certainly aren't rambling." Her mother tucked her napkin under the side of her plate. "It's fascinating, although alarming. And the dinner was every bit as good as you hyped."

August glanced at her wristwatch. Hopefully, golden Kurt wouldn't arrive early.

"But I must be boring your daughter." He smiled from one corner of his mouth.

"No, no. I just wondered what time it was." She almost wished she'd not followed through on the late date. Dessert, an after-dinner drink, and more conversation with Wolf wouldn't have been such a bad way to spend the remainder of the evening. "I've thoroughly enjoyed myself." His brow cocked again at her words. She wished he'd stop doing that. He probably knew it was a totally disarming gesture. "The food. Yes, the dinner, the cognac. Really good."

"Am I hearing you are not interested in dessert and a *Schnapps*?" he asked.

Totally up for it, but totally can't. "It's been a long day. Aren't you tired, Mom?"

Her mother darted a glance in her direction as if a shared secret could be exposed at any moment. Her gaze slid away, and she addressed Wolf without exposing her reason for retreat. "I'm pretty beat. Do you mind, Inspector?"

"Of course not."

Heidi appeared. "Are you going to have dessert?"

"No, not tonight."

She nodded and glanced at each of them. "I hope you enjoyed

your meal and were able to relax. With complements of Thomas and myself."

"Now, Heidi—" Wolf protested.

She waved a hand toward him. "No discussion. *Gute Nacht!*"

"Thank you so much," she and her mother chimed in as their hostess left the table.

August scooted her chair back. "Will you call us with any information you learn tomorrow?"

"I'm sure I'll see you at the estate. Are you still determined to stay there?"

"I think it best," her mom answered. "I'm not exactly sure what to do next. I'll call my lawyer tomorrow. And we want to help Eike any way we can."

"Well, then…" He tucked a finger into the breast pocket of his jacket and came out with two business cards. As they stood, he handed one to each of them. "Feel free to call me."

"Do you have an extra one?" She dipped into the side pocket of her purse and found a pen. He stepped closer. Her heart kicked up a notch as she took the proffered card and jotted her cell number on the back. "Here's my number. If you need to reach me—us."

"Marvelous idea, August." He tucked the card into his breast pocket, and she felt a ridiculous connection with him over the action. "I'll see you to the stairs."

Although Mom moved toward the patio door leading to the inside dining area, she lingered just long enough for Wolf to come around the table and step beside her. They walked in silence, a breath apart, into the restaurant and on to the stairs leading to their room. The faintest scent of sandalwood and cardamom drifted over her.

"I hope you both sleep well." He smiled and left them at the base of the stairs.

"Goodnight," she murmured.

Cardamom. The Arabs considered cardamom an aphrodisiac.

CHAPTER FIVE

Tobias needed to get his thoughts elsewhere and not on August. His job and his attractions had never been a problem to keep separate—she was testing his ability to do so now. He headed to the bar after she and Lacy went to their room. If Heidi's husband had arrived, he'd be serving drinks, and they could chat for a while.

Thomas shook a martini at the end of the bar. The back of his crisp, white shirt took on the color of the hot pink wall behind him. His tall, slender build gave no clue to his young-man days as a fearless hockey forward. Only the nose, slightly askew from more than one encounter on the ice, spoke to his past love of the sport.

Happy to see his friend, Tobias leaned a hip against an open barstool and nodded when Thomas looked up as he set the martini in front of his customer.

The owner-bartender's face broke into a wide grin, and he sidestepped over. "I hear you had double the pleasure tonight."

He smirked. "Your wife talks too much."

"You want a drink?"

Tobias slid onto the stool. "I'll take a cup of coffee."

"American relatives of Herr Luschin?" Thomas poured a cup and set it on the bar in front of him.

He sipped the strong, black coffee. "Remember his son who took off for the States and never made it back? He was killed in a plane crash. Lacy Meadowlark is his daughter."

His friend shook his head and wiped the counter below the bar. "Too bad. I take it she didn't know the lord died this morning before she arrived."

"No. She and her daughter, August, were shocked."

A movement to his left and a laugh caught his attention. The two men dressed in *Burschenshaften* uniforms he'd seen earlier left the building.

"Hmph." Thomas noticed them also. He wiped the bar next to the coffee cup and leaned in, his voice low. "The taller one's an *Amtsleiter*. New to the city council."

"I don't remember him running on his *Burschenshaften* credentials," Tobias muttered. "Getting damned bold, aren't they?"

"Who do you suppose is holding meetings around here?"

Tobias raised his cup to his lips as he glanced at the few patrons in the bar. Not knowing who might be listening, he decided to hold his comment. He had a couple of candidates in mind, but he would discuss his suspicions at the next meeting of *Der Neue Widerstand*. He and Thomas's involvement with the organization to combat the rise of the neo-Nazi movement was as secretive as the groups they were trying to stop.

The hotel owner appeared to sense his reluctance to carry the subject further. "Talk has it Herr Luschin committed suicide."

He sipped his coffee without comment. Even with his old friend, his speculations had to remain unspoken. "Too early for a final determination."

"Pretty strange." Thomas pronounced each syllable distinctly and set the rag on the counter below the bar.

"Yeah? How do you mean?"

He leaned on the bar, palms flat. "The old lord and his cronies were in here yesterday for lunch. They come in at least once a week. They're a jovial bunch of elderly guys, in spite of their old family, aristocratic attitudes. Herr Luschin seemed his usual self, from my vantage point."

"Your opinion is part of a chorus." Tobias drummed his fingers on the bar. "I have more questions to ask before the case is closed on Herr Luschin."

"I'm sure you'll figure it out." Thomas sniffed, his crooked nose wrinkling. "I'll miss seeing the old lord around."

He agreed, then moved on to other community news. Once his coffee was gone, he stood. "See you next week if not before."

"By the way, Heidi says you and the young American woman are, shall we say—"

"We *shouldn't* say. Your wife…" He raised his hands in the symbolic stop gesture.

Thomas laughed. "I know, I know. Good night, Tobias."

He exited into the cool night air, paused on the step to admire the stars overhead, then approached his car as he dug into his pocket for the keys. Voices at the far end of the building drifted over. Only half-registering the unintelligible conversation, he glanced in their direction as he opened the car door. The two *Burschenshaften* were climbing into a sedan, but it was a third man who interested him.

Polizist Kurt Gruber.

The young officer, off duty and in civilian clothes, leaned down and spoke to the driver as he settled in his seat. Tobias slid into his car and started the engine as Gruber straightened and watched the sedan pull out of the lot.

Interesting.

Was the policeman dealing out some advice on flaunting their ill-advised politics, or was he a friend of the *Burschenshaften*?

Tobias had no idea what political leanings Gruber had, and technically it was none of his business. Yet…

****

Once again at the bottom of the stairs, August scanned what she could see of the restaurant and bar. Dinner with Wolf had been more enjoyable than she'd expected and had dulled the anticipatory edge to a late date with Kurt. She spotted him at the far side of the bar sitting at a high, round table.

No longer in police uniform, his black, short-sleeved shirt exposed the fit arms she'd only guessed. Without the beret on his head, his white-blond hair shone brighter than the dim lighting of the bar. Dressed in black without the beret, muscles displayed, and with his short-cropped hair—he looked less cute and more cookie-cutter handsome.

He stood and extended his hand as she neared the table. "August. How wonderful to see you again."

"Hi, Kurt. Hope I didn't keep you waiting."

"No, no. I'm fine." His handshake was more of a caress. "I do not mind waiting for you."

She climbed onto the high stool.

He stood straight and formal not taking a seat. "What would you like?"

"A glass of white wine would be great."

"We have some very fine local wines. May I choose one for you?"

"Thank you, I'd like that."

While he waited at the bar, he glanced over his shoulder and smiled. The handsome Golden Boy still gave the impression of a policeman, even in civilian clothes. This morning, the cocky tilt of his beret had seemed in contrast to his position. Now, he held himself erect, and his youthful, fit body stood as if he was on guard at all times. Some women might be impressed but her—not so much. She found herself wishing she'd not been so quick to contact him.

Kurt set her wine on the table and slid onto the stool. "This is from my favorite winery in Klagenfurt. It's a bit sweet for after dinner."

She sipped, not particularly impressed, but then, she wasn't a sweet wine lover. "Hmm, nice."

His confidence shone in his smile. "Were you able to see any more of the castle?"

August sighed with pleasure at the remembered short tour with Wolf. "We received a mini-tour of the buttery, bottlery, and private quarters by way of a passageway behind the Great Hall." Her mind wandered more to Wolf than to the castle tour.

"Was that quite enjoyable for you?"

She blinked away Wolf visions, "Loved it," then sipped her wine. "Passageways and antiquated rooms. All this castle stuff and European art may be commonplace for *you*, but I'm fascinated."

He closed in on her personal space, resting his arm within inches of hers. "Is this your first trip to Austria?"

She tapped her foot on the rail around the bottom of her stool. Fatigue seeped into her muscles, and she stifled a yawn. "Yes. How about you? Have you been to the States?"

"No, I've not been out of Europe." He shrugged, then squared his shoulders, sitting even straighter if that was possible. "There is much to see and do in my homeland."

"Your homeland. That's such an old-fashioned word." There was something about the way Kurt said homeland that had an entirely different connotation than when Wolf spoke of Austria. Dinner conversation drifted across her mind.

"There are some who think I have…er…let me think…" His brow furrowed. "Yes, you are correct in using the term. They think I have old-fashioned ideas. Yes, that is it."

Old-fashioned might fit him with his close-cropped hair and formal demeanor, at least by the standards of American men of their age. What he thought that would put him in the category, she didn't understand, but the conversation was at least getting more interesting. "What do you mean?"

Kurt's jaw tightened, and his face took on hard lines. "Some believe we should move away from the ideas of our fathers. There is much glory in our past, and they do not understand the true ideas for the future are found in our history."

Austrian history was a recurring theme tonight, although Golden Boy spoke of glory while Wolf expressed sad sentiments and a cautionary tale. A vision of Kurt standing and clicking his heels like a Nazi soldier from an old movie brought a shiver to her arms. "The glory you speak of—"

He waved a hand of dismissal. "*Ach*. We are too serious. A discussion for another day." His shoulders relaxed slightly, and he leaned on the table. "Let me tell you about the wine you are drinking. We have great Austrian wine."

She listened to a verbal tour of the local wine country, which migrated into a discussion about sites in the area she should see. Although cute, as she'd decided earlier in the day, Kurt was a bit dull. She found him…young.

Her mind wandered yet again to Wolf—older, sophisticated, and anything but boring. How odd…must have something to do with the police vibe Kurt gave off. Or maybe Wolf's more *unique* connection to castles and history.

"August?"

She'd lost track of what he'd been saying. "Sorry, Kurt. I'm tired." With the last sip of her wine, she stretched and sat straighter. "I should probably get back to my room."

"Oh? So early?" His hand snaked across the table and clutched her wrist. "Can I not offer you one more or perhaps go somewhere else?"

"Thanks, but I'm beat."

When she moved her arm, his fingers gripped her wrist firmer. The touch was anything but flirtatious, and her lips pinched at the pressure.

"A more relaxing atmosphere somewhere else would help." His

dimpled smile might've been meant to charm, but came off too practiced.

She scooted from the stool and stood, extricating her arm from his grip. "I don't think so. This has been an emotional day for us, and I'm drained. I need to make sure Mom's doing okay."

He stood stiffly. "All right. Will you be staying long, or do you have reason to hurry home? Work or personal affairs?"

Ignoring his prying, she answered, "I really don't know when we'll leave."

"We will meet again?" He took her hand into both of his.

"Sure. You know where I'm staying, and you have my number. But I think we'll be awfully busy for the next couple of days with Eike and the affairs at the castle." She pulled her hand away, smiled, and shrugged. "We'll see." The fascination with golden Kurt left as quickly as it had come. "Thanks for the wine. Goodnight."

August left him standing by the table and dragged her feet to climb the stairs to her room. She was drained, no exaggeration there. One mystery had been solved today. Her attraction to Policeman Kurt was first impression, skin-deep only. Wolf would be a much more complicated attraction to decipher.

****

Tobias closed the book, set it on the nightstand, and switched off the lamp. His head sank into the pillow as his fingers drummed on his chest. The book's subject matter, the roles women played during the Hitler years, deeply interested him, but tonight, his thoughts wandered to other women.

Lacy and August.

Concern for the American women thrummed in the back of his mind like a distant drum roll he couldn't silence, no matter where he tried to steer his concentration.

Herr Luschin's death could be accidental, suicide, or murder. He'd have to wait for the toxicity analysis to make a better determination between accident and suicide. Like a puzzle piece being forced into the wrong slot, neither felt like a fit. The old lord seemed to have every reason to live. If Bauer killed him to gain his inheritance sooner, then staying at the castle could put Lacy and August in the wrong place at the wrong time.

He thumped the pillow on each side of his head and attempted to get comfortable.

If he'd read them correctly, Bauer and Eike were having an affair. Even if Herr Luschin found out, he didn't seem the type to kill himself over a woman. Eike…

He glanced at the book on his nightstand. The neo-Nazi party had been particularly active lately in this part of Austria, according to his inside sources.

He'd like to know exactly where Eike Luschin figured into the political stirrings.

If he couldn't dissuade Lacy and August from staying at the castle, then having them close to Eike could expose more facts about her activities outside of her duties as Frau Luschin. The women would hear and see things that might be helpful, even if they weren't aware of what they were observing.

Tobias shoved his hands behind his head and groaned. Using Lacy and August to further his investigation of Eike's involvement with the neo-Nazi movement was not…what? Honorable? Not using every means available to kill the spread of the Nazi cancer wasn't honorable, either.

He sighed. If the American women stayed at Castle Luschin, and as long as the investigation of the lord's death continued…he'd just have to spend more time at the estate.

August spends time with Eike; he spends time with August. He rolled to his side and smiled into the darkness. The excuse was certainly logical.

****

Eike watched the brush rake through her crop of short, spiky, platinum blonde hair as if her hand was a bodiless appendage moving in the mirror. Her mind drifted from gloomy thought to possible scenario, but couldn't grab hold of any uplifting outcome. She'd known this day would come, even as she stood in the private chapel saying her vows with Lenhard five years ago. A tear trickled down her cheek, and she batted it away.

She tossed the brush onto her dresser, finger-combed the sides of her hair, and with a deep breath, stood.

A tap on her door echoed behind her. She smiled, cupped her breasts to bring them higher in her lounging robe, and padded across the room.

Opening the door only enough to peer out, she smiled at the expected face close to the opening. "Fabian might yet be awake," she whispered.

"No. He's passed out. I can hear snoring through his door."

The golden-haired, young man lightened her mood. "And why are you here?"

"I saw your distress today. Once off duty, I knew I had to soothe your grief." He pushed lightly against the door. "May I, Frau Luschin? I am at your service." He clicked his heels.

When he slipped in, she closed the door quickly. "Yes, Kurt, I do need some comfort and a strong arm around me now." Leaning into him, she swept her hands over tight muscled sides. "I thought you'd be much later."

"The young American was tired. I learned very little." His hand slipped under her chin and brought her gaze to his face. "There really isn't much we need to know. They're standing in your way—our way—Eike."

She blinked. "I haven't had time to think." Another tear toppled onto her cheek.

He dashed it away with his thumb and pulled her close. "Relax for now."

With her head on his chest, she relished strong, young hands sliding down her back then cupping her bottom. His thumbs and fingertips gripped firmly and the pressure uplifted her mood, reminding her of her own strength.

His warm breath caressed the top of her head. "Your cause is my cause."

****

The next morning, August pushed away her plate and a half-eaten breakfast pastry. Her stomach churned with excitement, and the pastry wasn't settling.

Her mother sat on the corner of the bed, phone to her ear. "Yes, give me voice mail." After a brief message to her lawyer, she ended the call and stood. "Mark's left the office for the day. Well, it's actually the end of the day in Arizona. He's in court tomorrow. I don't suppose there's any huge hurry to speak to him. The estate isn't going anywhere." She closed her suitcase.

"And you'll know more after today, probably." August poured another cup of coffee and splashed in some cream. "One more cup and I'll be ready to roll."

Her mother strolled around the room checking drawers, peeking under the bed, and inspecting the bathroom. "I think we have everything." A rap on the door followed her words. "They're here for the bags."

With one last gulp of coffee, she stood. "I'm ready."

They followed the attendant to their car. Bright sunshine bathed the ancient city in warm yellow light. August's feet touched down on the cobbled street, and she wobbled on the uneven surface as she envisioned medieval carriages and horses traversing these same stones. Across from the hotel, a fountain stood in the center of a roundabout. Water poured from the mouth of a man's head carved in gray stone. On the other side of the roundabout, patrons sat eating breakfast at a sidewalk café. As anxious as she was to explore Castle Luschin, St. Veit invited her to browse. Hopefully, there would be time in the days ahead.

"You know I could drive, Mom," she volunteered while the bags were loaded into the trunk.

"Don't trust my driving anymore?"

"You *are* kind of crazy." She snickered. "But I thought if you're at all skittish about the road up to the castle…and just because. I really don't mind driving."

Her mom opened the door and slid into the driver's seat. "I'm fine."

During the twenty-minute trip to Castle Luschin, her mother mused about what history they might uncover in her grandfather's belongings. A tone of excitement had replaced the melancholy. There could be photo albums and keepsakes that would paint a picture of the father she hadn't known.

When the castle came into view, the gate stood open as if welcoming them. They drove onto the circular drive, around the bailey, to the side door leading up to the private quarters. As they stepped out of the car, Herr Bloch came from the family entrance and into the sunshine. Although overweight, the man looked fit with his ruddy cheeks and broad chest. She guessed him to be in his early fifties.

"*Guten Tag.*" He smiled broadly.

"*Guten Tag,*" August answered his good day greeting.

Her mother held out her hand. "Hello, Herr Bloch. Nice to see you again."

His smile grew wider as he took her hand, and he bowed his head slightly. "I am here to escort you to your chambers. You have luggage?"

"Yes. We'll take the small cases." Her mother opened the trunk.

With the two heaviest suitcases in hand, he led the way. August pulled the heavy wooden door closed then joined Herr Bloch and her mother in the center of the circular entry. The area was bare of any decoration or windows. Six electric sconces provided dim lighting. Stairs curved upward and disappeared into rounded, stone-brick walls.

"Please, come this way." The man led them to the base of the stairs.

She attempted to get her bearings as to where the staircase could lead. "Are the guest quarters in a different area of the castle from the solar?" August peered upward, but the curvature made it impossible to see anything except stone walls.

"No, they are down the hall from the guest rooms. This is the private entrance."

When they reached the top, she understood his meaning. If she looked to the left, the doors to the family chambers were down the hall and across from the staircase they'd traversed from the kitchen with Wolf yesterday. Directly to her right, on the opposite side of the hall, were two doors. Herr Bloch opened the far one. She supposed the other guest room was occupied by Cousin Fabian.

Bloch gestured for them to enter, and set the cases down inside the doorway. The room was sparsely furnished with a nightstand between two standard beds, a small wardrobe, and a two-drawer dresser. A deep-set fireplace took up half of one wall and a door next to that. A chair and tiny round table stood on the other side. A window and second door took up the outside wall.

"The private bathroom is there next to the fireplace. Next to the window is the exit to a small balcony." He bowed slightly. "Please make yourselves comfortable. There are bottles of water in the small cabinet next to the bureau. Would you like coffee or tea?"

Her mom shook her head then questioned August with her eyes.

"Nothing now, thank you," she answered for both of them.

"Herr Bloch, when can we meet with Eike?" her mom asked.

"Frau Luschin is still in chambers and asked me to show you to your room. She will be with you later. She is…not feeling well."

"Do you know if Fabian is around?" She decided a little meet with the cousin would be a good place to start.

"I'm sorry. I haven't seen Herr Bauer this morning." As he backed toward the door, he gestured to a large black telephone on one of the nightstands. With its circular dial and receiver, it could've been lifted right out of a 1950s movie. "If you need anything, please pick up the phone. Someone in the kitchen will answer." He left the room, closing the door behind him.

"Hmph." She set her hands on her hips. "Some grand welcoming this is for the new *Frauen* of the castle."

"I guess we'll get unpacked and then see what happens." Her mother pushed her suitcase over with an irritated shove. "If someone doesn't show up by the time we're settled, we'll do some exploring on our own."

She drove a fist into the air. "We'll storm the bastion and take no prisoners!"

Mom laughed and pulled clothes from her suitcase. "Not until we put our things away, okay?"

Wheeling her case around her mother's, she opened it and lifted a pile of tops and tees to the bureau. "There're no corners in this room." After she dropped the last of her things in a drawer, she headed for the balcony door. Once outside, she called back, "Mom, we've been banished to the tower."

With the family quarters down the hall, this must have been the lookout and now converted to a guest room. The balcony was not much more than a two-person viewing area enclosed in waist-high stone. Although they were on the second floor, the high ceilings of the first floor put the view up more than two stories of a typical house. She could see the edge of the bailey to her right, more castle to her left, and above it all the magnificent Alps.

"You need to see this view."

Her mother stepped out. "Oh, my!"

She moved over to make room. "Kind of makes the mountains around Scottsdale look like piles of rock, doesn't it?"

With a laugh, Mom rested her hands on the ledge of the stone wall. But as she leaned against the enclosure, a scraping noise interrupted her laughter. The top of the balcony wall suddenly gave way, sliding into the air.

"No!" She grabbed her mother's waist and yanked backwards. Stumbling, she fell beneath her as they tumbled into the open doorway of the room. "Umph." Her butt, then shoulder, landed on the carpet runner.

Mom bounced off her and ended up sprawled beside her. "Good grief."

August came up on her elbows. "Are you okay?"

Her mother sat up, inventoried her arms and hands and nodded. "Mostly. A little scrape on my wrist, but I'm fine. My heart's still in my throat." She took a deep breath. "Did I crush you?"

"Nah." Her heart pounded as she rose on her knees to glance over the railing. "Good thing no one was below." She took a deep breath, rolled her shoulders, and stood. Stooping, she examined the balcony. There were definite cracks in whatever the material was that held the stones together and missing chunks of rock here and there. *Old age. Ancient age.*

"This room must not get used too often." Mom stood in the doorway. "The castle *looks* well kept…"

August tested the stone along the rest of the enclosure. "The whole top layer is loose. That's dangerous."

"We'll tell Herr Bloch and limit our balcony use." Her mother retreated back into the room.

August peered from her high vantage point. A door opened farther along the castle below the balcony. Kurt Gruber's head appeared from behind the door. She stepped back and crouched, watching him scan in both directions before he exited. *How odd.* He was dressed in jeans and dark blue T-shirt. In a brisk gait, he ducked into the foliage at the end of the wall.

"What are you doing out there?" her mother called.

"I'm spying." She came back into the room, shutting the door behind her. "Guess who I just saw sneaking out of the castle?"

"Sneaking?"

"Very much clandestine. *Politzist* Kurt."

"He was probably here on police business. I highly doubt he's—"

"He's in civilian clothes, and he ducked into the bushes, making sure no one saw him."

Her mother stopped unpacking and stared at her. "That seems a little strange, but he probably knows someone here. Maybe Herr Bloch or someone. I wonder if there's a parking area or something on the other side of the bushes."

"Maybe, but why the secrecy?"

"*If* secrecy." Mom rubbed a length of hair across her chin. "You might have read him wrong. The door could lead to other living quarters, you know. For gardeners or maids or whoever else that might live on the grounds. The trek into the bushes could be a short cut to somewhere." She shook her head and smiled. "Your imagination is on overload."

"I don't know." Only a part of her believed that. "Maybe I need some fresh air. I wouldn't mind getting out and taking a hike around the grounds." She opened her small case and set cosmetics on the top of the bureau. "You haven't gotten a run in a couple of days, Mom. Aren't you missing it?"

"You bet I am. Maybe later we should—" A knock sounded. "I'll get it."

August glanced over her shoulder. Herr Bloch stood in the hall speaking to her mother. He frowned, nodded, and bowed slightly. More words, then she closed the door.

"What?"

"He seemed mystified about the wall." Her mother closed her suitcase and shoved it under the bed. "He's not sure when he can get it repaired. And it looks like you get your wish." She plopped onto the bed. "We're to meet Herr Bloch in the kitchen in an hour where we'll pick up our picnic lunch, and he'll direct us to a hiking path."

"Seriously?" Indignation tightened her stomach muscles. "We're being told to go take a hike?" She threw a thumb out in the universal sign language.

Her mom snickered. "Yes, I guess we are."

"And you're not pissed?"

"No, August, I'm not." She brushed long, ebony hair from her shoulder and gave a brief smile. "Eike is in chambers, quote-unquote, and will join us later this afternoon."

Her mother's empathetic nature was amazing.

"Excuse me?"

"She's upset, I'd say." Her mother's expression held nothing but sympathy.

Searching her own feelings, sympathy hadn't made much of a showing. "More upset than yesterday?" Eike had been teary but appeared more detached than sorrowful.

"Everyone mourns differently. I'm sure she was on some sort of relaxer yesterday. Our appearance was a surprise, don't forget. Lenhard's death may have just hit home this morning. It can take a while for something like losing a husband to sink in."

The memory of her father's death smacked her like a wet rag. "Oh, Mom, I'm sorry." It had only been about three and a half years since he was killed in a mountain climbing accident. Of course her mother could relate to suddenly losing a husband. Lenhard's death could be dredging up painful memories. She wrapped an arm around her mom's shoulder.

"No need for sympathy, kiddo. I'm only pointing out why we should give Eike some latitude. I doubt she means to be rude."

"Okay, I'll give her that." She opened her arms toward the mountains. "Besides, I think a walk in the fresh air with such a magnificent view can only do us some good." She opened a drawer to pull out shorts, but changed her mind. "I think I'll call Penny first." Plopping onto the bed, she grabbed her purse from the nightstand as her butt hit the mattress. "She'll be manning the hotel front desk at the Grand View right now."

"Can she take calls when she's working?"

"She's the lady in charge at night."

Mom unbuttoned her blouse. "After I change, I'll call Chance. If we stay much longer, maybe he could hang up his sheriff's badge for a few days and join us."

She smiled inwardly at the joy that crept into her mother's voice at the mention of her new husband.

CHAPTER SIX

Albert eased onto the leather and chrome chair beside Tobias's desk. "The preliminary autopsy report is back on the lord of Castle Luschin."

He dropped his pen and leaned back. The black leather squeaked with the shift in weight. "And?"

"An apparent overdose of a prescription drug." His partner brought his leg up and crossed his ankle over his knee.

"There was that much in his system?"

"Yes, there was. You think the old guy was losing it? Forgot he took it—twice—*and* took it a couple of more times?"

He rubbed the back of his neck and stared beyond Albert's head. From the second story window, blue sky and one wispy cloud filled his vision. "No. I do not." He hadn't seen Lenhard in a while, and all they had to go on was Eike's summation of his mental state. The staff felt differently, but…more investigation was needed. He regarded his partner. "At least it's doubtful."

"You didn't see him all that often, did you?" Albert spread his hands in question. "My father-in-law went pretty fast once his mind starting going."

Tobias gazed upon the bookcase that took up half a wall and thought about the few times he'd seen the old lord over the last few months. The antique clock on the middle shelf held his attention for a moment, a stark contrast to the modern office, and he was reminded of the estate where he grew up. A very old memory of his grandfather and Herr Luschin playing chess came to mind. "I saw him now and then. Besides, if his thought processes had become so jumbled, wouldn't his wife take over administering his medicines? Look at the statements you took and his activities the day before—no, I don't think he'd lost it."

"Then suicide?"

He leaned forward, elbows on his desk and shook his head. "Doesn't make sense." Then drummed his fingers on the desk pad. "He was excited to learn he had a granddaughter and great-grandchildren. He kills himself the day he's expecting them?"

"To me, there is no evidence to suggest anything else." Albert shrugged. "The only fingerprints on the med bottle and around his bed were the lord's and Frau Luschin's. As expected. No struggle. No dishes or glasses."

A flash flared in his head. "No there wasn't. Where was the glass? You think he swallowed all those pills without a glass of water? He would've choked to death before he overdosed."

Albert's bushy eyebrows pinched together.

"If you kill someone by poisoning them with their own medication, you'd make sure the glass or coffee cup, whatever, was washed and not leave any evidence behind. Or you'd leave a glass with the victim's fingerprints only."

"Holy Mother."

The first crack came, a sliver of light. "A total *lack* of evidence is suspicious."

Albert shrugged. "And yet proves nothing."

Tobias pushed back from his desk, stood, and grabbed his suit jacket from the wooden coat tree between their desks. "Lacy and August are staying on the estate as of today." He glanced at the antique clock again, remembering his love for his grandfather. The thought spurred his desire to find the truth about the old lord's death. "I'm going out, nose around, see how Frau Luschin is getting along. I need to get a more detailed statement from her. Talk to Bauer again, if he's sober enough."

"Want me to come along?" His partner shifted on the corner of the desk.

"No. I'd rather you interviewed Herr Luschin's doctor. Find out how he'd rate his mental state."

"You get the two beautiful American women and the sexy Frau. I get the doctor. The *male* doctor."

"They call me *Chief* Inspector." He slipped his arms into his jacket, buttoned the front, and stretched his neck while straightening his tie in an exaggerated movement. "And you would be the inspector."

"*Ach*." Albert waved a hand. "Good thing I'm retiring in a couple of months. I couldn't take another year of working with you."

"You're going to miss riding around in my Porsche."

His partner's face wrinkled with a smile. "I will."

****

"Whew, I feel the altitude." August's mom plopped onto the bed in their tower room, bent over, and unlaced her hiking boots. "I finally got used to Timberline, but I think we're even higher here—hard to catch my breath. Head feels a little woozy. But my legs feel good."

"Me, too, and I'm so awed by the beauty. It's everything I'd hoped—Alpenrose and Edelweiss, meadows, the Alps, a castle."

Her mother laughed. "And you, singing at the top of your lungs. You've seen *The Sound of Music* too many times."

"It was just one of those moments." She pivoted a half-pirouette and beamed with a natural high.

"It sure was." Her mother kicked off her second boot. "I need a shower, but first I'm going to relax, read, and if I doze off, fine."

"I'm going back out. I'll drop off the backpack in the kitchen and do a stroll inside the castle wall. Get a shower before dinner." Energized, she wanted to snoop around the grounds, maybe catch her cousin or Eike off guard and learn something.

Mom fell back onto the bed. "Have fun, kiddo."

She strolled down the hall, treading softer and slower as she passed first Fabian's room then the solar suite. Disappointingly, there was nothing to see or hear. Descending the spiral staircase, she continued on to the kitchen. No one manned the room, so she left the empty backpack on the butcher-block table, stepped back into the hall, and opened the door that led into the Great Hall. A slow stroll through the enormous room had her imagination on overdrive. The scent of centuries-old stone and fresco blended with smoky whiffs from the oversized fireplace. She walked with lords and ladies across the stone floor polished from centuries of use.

Wolf came to mind as her hand touched the door handle. He'd said he'd be around, continuing the investigation. It wouldn't be so bad to run into him while wandering the grounds.

****

The door of the Great Hall opened as Tobias slid from the leather seat of his car. When August entered the sunshine, shapely legs in khaki shorts and hiking boots, all thoughts of an interview with Eike left his mind. Her bare arms were smooth and tanned. The nipples of her small breasts, unhindered by a bra, dotted the front of her white T-shirt. There was an uncomfortable, yet pleasurable, surge below his belt.

She saw him, waved, and descended the steps with a bounce in her gait. Enjoying the view of shapely legs and perky breasts, he leaned against the front of the Porsche and waited.

"*Guten Tag*, August."

"It certainly is, Inspector." Her crooked smile outshined the sun.

"Are you going for a hike?" He couldn't help giving her one more full body appraisal as she stopped close enough for him to smell her honey scent, this time mixed with the heat of exertion. Changing his focus from her body to her eyes didn't help cool the building heat within. Their color was odd, brown rimmed in lime green, which matched her crooked smile on his seduction meter.

"I've been for a hike. And a picnic thanks to Eike. Now, I thought I'd take a walk."

"Perhaps I could walk with you. I know a little about the estate and could be your tour guide."

She tilted her head in a challenge. "Aren't you here on official business?"

"I'm sure the official questions can wait a little longer."

She gave him the once over, obviously taking in his Canali suit and Scheer oxfords with thoughts of inappropriate hiking attire.

"You did say walk, correct?" His clothing wasn't going to stop him from enjoying a beautiful woman on a perfect summer afternoon. He removed his suit jacket, slipped off his tie, and threw both into the back seat of the car. "Or is my understanding of the American vernacular failing me again?"

She laughed. "Yes, I said walk. But let's call it a stroll. If your walking is anything like your driving, we should take it slow."

"I'm wounded." He fisted his hand over his heart and swayed. "Will you ever let me off the hook?"

"I'll consider it." She laughed and stepped beside him, pointing to their left. "Let's go this way, around the tower we're staying in. I saw a path along the outer wall from our balcony that leads to a garden."

Their pace was leisurely, the air clear and bright, and his downturned mood from the autopsy report lifted by her company. Well-tended grass stretched before them and ahead of the path into the garden. The Alps loomed above, piercing a cloudless sky.

"You said you hiked and picnicked, thanks to Eike? I thought your mother would be combing through Herr Luschin's room looking for photos and anything related to Hartmut."

"That's what we would've preferred to do, although the hike was magnificent and the exercise needed. Eike wasn't up to company when we arrived." Her chin dipped, and she glanced at him through dark lashes. With a quick frown, her gaze shifted to the Alps. "Mom thinks the death of Great-grandfather hit Eike today, and she's too upset to see us. She said she's hoping to join us this afternoon, or at least by dinner."

The path of solid stone now changed to more of a pattern of stepping stones set in thick, green grass. Miniature rose bushes lined each side.

"Hmm. And Herr Bauer?"

"Who knows? He's been locked in his room." A smirk passed over her face. "Or locked in Eike's room."

He would suspect the latter. "Is that what you think?"

"Oh, come on, Wolf. Whoops." Although she comically grimaced, there were no signs of embarrassment.

He laughed.

"Okay, so now you know what I call you when you're not around."

Her easy familiarity gave him pleasure. "I give you permission to call me Wolf when I *am* around." And he'd like to be around her often. He couldn't remember ever feeling quite this way—more interested in a woman than his mission.

"Are you sure? It could speak to my impression of you." Her crooked smile teased and shook his foundation.

"Does it?" His shoes crunched on the gravel path, now leading into the garden.

"It does." Her smile fell away, and she feigned a perfectly serious expression. "But being an Austrian James Bond can't be an insult."

"Unless Bond is played by someone other than Sean Connery."

"Oh, the original. And I agree." She bent to admire a bush with deep red roses. "He's perfectly yummy."

She found him perfectly yummy like Sean Connery? His chest swelled. How oddly embarrassing...

Yet, oddly satisfying.

When she righted, her mouth clamped shut, and her cheeks pinked. Her squirming was adorable, but chivalry was called for to relieve the embarrassment—a condition he'd guess she wasn't accustomed to, considering her brash nature.

He continued to walk. "You were saying about Eike and Bauer?"

With a swallow and a chin lift, she continued. "My cousin Fabian didn't visit Castle Luschin to see his uncle, if you ask me. Although, I can't understand why someone as attractive as Eike would... Then again, he was supposedly the heir. Great-grandfather's death would've left her in the streets."

"And now?" Avoiding personal comments on his part was difficult.

"I don't know. She still seems to be hanging on to Fabian, doesn't she?"

"Does she?"

August abruptly stopped. Her beautiful eyes narrowed, and she perched her hands on her hips. "Look, Wolf, we need to start communicating. You might like to know what I hear and see—that is, if you're still suspicious about suicide. But if I'm going to be open with you, I'd like it to be a two-way conversation."

Ah, the feisty, lovely, young woman was showing her claws again; what had drawn him to her in the first place. But she had a point well taken. Preliminary facts pointed to suicide or accidental overdose of which neither conclusion satisfied him. He needed to expand the reach of his investigation. Plus, information on Eike's political activities could be revealed with an insider's observations.

"It is very likely Herr Luschin's death could be ruled an overdose, cause undetermined. There is no evidence to support suicide. There is no evidence to support anything. Which is part of my concern."

A hint of her crooked smile broke the fierceness of her expression. "So, we're talking?"

"Yes, we are talking."

The stroll continued.

"No evidence. Like someone wiped the crime scene clean?"

"If it is a crime." The inspector in him had to stick to facts, but his gut disagreed with his head. "I'm in agreement with you about Bauer and Eike. Not your typical family relationship. They both have much to gain from Herr Luschin's death." An uneasy twitch bothered his gut. "Or they did."

The roses ended, and the path led down two stone steps. On both sides, rocks of varying sizes seemed to tumble on top of one another with vines and flowers in every crevice.

August stopped and fingered a violet-colored flower. "But why move up the timetable? Lenhard couldn't have lived too many more years, and they didn't know about us." She tilted her head and questioned him with wide-open eyes.

Bauer had been Tobias's focus at first. On further speculation, he wondered if Eike's aspirations had anything to do with it, yet he couldn't figure out what. His dislike of her political activities could cloud his judgment, and he needed to keep those separate. "Impatient lover?"

"He might've had a nudge from Eike, but she couldn't know she was encouraging him to murder. I mean, if he was pursuing her, wanted the castle, and the sexy wife, but she complained that they were trapped until Lenhard died..." She let the flower go and continued to stroll. "I don't know. Her playing around with her husband's nephew sucks, but I can't help but feel a bit—just a bit—sorry for her. She could've had real feelings for Lenhard. Her distress could be real, I suppose."

"She possesses an engaging personality." He strained to keep the sarcasm from his voice. Eike did charm most people.

"I didn't *think* you liked her."

Her frown and direct gaze challenged him to answer, but he didn't want to elaborate. His opinion of Eike was complicated and not fully formed, driven by her political ambitions.

"Ah, the garden." And a diversion to avoid more exchange about Eike.

He gestured expansively with his arms. Opening his mouth about the death of the lord was fine. His side investigation concerning Eike would only muddy the waters for the inquisitive August. There was nothing illegal about the Frau's activities, only moral, and when it came to neo-Nazi aspirations, he could be judge and jury alone. His crusade was best kept close to his chest.

"This is the garden you viewed from your room."

His palm touched the middle of her back, prompting her to admire the garden and change the subject. The gesture came without forethought, yet satisfied an urge he'd been suppressing since she'd walked out of the Great Hall—to touch her. When his skin met the flimsy barrier of T-shirt covering her, heat fired his palm and satisfaction pulsed deep in his chest. He let his fingertips rest heavier against her.

She glanced at him, a hint of pleasure in a half-smile, before diverting her gaze to the garden.

He hoped her quiet reaction was from their contact more than the beauty of fauna. His fingers twitched, on purpose, and he read the slightest echo twitch on her lips.

"It's beautiful. I can imagine lazing on the bench beneath that tree with a book. Hartmut, my grandfather, might have played tag or hide and seek with other children through the grass and the trees over there. Unless this is new, but—"

"No, it is a very old garden. Several centuries, I'd say." A memory surfaced. "There used to be a table and chairs in that clear, grassy spot, there." He brushed against her, gesturing with his free hand. "My grandfather and Herr Luschin played chess occasionally, and I accompanied him a couple of times. I would sit on the bench, there, and read."

"You might have known my mother back then, if Hartmut and Kaya had lived." Her eyes had gone liquid and dreamy. She breathed softly and scanned the garden. "I wonder about the sculpture, over by that circle of white flowers." Sliding out of his touch, she wandered toward the naked, stone woman kneeling as if inspecting the garden.

He followed, feeling the draw of her more than the art. "Do you recognize it?"

"Not the actual sculpture, but the style is very much Arno Breker. Are you familiar with him?"

"No, sorry, I'm not much of an art connoisseur."

"I remember his work from an art history class I took. We covered wartime artists. Breker was a favorite of the Third Reich. But when the war ended, much of his public work was destroyed by the

Allies. I wonder how the family came to have…" Her fingers trailed over the woman's head and shoulder. "Oh, of course."

Their gazes met.

"The brief time this estate was taken by the Nazis," he said.

"Yes, exactly what I was going to say. And I'm so glad the Luschins didn't find the need to destroy it."

The expression of the carved face, even the positioning of the stone body, said she loved the garden. The proportions of her female anatomy were realistic and beautiful without being erotic in any sense. He was no judge, but this sculpture exuded emotion.

"It's a piece to be treasured." Moving to her left for a different angle, she said, "Breker died not too long ago at the age of ninety-one."

Wolf shook his head. "A Third Reich artist or not, it was a shame much of his work was destroyed."

She smiled. "I'm glad you feel that way." One more glance around the garden and with a sigh, she moved toward the castle.

"Yes, I need to get back, too," he said. "My interview with Eike and other inquiries."

"Try to find some of the evidence that doesn't exist?"

"Yes, that would be helpful."

"Is there anything I can do?" She made more than a cursory offer. Her tone held excitement.

"I don't think so. You know, August, your great-grandfather's death could be purely an accident."

"And better if it is. But still, wouldn't you like me to be a spy? I can be your eyes and ears when you're not around. I'm quite a good people watcher."

He pondered her proposal while they walked in silence. Why not let her? There were definite reasons. A death not yet solved. A woman whose aspirations included bringing the Nazi party back into power. And a young American woman who might not understand the scope of either, but had the brash personality to not care. Then again, he'd wanted to gain information through her anyway, and if she knew to keep her eyes open, the effort could have results as he stayed close in touch.

"All right—" She stopped abruptly, and he raised a hand to her eager smile. "But you are to only listen and watch. If you suspect or see anything unusual, you are to call me *immediately*." They continued on the path back.

"It's a deal." She snickered.

"What is funny?"

"Me. Working with a cop."

"Because?"

She looked at him sideways, the sun glinting off several earrings lining her ear. "I'll tell you about it someday."

He'd have to remember to ask again.

"Would Polizist Gruber be working on the case, here at the castle, today?"

"No. Why?"

"I saw him earlier, come out that door." She pointed ahead.

"Hmmm." The young *Politizist* seemed to be crossing his path at odd times. "No reason for him to be on police business. He must know someone here." Gruber did have a life outside the force. He reached back in memory, but had no recollection of where the door led. "Did you speak with him?" She'd seemed interested in the young policeman yesterday.

"No. No reason to."

Her answer pleased him.

"I was on the balcony inspecting the decaying railing that nearly had Mom going over when I saw him. He didn't see me."

"What? What happened? Was Lacy hurt?"

"No. She leaned on the wall and some stones came loose. I guess after this many centuries, it's bound to happen."

Curiosity about the condition of the guest quarters sprang up, but when she brushed against him with her next step, he pushed it aside. He let his feet wander slightly toward her to capitalize on her closeness.

They rounded the tower and stopped in front of the door leading up to the family solar and guest rooms before she spoke again. "I hope we get all the answers soon about Lenhard."

"Perhaps we'll find Herr Luschin's death was an accidental overdose." He had to reiterate. As much as he believed otherwise, there was still the possibility. "It would be best if that was the outcome."

"I know. Especially for my mother. She's had so much tragedy in her life in the past four years. It's bad enough he died before we met him, but suicide or murder?" She shook her head. "All the same,

I'd like to know for sure."

"As would I, August."

"We'll hopefully have dinner with the fam, and I'll have a report for you tomorrow. Will you be by tomorrow, Wolf?"

Her crooked smile beckoned him whether she realized it or not. She just might realize it.

"The investigation continues." If it didn't, well, yes, he definitely wanted to continue getting to know her.

He pulled the door open, waited for her to enter, and as she approached the stairs, watched nicely shaped calves flex as she walked. Pausing with her foot on the first step, she asked, "Hey, Wolf. What do you call me when I'm not around?"

"I call you lovely."

Her mouth fell open.

He chuckled, closed the door, and returned to his car.

Leaning on the fender, he dialed Eike's personal telephone number. She answered on the second ring.

"Good afternoon, Eike. Are you in chambers?"

"Yes, I am, Tobias." Her voice was tired, strained.

"I'm outside. Can we talk?"

A hesitation, then a sigh. "I'm always happy to see you, but—could we do this later?"

"Not really. It won't take long."

"All right." She sounded stronger when slightly perturbed.

He reentered the family entrance and climbed the stairs, the vision of August in his thoughts. She was making it difficult to keep a professional attitude up front.

****

"It's nearly five o'clock. I'm for going down and knocking on the door." August slipped on her sandals. Eike, or even Fabian should've acknowledged their presence in the castle by now. It wouldn't hurt if Wolf was still hanging around either.

Her mother closed her book and thought a moment. "You're right." She stood and motioned for her to follow. "I'd like to get a start on going through Lenhard's things before dinner. Maybe I can find some photo albums or family records to bring back to our room tonight."

As they opened the door, the old, black rotary phone rang. She trotted back and was greeted by Herr Bloch's voice.

"Ms. Myer?"

"Yes, Herr Bloch?"

"Frau Luschin would like to know if you and your mother would come to the solar now and stay for dinner."

She winked at her mom. "I think we can do that. Thank you." The weight and shape of the receiver felt foreign in her hand as she set it back on the cradle.

"What now? Are we being sent into town for wine and *Schnitzel*?"

August chuckled. "Good one, Mom. And you wonder where I get my sarcastic side." She joined her at the door. "No, we've been requested to join Eike in the solar and stay for dinner."

Her mother beamed. "At last."

She followed her mother who strolled toward the solar with purpose, which didn't give her time to admire the paintings. She did notice fresh flowers in the middle of a narrow table against the wall and the red and blue floral pattern of the runway carpet beneath their feet. Mom rapped on the door.

Eike greeted them with a flourish. "Lacy, August, please come in."

She wore a black shirtwaist dress, the belt cinched tight on her hourglass figure and black Ferragamo kitten heels with a pink bow on the toes. Mom had a similar pair in her extensive shoe ensemble only in monochromatic brown.

"I'm so sorry about missing lunch. Last night's pills prescribed by the physician left me so terribly groggy this morning. I would've been horrible company." She remained just inside the room, not offering them seats. "I do hope you enjoyed your picnic lunch."

"We did." Mom smiled sympathetically. "I appreciate you seeing us now. Are you feeling better?"

"I have my moments, but for now, I'm fine." She patted Mom's hand. "Would you like to see your grandfather's chambers and some of his photographs?"

"Very much."

"Good. This way."

They followed her through the sitting area and past the dining table, set with china and crystal for the evening meal, to the far side of the room.

As she swung open the deep red-brown, beautifully gnarled

door, August couldn't take in the antiquated ambiance fast enough.

"I'm sorry, but the room is very old and musty." Eike's nose crinkled. "I left the window open all day." She glanced toward the ceiling. "There are vents and the temperature is adequate year-round." She continued to the far side of the room where an armoire made of the same wood as the door stood.

Her mother followed, but August stopped a third of the way into the room and breathed deep. She thought Eike's appraisal might be more an opinion of the furnishings than the air. There was nothing musty about the room. It smelled of old wood, ancient stone, and ashes in the fireplace. The bed was a four-poster, and although the mattress would barely qualify as a standard size, the posts and frame were the same thick red-brown wood, unadorned, but made to last. Her great-grandfather's bedcover was a tapestry of deer and forests. A painting over the fireplace depicted a scene similar to the cover.

"Lenhard used this old cabinet for his keepsakes." Frau Luschin tapped the door as she spoke.

The term old hardly did justice when describing a piece of furniture built centuries ago. Such a nameless piece of furniture was still a work of art in that it had lasted the ages. The wood had to be at least three inches thick. The cabinet wasn't big enough for a modern man's amount of clothing, but ample in the past. August glanced around to see where he would've kept his clothing if this cabinet was used for other things. Her survey lighted on another door. "There's another room?"

"Yes, that's the wardrobe. We can look in there." She gazed without focusing as if trying to recall the room. "I really don't know what all might be in there besides his clothing."

"Eike, this is so generous of you to allow us here, in Lenhard's room, after such a short time."

"Well, he was your grandfather and…there's nothing here but his past. Nothing of mine." With a shrug, she retreated toward the door. "I'll leave you now so I can make dinner preparations. We'll dine in two hours." A small smile and she closed the door behind her.

"She seems to be doing better." August walked to the fireplace to admire the painting. "Hmmm. Not sure who this is."

Something crashed behind her. She spun, then ran to her mother now lying on the floor. "Are you all right?" She dropped to her knees beside her. "What happened?"

The wooden door to the armoire lay on the floor next to her.

"It came toppling toward me when I opened it. Stupid thing came off the hinge." She put her left hand down to lever upward. "Ow!"

"You're hurt."

"I must've wrenched my wrist. Damn door's heavy."

"Do we need to get a doctor?"

"No, no. Not that bad." Her mother's mouth pinched. "Am I accident prone or what?"

"Why would the door just fall off its hinges?" She rose and squinted at the metal. "The thingys that go through the hinges are gone."

Her mother sat upright and scooted closer to the cabinet to examine the lower one. "Sure are." She levered up. "This place needs some attention."

"Mom. They're not broken. They're just gone." She stared into her face, but the same thought flashing through her mind didn't appear to bother her mom. "Why on earth would Lenhard remove them?"

Mom leaned into the cabinet scanning the contents.

"Eike did say this room was all his. Maybe he booby-trapped it in case she came snooping."

"August, you have the darnedest way of thinking sometimes."

"It's that or someone is trying to scare you." When her mom stared at her, she hastily added, "First the balcony and now this! Inheriting the castle could be a curse." Nervous tremors shocked her neck muscles and tingled her fingertips. She was only half-joking. "You could've been really hurt with either accident."

"August, please. Don't be so dramatic. It's more likely the door was removed to be polished or repaired in some way and whoever put it back on got interrupted and forgot to put" —she scooped up some screw-looking thingys from the corner inside the cabinet— "these back in. And the balcony is a case of deteriorating stone work."

"Mom—"

"Look." Her attention was back on the contents of the cabinet. "Boxes and photo albums. Why don't you go look in the wardrobe.

See what's in there."

Discussion closed as far as her mother was concerned. She pushed concern aside…for now…moved toward the other room. "All right. But be careful of anything heavy, and keep your eyes open for booby traps."

The two hours flew by while she nosed around the wardrobe filled with clothes, a collection of ceramic and wooden deer, and toys that looked to be from her grandfather Hartmut's era. She and her mother leafed through several photo albums dating back to Lenhard's youth. A bundle of letters from Hartmut to Lenhard was of particular interest.

Her mother opened a letter. "It must be near dinner time. I'll read letters until Eike calls us, then take the rest of these back to the room to read later."

August sat on the bed, delicately and without comment, in case someone had booby-trapped it. Mom might classify falling-apart balcony walls and cabinets as accidents, but she had an edgy sensation.

CHAPTER SEVEN

"*Mein Gott!*" Eike dropped her fork. "You could've been hurt."

August winced at the sound of metal hitting china and the disregard Eike had for the antique dinner plate.

"I found out about the accident on the balcony only moments before you came to the table. And now this. I'm…I'm so sorry. I hope you're not nervous about staying on."

"I'm fine, Eike." Mom lifted her hand and rotated her wrist as if to prove her fitness. "Accidents happen." She took a sip of wine. "Of course, this won't deter us from our stay."

The candles on the table flickered, and the Frau's eyes glistened as if tears threatened. "Oh." She lifted a platter from the side table Herr Bloch had wheeled in and positioned alongside her. "Please. *Tafelspitz.* Beef." She passed it, and a dish of what looked like creamy horseradish followed.

August hadn't gotten halfway through her salad yet, but took the offered platter. She glanced at Fabian, who had barely touched his salad. He seemed far more concerned with pouring more wine.

If her mother was miffed about the rush with the meal, she didn't show any signs. "I was wondering if either of you knew anything about the relationship between my father and Lenhard at the time Hartmut left for the States. There were pictures of him that appeared to be taken while he was at a school. Maybe college. Inspector Wolf mentioned a restaurant on the estate that closed when my father left Austria."

Eike dabbed at her eyes with fingertips. "I don't know the entire story. I do know Hartmut had been in college in Vienna studying business, specifically for tourism, and I suppose restaurateur. Something happened between father and son. Lenhard never revealed to me what it was. That was long before my time, of course." She picked up her fork and poked at the beef dish.

August dipped a forkful into the horseradish sauce and chewed. The meat practically melted in her mouth while the burn in her nose left no doubt about the main ingredient in the sauce.

"There was family gossip." Fabian didn't look up from his meal as he interjected his comment.

"Gossip?" she asked around her chewing. "Family gossip can be very revealing."

He glanced from her to her mother. "Did you know Lenhard had a daughter?"

This stopped her mid-chew.

Her mother's forehead creased, fork paused over her plate, and she stared at her cousin. "What? No. Who? Where—?"

"Emma. She died many years ago. I think she was four years younger than Hartmut. The story goes that Hartmut really didn't want to go to school for business, didn't care a bit about a restaurant. This would've been the year Emma died in a skiing accident. Hartmut and Emma were very close, and her death upset him terribly. In the middle of dealing with his daughter's death, Lenhard's son announced he was quitting school and going to the States. They broke ties, you might say."

Another relative that might've been. She wanted to give her mother a hug, and she would when they talked later, alone. "Mom, you said after the airplane crash, authorities ran ads or tried to find Hartmut's relatives in Vienna, right?"

"Yes. That was his last known address. But no one responded, leaving Arlo and Sarah able to adopt me."

She wished her grandfather hadn't kept his secret about her mother. "He never told his father or anyone about you." She spoke quietly, her heart taking on the now accustomed ache for her mother.

"Apparently not. His plan was to come back to Austria to be married and *surprise* Lenhard. But the crash…"

"Unfortunate." Fabian tilted his head and gazed at her mother. His thin, reddish brows puckered over blue-gray eyes.

For the first time, she caught a hint of emotion from the man.

"Very unfortunate. So much sadness," Eike chimed in with a

tsking noise. With a shake of her head, she asked, "Would anyone care for dessert?"

****

Albert ambled up to Tobias's desk and perched his butt cheek on the corner. "Why are you still here?"

"I might ask you the same thing."

"Wife's having a hen party at our house tonight. Last place I want to be, so I stayed here and got my reports and files in order. Can't retire leaving a mess. That's my story, but you—you should be out with some beautiful young woman."

August came to mind, and he shrugged. "I've got your report from Herr Luschin's doctor. No way in hell was the lord getting Alzheimer's. Or any other memory loss problem." He crossed his arms over his chest with finality. "And I'm equally sure he didn't commit suicide. No one working on the estate gave any indication they'd noticed mood problems. His schedule hadn't changed. He was excited when he spoke to his newfound granddaughter. Nothing to indicate a man in a state of mind to want to end his life."

Albert scratched his chin. "Now what?"

He'd asked himself the same question, several times. "Can't get a search warrant without probable cause. And I'm not even sure what more to search."

His partner peered down his long nose. "So, who killed him and why?"

"There are only two suspects. Only two people who had enough access to him to do the job or have any reason."

"The sexy, younger wife and the heir-apparent nephew."

Tobias nodded. "There's no reason to assume Eike had anything to do with it. I got nothing from her statement today. Her emotions seem real enough. But if she's having an affair with Bauer…August proposed she might've planted the idea in his head without knowing."

"Without knowing? I suppose a woman could do that."

"Maybe, and we're dealing with Eike. She's a zealot." He knocked Albert's knee with his elbow, dislodging his butt from the desk, and stood.

His partner frowned, doubt apparent. "You think her Nazi activities have something to do with the lord's death?"

"I haven't put it all together yet, but everything she does has something to do with the neo-Nazi movement."

"Hmmm." Albert gave a more emphatic chin rub. "Are the two American women at the castle?"

"Yes, unfortunately." Always a vein of worry niggled when he thought of Lacy and August on the estate, unfamiliar to them and certainly not invited guests of Eike or Fabian.

"Or fortunately."

Albert implied exactly what Tobias had already considered. "August wants to be my spy."

"Ha!"

More of an exclamation than a laugh, his partner's amused expression didn't bring any amusement to Tobias. "But I'm afraid they're both in danger." The roil of his stomach confirmed his words.

Albert cocked his head. "I wouldn't be so sure. There are now three people in Bauer's way—Lacy, August, and Lacy's son. Poisoning one old gentleman is one thing. Knocking off three people, one not even in country, would be quite a feat."

"The son is young and years from being a threat as heir to the estate." Tobias pulled the jacket from the back of his chair and slipped into it. "I'm heading home. I'll see August tomorrow and attempt to convince her to move back into town until a ruling is made."

****

August strolled along the hall, past Fabian's door and the family's private solar of suites, glancing at the oil paintings of long dead relatives. Electric lanterns illuminated the stoic faces, one of which bore a striking resemblance to her mother across the eyes. She didn't stop to admire the artwork; she was on a mission. Coffee hadn't been offered after dinner, which was rushed with a forced social atmosphere. Eike claimed stress and fatigue while Fabian grew increasingly quiet and intoxicated. She hadn't minded an early escape to the room. Her mother climbed into bed with letters from son to father, but she craved coffee. Maybe someone in the kitchen could brew a cup.

A click came from behind her. She paused on the first step down the spiral staircase and glanced over her shoulder. Fabian froze like a mouse caught with cheese, one foot in the hallway and a hand on his doorknob. Perhaps he was on his way to his lover's room, and he had enough conscience to feel guilty. His jaw dropped, his mouth twitched, a foot danced forward then back.

"Hi, Fabian. I'm on my way to the kitchen for a cup of coffee.

Would you like to join me?" Upsetting a probable tryst with Eike brought her a little mischievous pleasure.

His slow blink and wrinkled brow made him look as if she'd asked a trick question. Or maybe the thought of something to drink besides alcohol was such a novel idea he had to consider the sense of it.

Then again, the man was an unofficial suspect in the death of her great-grandfather. Inviting him to accompany her down a narrow staircase and deserted passageway might not be the wisest thing she'd done today. "Or not. Maybe you're on your way somewhere else." She descended two steps.

"I'd like to join you...if you don't mind."

Her pulse kicked up a notch. How stupid to purposely get trapped with the man, alone and probably out of earshot from anyone. She peered into the staircase passage, scrutinizing the thick, stone walls that could deaden any sound. A glance back smoothed her overactive imagination. He looked harmless enough, and swayed slightly as he approached her. She could probably knock him on his skinny, middle-aged ass, if she had to. She swallowed. Still…

"Come on, then." She descended two more steps and stayed ahead of him on the trip down. The cool air in the circular stairway chilled her arms more than it should have, but each step farther into the narrow way inflamed her nerves.

"Your English is really good." If she kept him talking, she could gauge where he was behind her.

"Most Austrians speak English. I sell quite a few cars to Englishmen, as well as Americans living in Europe. It's a necessity of my business to speak a couple of languages."

"How interesting."

"Just business."

At the bottom, she paused. He'd trailed farther behind than she'd thought, and when she looked over her shoulder, he smiled. She took a relieved breath. He didn't appear particularly menacing. If she wanted to sleuth for Wolf, she needed to get ballsy.

"Do you think there'll be anyone in the kitchen? I can make my own coffee, if that isn't overstepping the hospitality."

He drew up beside her. "There will still be staff on duty."

She didn't hesitate to continue on, and he now kept pace with her. If there were people in the kitchen, she wanted to be there. "Isn't it Austrian custom to have coffee after dinner?"

"We could've had an after-dinner drink or coffee, if our hostess had offered." He cleared his throat. "And so we find ourselves getting our own refreshment."

"I guess Eike is still distressed." She had to take her mother's word on how the Frau's emotions might be affecting her.

Her cousin's face gave nothing away. "So it would seem."

"Are you two close?" A ridiculous question, but it was worth sounding like a fool if she could get him talking.

"I met her when she married my uncle."

Although he avoided looking directly at her or answering her question, she caught the corner of his eye tick twice.

"And you formed a close friendship? She's certainly too young to be your aunt."

He didn't say anything, but clasped his hands behind his back. Out of the corner of her eye, she studied his profile as his shoulders sagged and his gait slowed. When he failed to elaborate, she pressed on.

"Did you like my great-grandfather?"

He nodded and sighed. "Yes, I did, August."

His downtrodden face and meek posture fueled her bravery. You don't take the wife of a loved uncle as your lover. And if you do, you deserve to be raked over the coals.

"Then why did you betray him?"

With his hand on the doorknob, the question, not the closed door, stopped him. She caught her breath, and tensed with a readiness to vault if he angered. Blue-gray eyes regarded her. She put a lot of stock in the expression of a person's eyes. Fabian's were sad, not mean.

She let go of her breath and relaxed at his lack of response. The question could go unanswered for now.

He opened the door. "Let's see if there's any coffee already brewed."

She might be an amateur sleuth, but Fabian didn't give the impression of being a heartless, coldblooded killer. As much as she'd believed he'd played a part in the death of her great-grandfather, he seemed far too timid and...sad. But there was always the possibility the regret she saw on his face meant he was now weighed down with remorse.

The man who appeared to be Eike's personal assistant stood from a table as they entered, coffee cup in hand.

"Now, that's what I'm looking for. Have you got anymore coffee,

Herr Bloch?"

He set his cup down. "Yes, Ms. Myer. In the future, you should ring, and I can bring it to you."

"I felt like stretching my legs." She followed him to the coffee pot on the wooden countertop. It wasn't the delicious espresso found in the buttery, but she didn't need anything that strong this time of evening. "Can I get some cream?"

"Of course." He poured from a delicate, porcelain pitcher next to the coffee pot. "What may I get you, Herr Bauer?"

"I'll take the same, please."

The small hesitation from the older man matched her surprise. She'd known her cousin only two days, but she hadn't seen him drink anything non-alcoholic.

"Would it be okay if I took my coffee to the Great Hall?" she asked Herr Bloch. "That is, if the lights are on and it's not putting anyone out." With the castle employee aware of her whereabouts there was a sense of safety just in case her cousin's eyes led her to the wrong conclusion. Fabian on coffee could be a good source of information, if she could get him to relax and chat.

"There would be no one to remove from the room at this time of night, so you will be fine."

August snickered to herself, but let the miscommunication go.

"The lights are always on in the Great Hall."

"Thanks, Herr Bloch." She saluted him with her coffee cup. "Would you like to join me, Fabian? It's a beautiful room. Well, I guess you know that."

"Actually, August, I haven't spent any time in the Great Hall." He crossed the kitchen and opened another door.

"Why not?" With her cousin close behind, she entered through the door that Kurt had pointed out the day before when they'd been in the Hall. The table on the raised dais was only a few feet inside the room. The beauty of the high backed, gnarled wood chairs beckoned her, and she stopped behind one of them.

"It's not a family room. It's"—he glanced beyond her—"rather large and impersonal."

"But *so* historic and beautiful." Her hand caressed the aged top of the chair. "Do you suppose we could sit here?"

He shrugged. "I don't see why not." He raised his coffee mug to his lips, but spoke before sipping. "It's yours. Or your mother's at any rate."

She clasped the chair back more tightly, then studied his expressionless face. It came to her that she and her mother might have dashed some dream, some vision of his future, and for a moment, his sadness was hers. Then again, had he been willing to kill for his vision? Hard to imagine, considering his droll sadness and the lack of enthusiasm he showed for the Great Hall.

"What does that mean to you? That my mother inherits the estate."

He set his mug in front of the next chair and pulled out one for her. "Your coffee is going to get cold." Not waiting for her to sit, he slid into his chair and cupped the mug in both hands. "You are a curious sort, aren't you, August?"

Annoyance pricked her at his penchant for ignoring her questions. "If you mean I want to know more about my great-grandfather, about how he died and about you, my last *living* Austrian relative, then yes, I guess I am."

His gaze flitted around the oversized room. "Suicide." The word was more a spoken thought.

"You think he committed suicide?" She watched him for a reaction.

"Yes." There was no hesitation in his quiet answer.

Her fingers jerked on the cup handle. "Really? You don't think he could've made a mistake or perhaps—"

"My uncle was robust, active." He lifted his chin. "And not stupid."

"Not stupid?"

Another swallow of coffee delayed his answer. He pinched his lips in a thin line, as if pondering his next words. "You asked why I betrayed him, and you're most certainly referring to my relationship with his wife." His fingers fidgeted along the handle of his half-empty mug. "No, he wasn't stupid, but I am."

"Why, Fabian? Did you think you could have…did you want *all* that he had?"

Her bluntness was answered with a half-smile. "I'm quite happy in Vienna, August. My auto dealership does well, and the city is more to my liking. Owning and managing this estate was *never* my intention." His smile grew tighter. "I wish you and your mother the best of luck with that."

"So, you and Eike—"

His hand jerked from the table, palm flattened in the air with a finality she couldn't breach. Apparently, his relationship with Eike was a closed subject. Did he think his affair with her had driven his uncle to suicide? That's the load weighing on his shoulders. Guilt.

"Please." He cleared his throat, tightened his jaw, and changed the subject. "You are entranced with Castle Luschin, aren't you?"

"It's amazing." She'd go with his abrupt change of subject for now. He'd already revealed more about himself than she'd imagined he would. "The history is fascinating." She glanced around the Great Hall. "The grounds, the Alps are breathtaking. And the art and artifacts here in the castle are nothing short of marvelous."

"You make our little piece of the world sound quite enticing. I wonder if I spent enough time around you, cousin, I'd catch some of the enthusiasm you have for our everyday surroundings."

"I'll see what I can do." She meant it. A little sympathy was growing for her cousin.

"I'm sure Lenhard would be happy his beloved estate will be left in your hands."

"And Eike?"

He shook his head and stared into his coffee. His lips were apparently sealed when it came to his lover and the affair he thought drove his uncle to suicide.

That's all she'd get.

She slumped back in her chair and stared at her cousin lost in his thoughts. Fabian believed Lenhard had committed suicide. If he was right, had the elderly man timed his death so their arrival was an added slap in the face to the nephew who'd upset his world? How would her mother react to this news?

"I better head back to the room. Would you like to walk back upstairs together?" She stood, hoping he'd follow and elaborate more.

"I think I'll sit here for a while, finish my coffee, and try to gain some appreciation for the art and this room that you have so much enthusiasm for."

"I'll see you tomorrow?"

"Yes." He glanced up, his expression softened. "Thank you for a most enjoyable visit and after dinner coffee." Sincerity colored his words. There was a slight flush to his pasty skin that hadn't been there before. "I think I'll like having relatives again."

"Thank you, Fabian. Goodnight."

Back in the kitchen, Herr Bloch tidied the counter. "Did you want more coffee, Ms. Myer?"

"No, thank you." She put the mug in his outstretched hand. "Good night."

"*Gute Nacht*, Miss."

The walls of the short hallway were cool to her touch as she trailed fingers over the uneven stones. What a feat it must've been to build the castle centuries ago without any heavy equipment found at construction sites nowadays. She paused and breathed in the slightly musty air of centuries-old stone. What a feat it must be to maintain an estate the size of Castle Luschin. Mom had a lot to consider.

She touched the stone again. The art, the beauty, the history. It seemed like Cousin Fabian didn't know what he'd almost had. And didn't care. Except for Eike. She had the impression he'd found out the woman's attraction to him had more to do with the estate than anything he had to offer. Her chest ached a little for him. Instead of a snobby drunk who'd probably poisoned his uncle to gain control of Castle Luschin, he now seemed a pitiful, lonely soul who had to face unrequited love. Suicide? She'd rather Lenhard's death was accidental. For her cousin's sake.

Wait until Wolf hears about my rap session with Fabian. Her pace lightened, and she smiled at herself.

As she put a foot on the first step of the spiral staircase, pain spiked against her head. Her knees buckled, then blackness.

****

August rose on her hands, sat, and leaned against the cold, stone wall. "What the hell?"

"August?" Her mother's voice echoed in the staircase, her shoes clicking quickly on the stone steps. "What's wrong?" She kneeled. "What happened? Are you okay?"

"Yeah, I guess." She touched the back of her head with a wince. A knot was forming. "I was conked on the head. I guess."

Her mother felt her face, looked closely into her eyes, and kissed her cheek. "I think you slipped on the wet floor and hit your head."

"Wet floor?" She scanned the stone around her, rubbed her hands together, and only then noticed the dampness.

"There's the bucket. Someone must've been mopping."

To one side of the stairway entrance, a yellow pail stood with water and a rag.

"I don't remember..."

"Let me help you up."

She propped herself against the wall, bump aching, but no other effects. "I didn't see the bucket. I'd have noticed."

"Well, you didn't. You must've been deep in thought."

"Mom, a yellow bucket. There. How could I miss it?"

"I don't know." Her mother shrugged. "What are you saying?"

"I'm not sure." She levered away from the wall, glanced down the hall, then back at her mother. "What were you doing here, anyway?"

"I thought you should've been back by now. I went looking for you."

She smiled. "You and your mother's intuition."

"Something like that. How's your head? Do we need a doctor?"

"Nah. I think I fainted for only a few seconds." One more glance down the hall, at the pail, and the floor, and she heaved a sigh. "Let's go to bed."

They took the first few steps in silence. She had a bothersome tightness in her chest, and not from the fall. "Mom, we've had three accidents today. Don't you find that odd?"

"I was just thinking the same thing. But accidents happen."

"We've had enough *accidents* to last us a year."

At the top of the stairs, they continued to their room, steps muffled by the carpet runner, the quiet of ages surrounding them. Her mother's words came softer, as if she'd entered a library and tempered her volume. "But each incident is perfectly explainable."

Touching the already sore bump on her head, she pondered on a possible explanation to this last mishap. "I didn't see the bucket. And, although it happened fast and unexpectedly, I'm pretty sure I fell *after* I conked my head."

"How could you—?"

They stopped in front of their door. She lowered her voice. "I mean, after my head met with the bonk."

Mom's eyes widened.

She put a finger to her lips, opened the door, and waited until her mother was inside, then closed the door.

"You're saying someone hit you?" The pitch of her voice rose.

"That's the only explanation."

"Okay, kiddo." Her mother paced a few steps forward, then back.

"You're making quite a jump there. I know this whole Lenhard dying and ancient castle surroundings has us out of our element, but to think someone would try to…hurt you? Us?" Mom plopped on the bed, lifted a tendril of hair, and ran it over her chin.

The bump on the back of her head ached. She tested her neck and shoulders with a stretch while she waited for the wheels to quit turning in her mother's head. No damage. Had Fabian snowed her? The only other person she'd seen on her coffee excursion was Herr Bloch. What possible motive?

Her mother's startling green eyes narrowed in a frown. "We have reason to believe we're targeted. But—"

"But whoever it is isn't too serious about harming us." August finished her sentence. "It's more as if they're trying to scare us."

"Not what I was going to say, kiddo. I question our jumpiness…and your imagination."

She rarely became irritated with her mother, but now was one of those times. Sometimes Mom had the market cornered on practicality. "Whatever." Opening a bureau drawer, she pulled out pajamas and tossed them on the bed. She'd run her ideas by Wolf tomorrow. He had more concerns than her mother wanted to believe.

"Okay." Mom drew her hands together and scooted to the edge of the bed. "I have a plan, kiddo. If you're right, then maybe we'll get a reaction."

She stopped to listen. "A plan?" Hope welled, and anticipation for action ramped her pulse.

"We need to decide exactly what we're doing with the estate. Regardless of how my grandfather left this world, I now have a castle and all the responsibilities attached to it to deal with." She stood and turned back the covers. "I can't live in Austria or even want to. We need to meet with whoever takes care of the finances, the business aspects, and the day-to-day maintenance of the personal side of this estate. Plus a myriad of other things we need to know." She lifted her pajamas from the drawer and faced her, a brow cocked and a mischievous slant to her lips. "If I make it clear I plan to retain this estate and, I don't know, say I'm going to use it as a second home for my family, even imply there could be changes to suit us, then maybe we'll force whoever's hand you believe is trying to scare us away."

"All right!" She pumped a fist. "Force their hand." Doing a pirouette to the dresser, she opened a drawer. "But I have to tell you,

I'd ruled Fabian out after our little coffee time this evening." At her mother's questioning expression, she continued as she stuck one leg and then the other into pj pants. "Yeah, I ran into him, and we had coffee in the Great Hall. He seems so pathetic. Unrequited love for Eike and no real ties to this estate."

"But now?"

She slipped under the covers, doubt and puzzlement swirling her thoughts. "Besides Herr Bloch, he was the only one I saw downstairs. Makes me wonder."

CHAPTER EIGHT

August rolled to her side for the sixth time. Maybe jet lag finally caught up with her, but more than likely the events of the last couple of days were to blame. The more she thought about her fall, the clearer the memory. She'd been hit on the head and *then* fell.

And the floor hadn't been wet.

Either Fabian was a great actor or a psychopath. She shivered and clutched the covers to her neck. Or not. He'd seemed so real, so heartbroken. But with him out of the picture as a suspect, Eike stepped up front and center. That thought kept her awake more than any other. *Or* her great-grandfather really had committed suicide. Fabian implied his affair with Eike the cause, but that scenario left her unsatisfied. Lenhard didn't seem the type of man to practically lure his granddaughters to Austria only to commit suicide and use them to further torture his nephew.

So, did Eike murder her husband? This scenario was a bit outrageous even for her to consider. She appeared genuinely upset, although overly dramatic, over her husband's death. Why kill the lord for a man she didn't love in order to keep the castle she already had? Yet, August couldn't see Fabian as the instigator much less a murderer. The affair could've continued until Lenhard died of natural causes. But if Eike intended on marrying Fabian and keeping the castle, she, her mother, and her brother now stood in the way.

She sat and patted the knot on the back of her head, then darted a glance at her mother in the other bed. Sleeping soundly.

Rising, she slid her feet into slippers, padded to the door, and eased it open. A chilly breeze caught her when she opened the door, and she reached back to grab her robe. Outside, the stars made more light than the half-moon. This sky could rival Timberline. She reclined her shoulders against the tower wall, breathed deep, and hoped that tomorrow Wolf could make more sense of her garbled musings.

Wolf.

Her stomach fluttered and warmth came over her in spite of the cool night air. This man was all wrong. Too old. Too foreign. Too...*hell, he's a cop.* She smiled. Age really had nothing to do with it. The slight crinkle at the corners of his eyes, the quirky been-there-done-that smile, and his self-assuredness made her heart palpitate. As far as being foreign, well, yeah, he lived a long was from Tucson, but holy shit that accent made her tingle in all the right places. And he wasn't exactly a cop. An inspector, Chief Inspector, was a whole 'nother category.

A noise, steps crunching on gravel below the balcony jarred her. She leaned forward and caught sight of golden-haired Kurt approaching the castle, then quickly jerked back.

Pretty strange time of night for him to be here.

She edged away from the building just enough to peek over the wall, yet careful to not touch the unstable top. He stopped in front of the door he'd exited earlier in the day, looked behind him and to his left and right, then opened it and slipped inside.

She slumped back against the wall. The shock of seeing him left her puzzled, but his wardrobe puzzled her even more. She hadn't seen his entire front, but...why was he dressed like he belonged in a high school marching band?

****

Eike nodded at each individual of the group as they trudged silently up the steps after the meeting. Each man peered out the door at the top before slipping into the darkness. The members of the Council *Burschenshaften* would walk from the estate grounds to where they'd parked their cars on the other side of the wall.

She closed the door behind them and descended the steps to where Kurt waited in the meeting room.

"Schuler's accounting tonight was exciting. He's made great inroads into the Social Democrats. Add them to the thirty percent backing in the last election, and those numbers will explode next time. If we even need them by then." She clamped her hand around Kurt's strong forearm. "We are living in an exciting time, *mein Liebling*. My great-grandfather would be so proud."

"Your great-grandfather would be proud of *you*."

She put her arms around Kurt's neck, her fingers tickled by his bristly hairline. "For someone so young, you are a master at leadership. I'm very happy to have you by my side, darling."

"You have my loyalty and my undying admiration." His arms wrapped around her waist. "I am most pleased to be so honored to stand beside you, behind you." He clicked his heels and stood straighter.

She chuckled and acknowledged the ripples between her legs. Kurt was not just a good-looking young man. His dedication to the new Nazi power that would soon rise and take control—with Eike Buchleitner leading the revolution—thrilled her far beyond his physical appearance.

He ran a finger along her jaw line, the pressure noticeable as his other arm's muscles grew tighter at her waist. "You must not let the American women stand in your way. This estate should belong to the Homeland."

"I know, I know." She pressed her face against his chest. The truth of his words echoed in her head. "I think they'll make plans to return to America soon. I gave them full access to Lenhard's things. That's what they're here for."

"Don't be so sure. The daughter longs for possession of the castle. I can tell."

"You could've hurt her, you know, if she had tumbled down the steps—"

"Would that have been so bad?" The muscles of his chest flexed against her cheek.

"Kurt…"

He pulled her tighter. His undying affection pushed against her belly.

"Do not be fooled by their friendly manner. They are American." He spat the word. "Action is needed."

"I'm convinced after tonight they will run back to their safe little existence across the ocean. Our new order will not allow Americans to own any part of the Homeland, voiding their deed. Castle Luschin will be Castle Buchleitner…again."

His breathing came heavier, the heat of it searing her ear as he spoke. "Eike, *mein Fuhrer.*" His hands dropped low, smashing her hips against him.

"Kurt, *mein Liebling*, it's very late. Fabian has been known to wander out for a drink even at this hour."

He backed her up to the long, oak table. "I didn't intend on taking you upstairs."

She couldn't fight the strength of her young Nazi. Nor did she care to.

****

A shrill tone startled August from sleep. She opened her eyes, shut them, then opened wider, this time disoriented with what she first glimpsed. *Oh yeah. Castle Luschin.*

"You're closer." Mom's groggy voice joined the next ring. "Answer the damn thing."

"Ugh." She rolled to the edge of the bed, grabbed the black receiver, and moaned into the mouthpiece. "Yeah?"

"The Frau asked me to say that the…breakfast will go at eight." The voice was female and heavily accented.

"*Danke.*" The receiver clunked loudly as she dropped it in place then relaxed back on her pillow.

"How's the head, kiddo?"

August ran her fingers over the bump. "I remember you once calling me a stubborn, hard-headed little brat. Still holds true."

"I did not call you a brat!"

"Was it another B word? After all, I was a teenager."

"Most certainly not." She sounded genuinely indignant. "Who was on the phone?"

"Kitchen staff, I assume. Breakfast at eight." She wondered if anyone would give off guilty vibes around the breakfast table.

Her mother noisily yawned and swung her feet to the floor. "Good. I intend on letting Frau Luschin know about the carelessness of whoever mopped the floor at such a ridiculous hour last night."

August rose on her elbow, head propped on her hand as her mom grabbed her robe and headed for the shower. "You can complain, but I don't think anyone was careless."

She stopped in the doorway, frowned, and took a deep breath. "I know. And that implies someone is trying to harm us. That leads me to think Grandfather's death wasn't an accident. I feel like I need to get Chance here on the next plane and move to a hotel."

August kicked back the cover, sat, and crossed her legs yoga style. "I have another theory."

"Oh great."

She raised her palms. "Hear me out. I couldn't sleep last night so I went out on the balcony. Guess who I saw sneaking *into* the castle?"

"Must be Kurt."

"Yes, and he was dressed like the burkowhatever guys Wolf pointed out at the restaurant. I think we're sitting in a Nazi stronghold."

"Stronghold?"

"Okay, I might be overstating it, but blond-haired, blue-eyed Kurt is here a bit too often, and now I see him late at night in *the garb*. Look at Eike. Arian all the way. This may have nothing at all to do with Lenhard's death—which could've been accidental. But it has everything to do with scaring us off."

The way her mom leaned against the doorframe, narrowed her eyes, and swished her mouth to the side spoke to her disbelief without uttering a word.

"I can see your doubt. But think about it. They need us to go away. I'll have a meeting with Wolf today and see how he feels."

That brought a smile to her mother's face. "Yes. You meet with Wolf today."

"Strictly spy business."

"Of course. Meanwhile, let's go forward with the plan we discussed last night. At breakfast, I'll tell Eike I need to meet with the business manager, if there is one, and with the Luschin lawyer. This is truthful. I can't call Mark until tomorrow, and I'm sure he'll have some research to do. In fact, no real decisions can be made until after my grandfather's funeral, and we return home to make some plans, but she doesn't need to know that. I'll imply there will be changes very soon. Castle Luschin will be our second home. We'll force someone's hand."

"Whether it's Nazis or murder, we should get a reaction."

Mom winced and retreated for her shower.

For her mother's sake, she truly hoped it wasn't murder. And if Wolf let her continue spying, for the sake of his anti-Nazi activities, alongside him—that wouldn't be so bad.

****

Eike dabbed her mouth with a linen napkin as Fabian opened the door of the solar. She pushed back from the table. "You missed breakfast."

"I guess I wasn't hungry. I was up, but fell back to sleep."

He drifted toward the bar then stopped near the table. His pants were rumpled, but he'd smoothed his thin, reddish-brown hair. "We're alone."

"We're often alone, darling." His meaning was clear, but she enjoyed making him work for her understanding.

"You know what I mean, Eike. Alone. Really alone. No more need to—" He shrugged and ran a hand across the back of his neck as if releasing tension.

She rose and sauntered to him, satisfaction filling her when his eyes lit with her approach. His lips twitched as she trailed her index finger along his pale cheek, over his mouth, and down the other cheek to his chest. "Yes, dear nephew, we can—"

"I'd rather you didn't call me that." His tone was defensive, but his body leaned toward her, defenseless.

"*Now* you're getting a sense of propriety?"

"It seems a bit disrespectful, don't you think?" His arms slipped around her waist.

The usual warmth a man's arms brought on never came with his embrace. Deeper emotions than warmth came with Fabian's touch—as a Luschin and eventual heir to the estate, he held the key to her future, to Austria's future, and that far outweighed any sexual attention he offered. In fact, she'd rather refuse him, but meeting his base needs was for the good of all of Austria.

With that thought, she pressed her body against him, excited by her mission. "Or is it guilt?" She toyed with the buttons on his shirt, stared into his blue-gray eyes, and batted her lashes like an innocent schoolgirl.

"No more than you, I would imagine."

She flinched. "I'm not."

His grip tightened.

Choosing to overlook his rare show of backbone, she relaxed into him, and dropped her hands to his hips.

"It would've been helpful to have you by my side this morning at breakfast. You are, after all, the only living relative of my late husband. You should be the one inheriting his estate."

His arms stiffened. "Eike—"

"It's true. They're *Americans*. What do they know of Austria? Lenhard's son disowned his father and his country and his right to this land when he ran off to America. He never even married the woman. Now, the bastard child wants to meet with our managers and financial executors."

He released her and rubbed his temples. "This is all too much."

She patted his hip. "Yes, poor Lenhard is one thing, but we can't let your so-called relatives stand in *our* way." Holding him to a united effort was tantamount to her plan. The implausible man had to be guided constantly. "She wants *meetings*. Her plans are forming, and she intends on taking over our home, Fabian."

He paused in thought a moment then sighed. "They're Americans. They aren't going to want to live in Austria. I'm sure we can come to some sort of agreement."

"What agreement would that be?"

"They'll need someone to oversee the estate and—"

"Oversee?" Anger rose from the pit of her stomach, and she reared back to stare at him. "I am not someone's *employee*. I am the Frau of Castle Luschin. And soon…" She clamped her mouth shut.

He faced toward the bar. "And soon what, Eike?"

She remained silent. Her intentions for the estate, for all of Austria would be beyond the dolt's understanding. Better he think her a treasure hunter, a seducer of the late Herr's self-proclaimed eligible bachelor nephew.

His bony hand cut the air above his head. "I'm not the heir any longer." A glass clinked as he set one on the bar then splashed Lenhard's best cognac into it.

Of course he'd give up so easily. How could Lenhard's only male relative be such a flimsy man? As old as her late husband had been, he had a strength Fabian would never have.

Ah well, that's why the weak man needs me.

"It's not that simple." Clasping her arms around her waist, she made an effort to control her rising anger. Her nostrils flared, releasing hot air that bathed her upper lip. "From the waste, new and more determined plans shall rise."

His brow furrowed. "What the devil are you talking about?"

If only he was as dedicated as she. At least his lack of strength could work to her advantage. Her shoulders relaxed, and she held her arms out in invitation. "Come here, pet. You don't need that drink."

When he reached her, she took the drink from him and set it on the table.

"Eike, I'm—"

"You're in need of some company, darling." She led him to the sofa. "We have much to do over the next few days. We must lay Lenhard to rest." She pulled him down with her.

"I know you didn't love him. Did you tell him about us?" Watery eyes stared into her face.

"I might've slipped. Said something that gave him a clue."

His chin slumped to his chest. "And yet, he didn't come to me…"

"He really had been out of sorts lately, Fabian." She ran a hand down his arm, soothing. "Stop obsessing. What is done is done."

"You might not be able to stay on here, Eike. We can go to Vienna. My home—"

"Don't be ridiculous!" She shivered at the thought. "I belong here."

"Lenhard's granddaughter might feel differently."

"It won't matter how she feels." Lacy and August were a problem, but one that could be dealt with.

"How can you say that? They do have their rights."

"Really, darling?" She dropped her hand from his arm and ran it through her hair. Where was this sympathy coming from? "You're going to tell me about the rights of some unknown granddaughter whose claim to my inheritance is some meaningless ancient piece of parchment? Those fortune-hunting, money-grubbing Americans don't belong here."

"The ancient piece of parchment is far from meaningless, and I think you've read them wrong." He fussed with the pleat of his trousers, not meeting her gaze. "They seem nice enough, and they're only trying to connect with family."

"Oh Fabian, really." Every muscle in her body tensed with barely restrained anger. "First Vienna and now you're blubbering about your newfound cousins."

"What about us, Eike? I thought…"

"Us?" She plucked his hand from his knee with one hand and tipped his chin toward her with the other. "Why, that's what I'm concerned about. Us. Our home."

He stared into her face. "An autopsy." His frown deepened. "They're actually doing an autopsy on the old lord."

She pulled her legs under her, scooted so close to him that her knees rested in his lap and patted his chest. "Don't fret, Fabian. They'll find nothing but a drug overdose and release him to us soon." The weakling required so much attention…a tiring endeavor, but the result would be worth the effort.

"You sound as if you know for certain."

Skimming her fingers over his forehead to smooth his brow, she silently acknowledged enough confidence for both of them. "Let's not talk anymore." She stroked his thigh. "Relax, darling. No guilt, no worries about our future."

****

August enjoyed the sun on her arms, the blue of the sky, and the lyrical, yet sometimes harsh, sound of the German being spoken around her. When Wolf pulled his car alongside the curb, her day got that much better. She smiled and waved. She'd been waiting for him at the sidewalk café, across from the Hotel Karnten and the fountain in the middle of the roundabout.

"*Guten Morgen*, August." A lingering smile accompanied the greeting as he took the other seat at the table for two.

A nervous skitter tripped across her chest when he scooted the seat closer to her as he sat. His suit was the same brown as his toasted almond eyes, and the sun bounced off the slight sheen of the material.

"Where's Lacy?" He leaned toward her when he spoke.

"She wanted to go exploring. Mom's used to running every day, so she needed to stretch her legs. She'll grab a bite to eat somewhere."

"How are you today, August? You sounded quite mysterious when you called."

"I have tales to tell. But let's order lunch first?"

He hailed a waitress, and they ordered sandwiches and colas. He rested his arms on the table. "Are you enjoying your stay at the castle?"

"We've been able to go through some of Lenhard's things. Perusing old photographs and memorabilia is fun. Watching Mom's reactions and excitement makes it all the better." She toyed with the three earrings of her right ear, a slight flutter in her stomach as she stared into Wolf's brown eyes. "She's been reading letters from her father to her grandfather. There's a lapse of correspondence when her father went to the States. Probably why Lenhard didn't know about her."

"That was unfortunate." He glanced away for a moment.

"Families...the dynamics...who can explain?"

There was a story with Wolf, but she'd let it pass for another day. If it was sad, she didn't want to go there. Not right now.

"Yeah, who can explain?"

His gaze came back, and with it, his smile. "You have tales to tell?"

"I certainly do. Accidents do happen, but it seemed every time we turned around yesterday, we ran into trouble."

His perfectly shaped brows drew together. "You turned round? What did you run into?"

She chuckled. "That's a phrase. Just means...oh never mind. We've had two more supposed accidents."

"Why did you not call? I told you to call me if there was any reason—"

"*Hier, bitte.*" The waitress set their sandwiches and colas on the table.

"*Danke.*"

Wolf didn't take his gaze from August's face, and the concern on *his* face gave her pause. There was a personal slant to his interest. She swallowed her pleasure and jumped in as soon as the waitress left tableside. "We're fine, honestly. Mom swears it was just a string of accidents."

"But you think differently."

"Well..."

"Which is why I should've gotten a phone call." He ignored his sandwich, thumped the table, and tipped his chin downward. "Explain."

After relating a more detailed description of the balcony giving way and the wardrobe door coming off and toppling her mom, she paused and took a bite of her sandwich.

"When we took our walk, your description of what actually happened with the balcony was incomplete." His hands came off the table in a gesture she could only call frustration.

"It hardly seemed important at the time. Just an old wall—"

"August, if we are working together, you have to tell me everything, and let me be the judge of what is important."

She stopped eating and stared into his face. He was the inspector. "You're right."

He appeared speechless for a moment. He probably hadn't expected her to agree so readily, but she had to. Working with Wolf was exactly what she wanted, and she couldn't risk him shutting her out.

"Good." He pulled his plate closer and picked up his sandwich. "On the surface, they do appear to be common accidents." He chewed, sipped his beverage, and took another bite.

"I suppose. If no one has stayed in the guest room for a long while, needed repairs might go unnoticed. Mom explained away the door, too. But there's more." She went through her visit with Fabian and her fall on the stairs.

He rubbed a hand over his eyes and down his chin.

"I think someone wet the floor around me after knocking me out. Made it look like another accident to anyone else. Except me. Which then makes me seem like I have an imagination gone wild."

"And you're sure—"

"I've had a restless night and all morning to think about it."

He waved a hand then pushed his plate aside again. "This is bothersome, August. These feel a little more than incidents intending to frighten you. Anyone of them could have brought you or your mother harm." He slid his hand to hers and brushed his fingers lightly over her knuckles.

The ripple his touch sent up her arm was over the top for such an innocent gesture. A vision of leaning into him for a kiss flashed through her mind. She swallowed deeply and hoped her face didn't give away her thoughts.

"B-but they didn't."

"Hmm."

"After my visit with Fabian, I didn't see him as a threat. Would he try to scare us away? Maybe. I don't know. Loosening the ledge on the balcony is rather…extreme. Premeditated, for sure."

Wolf studied her face for a moment then lost himself in brushing breadcrumbs around the pale pink tablecloth.

"We saw him this morning as we were leaving. He didn't look…guilty. In fact, he was the most cordial he's been. It's like our little talk bonded us or something."

"Hmmm. Maybe. Or he's clever."

"And speaking of a restless night—I wandered out to the balcony and saw the late-night appearance of Kurt, in uniform, entering the door I'd watched him come out of earlier in the day."

"*Polizist* Gruber?"

"Not in *police* uniform."

"*Burcheshaft?*"

"Yes. How did you guess?" Her pulse pattered in her temple. *I knew this meant something.*

He muttered something under his breath in German.

"What? What is it?"

His full lips grew thinner in a momentary grimace.

"Wolf, tell me."

He scooted his chair closer to her, folded his hands on the table, and released a low groan. "Eike is active in neo-Nazi politics."

"I knew it!" A thrill overcame her, pleased with her detective skills. "But why didn't you tell me?"

"Why would I? It has no bearing on why you're here. I didn't feel it necessary to discuss the Frau's politics when you aren't Austrians and have no reason to interact with her on that level."

"But…but it makes her seem so much different." This had to be why she picked up on an unspoken low opinion of Eike. "Are her politics why you don't like her?" Politics and Nazis—he'd been so serious at dinner the first evening.

"They don't help."

"Before I got conked on the head, I was convinced Fabian couldn't be involved in Lenhard's death. It seemed your reservations to accept his overdose as suicide or accidental were unfounded. Then the conk, and he had the perfect opportunity to come at me from behind. Then I got to wondering about Eike. If my great-grandfather was helped into the afterlife, and Fabian was innocent, his wife would be the logical helpmate."

Although his brow held the slight wrinkle, he remained silent.

"Now this Nazi stuff. It's messy. Maybe Lenhard did accidentally overdose, and all we have is a cheating wife who also happens to want to keep her Nazi ties secret. I don't see how Lenhard's death has anything to do with it."

Wolf's eyes stared unfocused at his fingers, while he again brushed crumbs around in a circle on the table. She left him to his inner musings while she took her last bite of sandwich.

After a drink, and he still remained silent, she plunged in impatiently. Hell and be damned, she'd force him to share more if she divulged what most certainly he wouldn't approve of. "Well, perhaps we'll find out soon if it's Eike or Fabian, maybe both, trying to scare us away."

He glanced up slowly, his eyes narrowing. "Why?"

"Mom announced at breakfast that we need to meet with the property managers or whoever handles the estate. She mentioned we needed to get the estate in order, and she requested she receive everything that our lawyer would need to see. I might have mentioned that Castle Luschin would make such a lovely summer home. Eike looked a bit shocked. Fabian didn't come to breakfast, but I bet she'll update him."

He abruptly flicked at the crumbs and sat back in his chair.

"What? We have to *do* something." Her neck heated. His insufferable silence was annoying. "You're not telling me something or you wouldn't look the way you look. I can't observe what's going on at Castle Luschin if I don't know what I'm looking for."

"I don't want you observing anything more. I think it's time you and Lacy moved back to the Hotel Karnten."

"Why? Are you afraid the Nazis are going to get us?" She snickered irritably at his demanding voice. "It's not like Hitler is in the next room."

"You jest, August, but until we know exactly—"

"You would never have known about Kurt unless I was there." She slammed the table with an open palm. "I'm at least helping your Nazi hunting efforts."

He flinched and drew closer. "Could you keep your voice down? I am Chief Inspector, not a Nazi hunter."

Her rising irritation cooled as he closed the distance to inches between them. She breathed in his cardamom-tinged scent, enjoyed the rub of his suited bicep on her bare arm, and the bump of his knee against her leg. She answered him in a loud whisper. "Sorry. But we're not ready to leave the castle. Mom is learning so much about her father."

"She can make day trips, gather items, and go back to the hotel to study them." He mimicked her exaggerated whispering with a slight smile.

She brought her lips so close to his ear that the downy fuzz tickled her lower lip. "I'll take your suggestion under advisement to my mother." The heat he gave off bathed her face, and she wanted to melt into him.

Slowly, he rotated his head, brushing his nose against hers, and stared into her eyes. "I do like the fire in your eyes, but the fire in your attitude—"

The shrill chime of his cell cut him off.

She held her breath, her mouth so close his exhale kissed her lips.

He drew back on the second set of chimes and plucked the offensive equipment from his suit coat pocket.

While he listened, she concentrated on getting her heart to slow down and her head to clear.

"Thanks, Albert." As he replaced the phone in his pocket, he scooted his chair from the table. "Duty calls."

"Sounded like Albert to me."

He chuckled. "Yes, well, I have to get back to work." He canted toward her, his voice low. "I'll follow up on everything you've told me. I'm sorry I missed Lacy. Maybe she would take my advice more seriously."

She pursed her lips and did an eye roll. "You're going over my head?"

No reaction. He stood and made a motion to leave, but stopped. He ran a finger along her ear, touching each of the loops then drew back. "Please convey my greeting and concerns to your mother."

Her ear tingled long after he slid into his silver car and pulled onto the street.

CHAPTER NINE

Tobias opened the heavy, metal door of the *Landespolizeikommando*, his partner a step behind.

They'd reached the stairs when he said, "I'm going to locate Gruber. Can you see if there's any more evidence come to light on Herr Luschin's death?"

"Sure." Albert peeled away and headed upstairs as Tobias strode down the hall to the duty officer.

Dorner waddled from the coffee pot to his chair when Tobias stopped in front of his desk.

"How are you, Franz? How's the wife?"

Hips twice as broad as his shoulders spread over the brown leather seat that groaned in protest. "Nothing to complain about." He rubbed the cropped hair atop his head, so thin and short it was nothing more than a few quarter-inch spikes. "Can I help you, Inspector?"

"Need to speak to Kurt Gruber. Would you look up what hours he's on today?"

Dorner punched some keys on his computer. "He's not. Off duty for three days. Cycles back on Sunday."

Tobias shook his head in irritation. "All right. Thanks."

Back in his office, he removed his coat and settled onto his chair. Albert didn't look up as he listened to someone on the other end of the phone.

Something niggled just below the surface. Something he'd not thought of that would make what August had told him, Eike's activities, and the death of Herr Luschin all fit together. Now young

Gruber was added in the mix.

His partner hung up the phone and swiveled his chair to face him. "Nothing new. And the final autopsy report will be a couple of more days, but Lena stands by her preliminary conclusions. Too many prescription meds and no sign of foul play."

"Too many pills *is* foul play." He and Albert stared at each other for a moment. "He'd been on the medication for years. Refilled it on time. Doesn't seem to line up with getting confused about his dosage."

Albert nodded. "His doctor felt his mental state was good for a man his age."

Tobias drummed his fingers on the desk. "August and Lacy have had a few accidents at the castle." He relayed what she'd told him at lunch. "But she's on the fence as far as suspecting Fabian for having anything to do with the lord's death."

"He seems the most likely to have knocked her out." Albert's shoulders rose in an exaggerated shrug. "If that's what happened."

"That's what makes her unsure, although after their chat she felt certain he's innocent of any wrongdoing—other than sleeping with the lord's wife. But if not Bauer, and unless there's reason someone else would want to do away with Herr Luschin, we're left with Eike. Bauer's motives to gain early access to the estate and the wife are clear. But Eike?"

Albert's chair squeaked as he leaned back with his full weight. "They could be equally guilty. What if Herr Luschin found out about the affair? Bauer and Eike had to get the old lord out of the way before he threw her out."

"Maybe." The simple explanation didn't sit right with him. "There's something I'm not getting. Something we're missing." He ticked through the key points. "Got rid of an old husband. The lover was the supposed heir of the estate. Castle Luschin, once a Nazi holding. Eike's political aspirations for the neo-Nazi party."

Herr Luschin would never have stood for that.

"Maybe there's a connection." He lifted the telephone and punched an extension. "Hello, Carl. How busy are you?"

Carl Hirsch, upstairs in IT, yawned in his ear. "Not. Got something?"

The IT specialist was always short on words and long on ability. He also had a nose for finding details others might miss. "I need some family history on Eike Luschin."

"You mean like a family tree?"

"Yeah. Go back a couple of generations, some time before World War Two. See if you can find out which side of the fence her grandparents, make that great-grandparents, chose. Her maiden name is Leitner."

"Will do, Inspector." He could almost hear Hirsch sitting up straight and poising his fingers over the keyboard.

"Thanks, Carl."

"Nah, thank *you*. Tired of sitting around with my thumb up my butt."

"Appreciate the visual." Tobias disconnected.

His partner stared at him for a moment, as if considering his words carefully. "You might be reaching to connect Eike's politics to murder. Why the family tree search?"

"It's too coincidental that the estate was bound for SS glory during the war, and now she's heading up a push for the Nazi party's power." Tightness in his chest told him there had to be some connection. The dots were there—just no logical way to connect them yet.

"Tobias." He rubbed his chin. "Tobias, you've been pretty mired in politics for over a year. Are you sure you aren't confusing the facts of this case with your…need…to halt a fascist uprising?"

"I've got to consider Eike as a suspect. We haven't found any reason to point the finger at any of Herr Luschin's business and social associates. No one had cause to wish the man dead." He opened a drawer of his desk, tipped back in his chair and propped his feet on the edge of the drawer. "Eike's a Nazi. Herr Luschin wasn't. She happened to marry the lord of Castle Luschin. I don't believe in coincidence."

"How are you so sure about her connections? She hasn't gone public. Never see her in any of the news stories when there's a rally. You sure your sources are right?"

His sources were more than sources. He was on the board of *Der Neue Widerstand,* and they fought the resurgence quietly and secretly. Exactly the way Eike worked.

"They're right, Al. It's easy to keep an eye on the ones out front, at rallies, voting, running on neo-Nazi platforms. Covert party members like Eike are to be feared the most."

Albert leaned back, folded his arms across his chest, and appeared to consider his words. "What exactly do you think Carl will find?"

"I don't know—exactly—I just know there's a piece missing." He gazed beyond his partner's head to the strips of bright sky wedged between slats of the blind on the window. "And until I figure it out, I don't want anyone hearing that we're looking at Eike. I want her to feel confident."

"She could be trying to scare them with the accidents. Send them running back home."

"That seems likely. But Lacy is still the rightful owner and August the next in line to inherit the Luschin estate. Eike isn't a tenant kind of woman." He removed his feet from the drawer and sat forward. "That bothers me."

Tobias took a key from his pants pocket and unlocked a drawer on his desk. He drew out two files: one on Eike Leitner Luschin, and one slim file marked Austria, 1938-1945. He and the committee focused on today's activities of the neo-Nazi movement, not the history. Tobias believed knowledge of the past could help him in the present, plus it interested him.

"There's something I'm missing, Al. Something…" He'd read through the files again, maybe add to his research. Something might click.

****

Eike paced beside her bed, a silky bathrobe flowing around her ankles with each turn. An afternoon bath had done little to relax her. She had no desire to entertain the *temporary* Frau of Castle Luschin at yet another evening meal. They could rifle through Lenhard's things all afternoon without her, then she'd have a lapse into sorrow and miss dinner. Let them dine alone in their room.

Lacy Meadowlark might be the deeded owner, but that sense of entitlement wouldn't last long. And her daughter couldn't lay claim for another year. Oh yes, she was well aware of the terms of the inheritance of the estate set up by the first Lenhard Luschin in 1847. Bloodline inheritance, yet, only able to take possession at the age of twenty-five.

A son—in Paris, did Lacy say?—would pose no threat for five more years. By then, Austria would be the German National state it should be, and the deed would have no relevance. She'd be the rightful owner.

These last five years…five long years…had been so trying. With a rub to the temple, she slowed her pacing. She hadn't realized how fit Lenhard was when they'd married—and how vain to think he could marry a woman like her, of her age, and keep her happy.

The plan had been good. Much had been accomplished in five years. Fabian, the drunken dolt, would be Lenhard's successor, and he'd have married her. Castle Luschin would've remained hers, and in her family, as it should. She could've accomplished so much in the next five years, perhaps even three years. Now, he was no longer the first in line for the estate.

But he could be.

In front of the mirror, she paused, tilted her chin upward, and clasped hands in front of her breasts. She was on the cusp of achieving her political goals, and soon she'd hold a position in the party that would allot all the privileges she deserved. Her eyes misted over, and she blinked back tears. She'd be able to correct history for her great-grandfather who'd been robbed of his accomplishments and her inheritance. A single tear escaped. Not only had her family's status and wealth been stolen, but also their name. Her grandfather's spineless action of changing the family name to Leitner would be righted. And Eike Buchleitner, great-granddaughter of Franz Buchleitner, SS, would hold her deserved place in history.

A rap on the door rudely interrupted her daydreams. "What?" She glared at the closed entry, brushing the tear from her face.

"Eike, sweetheart, it's Fabian."

She rubbed the ache of remembrance from her chest, closed her eyes for a moment, and answered. "Come in, dear nephew." With a mood just foul enough, she took enjoyment in rubbing the sniveling man wrong.

"I told you not to call me that."

"Close the door and stop being such a sissy."

"Sissy?" He sauntered toward the bed, yet he scowled.

His downturned mouth, pasty skin, and lifeless gait brought an angry tremor to her shoulders. She couldn't face a boring tryst with him today. "Why don't we have a small liqueur? I need a pick me up."

He glanced at his watch.

"I know, darling." She moved closer, batted her lashes, and smiled inwardly at his now expectant expression. "I'm a stickler on you not imbibing so early in the day, but I don't think a teensy bitter counts."

The bed didn't get a second glance as he took her hand and strode out of her chambers to the liqueur cabinet.

After pouring a thimbleful for her and a double amount for him, they lounged on the sofa. It would be best if he passed out before dinner, which she could ensure with a few more drinks.

"I've set in motion a chapel memorial for Lenhard in the morning. A notice has already gone out to anyone of importance." She wet her tongue with the bitters.

Fabian took a healthy sip of his drink. "They've released his body?"

"No, but I'm having a memorial, a tribute." She tapped the rim of the glass with her index finger. The community needed to see her sorrow. Sympathy would be called up for the grieving widow. "I should call Tobias today and insist they release Lenhard so final arrangements can be made. I can't be kept on hold for planning the funeral."

"Why not wait for a funeral? Why the memorial service?" He cocked his head, as if studying her.

His blue-gray eyes were grayer today. She didn't care for the way they stared.

"He's an important member of this community, darling, and we shouldn't let the town speculate about his death. It isn't respectable. He deserves a memorial as soon as possible. Inspector Wolf is dragging his feet for no reason." Her tongue darted a quick taste of the bitters. "Besides, I don't like the overtures your relatives are making. A memorial can help to get them on their way."

He avoided her gaze. "I rather like them. They're nice people."

"Nice people who are stealing your inheritance."

"Well, then, I guess it never was mine to steal, was it?" He gave her a sideways glance.

"Oh hell, Fabian, get a backbone." She slammed her glass on the table. "Why should someone who never knew Lenhard, only found out about Castle Luschin a few months ago, and are *not* Austrian, have any claim to this land?"

He threw down his bitters, scooped her glass up, and polished it off. "You don't think a deed that's endured for nearly two hundred years has any bearing on the matter?"

She stood and paced beside the sofa with clenched fists at her sides. "No. This land...this land..." The man could never understand.

"I don't suppose you want to marry me now, do you?" He slid from the sofa and stalked to the liquor cabinet.

A laugh rose in her throat, and suppressing the near outburst choked her. *Hell, no,* she wanted to scream. She wasn't marrying *him*.

Claiming her heritage was her one and only goal.

He unscrewed the top on a club soda, put a handful of ice in a tall glass, and splashed in the liquid, topping it off with a heavy dose of bitters.

"Oh, darling, of course I want to marry you." With effort she outstretched her arms. *For the sake of Austria.* "I'm only looking out for your well-being."

"I don't do so badly in Vienna."

With her arms still outstretched, she wiggled her fingers come hither. "Of course you don't. You're a respected businessman. But you deserve so much more."

Settling against her, he sipped his drink, and listened.

Always, he listened.

****

"The food was great and the company exceptional this evening." August threw her napkin on the table that kitchen personnel had set up in their room earlier. She raised her coffee cup as if toasting her mother, who'd just hung up from a conversation with Chance. "What did my new stepdad have to say?"

"He agrees with Inspector Wolf. In fact, he'd prefer we pack our bags and head into town right now."

"Men! No, I should say men with cop mentalities. *Sheriff* Chance Meadowlark and *Inspector* Tobias Wolf are a bit macho, don't you think?"

"I don't think machismo has anything to do with it. Chance had some valid points. They can read these things a lot better than we can, August."

"It's not that they're worried we can't take care of ourselves?"

Her mother's green eyes twinkled. "That might have something to do with it. Inspector Wolf does seem to be taking a personal interest in your safety."

She wouldn't deny it or the excitement that thought brought her. The mutual interest idea sent a pleasurable sensation across her chest, and she allowed a smile to answer her mother. "But, Mom, shunning us for dinner is obviously in response to your subtle needling this morning. Nazi Eike is pouting in her room, not mourning, I'd bet you anything."

"I wouldn't bet. It's a tossup. She did avoid us all day. Yet, she looked quite distraught when she told us about the memorial service tomorrow." She set her cell on the dresser and picked up a stack of pictures she'd taken from Lenhard's room. "We aren't really accomplishing anything here that we couldn't accomplish staying in town. The drive is short."

August huffed, realized she had her daughter-disagrees-with-Mom frown on when her mother narrowed her eyes, and bit her lip.

"We can go back and forth as much as we want. I'll be able to talk to Mark tomorrow and find out what more he needs me to achieve on the legal front."

"I've made some *late-night* discoveries that have been eye-opening for Wolf."

Her mom's gaze held a tinge of sadness. "But they don't have anything to do with why we came here."

A few tentacles of guilt slid around her heart. "I know." Spying on Eike and conferring with Wolf was enjoyable, but did nothing for her mom's main purpose in this trip. "Have you found enough in Lenhard's things to learn all you can about your father?"

"I've got a pretty good picture." She sat on the bed and glanced at the photographs in her hand. "I'm going to box up some things to be sent back to the states. Then in a few months come back and do some more browsing. I'm not sure how much longer we should stay." When she lifted her gaze from the photos, she set her shoulders as if she'd made a decision. "I feel certain we could leave, and the estate would be maintained as it is now. Mark may need to come back with us, assuming this is all in his realm of expertise. He mentioned finding an Austrian lawyer."

"What?" She stood. "Leave before we know exactly what happened to your grandfather?"

Mom shrugged. "We may never know for sure."

"But can we trust Eike to not sell off stuff or...or..."

"We have a few more days until our flight back. Let's see if she tries to pull anything. See what more the inspector learns." She raised a palm when August made a move to protest. "Yes, we'll need someone to keep the status quo, but that's probably the financial people. Eike's supposed to supply us with info tomorrow."

"Then we should hang here, watch, and wait." When her mother shook her head, rebellion tightened her stomach muscles. "Mom, I haven't gotten to study even one percent of the art and antiques. This Nazi thing is high priority on Wolf's to do list, and I'm enjoying the hell out of sleuthing."

"He told you to stop. I'm inclined to listen to him. August, you're an adult. I can't tell you what you should do, but I'd really like you to move back to the hotel with me tomorrow after the memorial service. Let's see what we can do to enjoy ourselves and stay out of the inspector's way for the balance of the week."

The last thing she wanted to do was stay out of Wolf's way. Yet, the police station was *in* town. "I suppose I can sleep in town if that'll make everyone happy."

****

The lights in the solar were out. Only one lamp provided dim lighting in Eike's bedchambers. "The car is ready?" She rose from her bed, shrugged into her robe, and wandered to the window.

"Yes. But a car crash is risky." Kurt slipped from the bed to stand behind her. His hands rested hot on her shoulders. "I can handle the disappearance of the two American women much quicker."

"I know, but this will keep us out of it. An *accident*. We'll trust the steep incline and mountainside will take care of our problem."

"You are trusting fate. This is not like you, *mein Fuhrer.*"

She whirled to face him, exalted by his pet name for her that also held foretelling of their future. "We must avoid any further scrutiny of our headquarters or me. They may die, or they may not, but such an accident will send them home."

His hands slid from her shoulders, and even in the dim lighting she could see his beautifully formed face surveying hers.

"Do you have reservations about removing obstacles that—"

"Do not question my motives." Her jaw clenched, and her eyes burned with threatening tears. How little he knew of sacrifice. She saw it in his eyes—the excitement of a man who relished death at his hands as a solution. The Americans had no right to her inheritance, but certain death? One day perhaps…tomorrow, perhaps. "Do not forget who I am."

He nodded, drew up straight and tall, and expanded his chest with a deep breath. She stared into his face, not blinking. His chin inched up, and a growing hardness pressed on her stomach.

A thrill tingled over her shoulders. Every obstacle was so easily handled. She had complete control. Even of the perfect specimen of man who stood erect before her. She snickered inwardly at the double entendre. "But now, leave, and wait for my call tomorrow."

When I'll be rid of the American women.
****

August stepped into the sunshine the next morning. "Things keep getting stranger and stranger around here, Mom. First Fabian turns out to be a nice guy who so much as said Eike is an untrustworthy bitch, and then flirty Kurt turns out to be a Nazi. And a Nazi having an affair with Eike. Then you announce we're forging ahead with plans for the castle, and we're shunned for an entire day. Now suddenly, we're invited to a memorial before anything is settled about Great-grandfather."

Her mother gave her a sideways glance. "First off, Fabian didn't use those words. In fact, it sounds like he didn't use any words at all about Eike—as much as you tried to pry some information out of him. And secondly, Kurt could be having an affair with a kitchen maid."

August opened the door on the rental car and peered across the top at her mom. "Really? Do you always have to be so…exact? And right?" She slid onto her seat as her mom settled behind the wheel. "I like my version much better."

Her mother chuckled, started the engine, and pulled around the circular drive. "I'm sure we'll learn more over the next few days, even though we're moving to town after this service. I'll call Mark this afternoon, about the time he gets in his office. I should be able to get the name and number of whoever is handling the estate from Eike by then."

The cool air, sparkling green grass, and abundant red and purple flowers contrasted with the reason for this early morning outing. A tribute to her great-grandfather would be at the very least somber.

"Maybe. Funeral plans are bound to be her next excuse after this memorial. And Wolf's investigation. Eike has lots of reasons to drag out the drama." Her stomach clenched. "What if she really had something to do with Lenhard's death?"

"Maybe by later today, Inspector Wolf can throw more light on that. I'm just glad we both think Fabian doesn't appear to have had anything to do with Grandfather's death," her mom remarked as they drove through the castle gate. "In spite of having an affair with Eike, I hope we get a chance to know him better in the next few days. At least he's a relative." They rounded a bend in the road and began a slow descent. "We spotted the chapel when we were hiking yesterday. The turnoff should be on our right. Eike said we couldn't miss it, and she'd be along shortly."

"The grand Frau wants to make a dramatic, tearful entrance, no doubt." After lunch with Wolf and his revelations about Eike's politics and then her moods swinging from ignoring them to playing sweet, she'd formed an opinion of the woman her mother didn't entirely share.

"When did you get so cynical, kiddo?"

"I don't think I'm cynical. And after what Wolf told me about her politics, I'm seeing her in a wholly different light. I'm realistic." If Eike *had* played a nasty part in Lenhard's death, someone so phony might be easier to catch in her own web. "Realistic?" Her mother chuckled. "You do see the dramatic—" She leaned forward and scanned the dashboard lights. "What the hell?"

"What?"

"The brakes seem—"

"Mom, what?" August fell to the right as the car sped around a curve. "Slow down."

She pumped the brakes. "I can't." Her mom darted her a wide-eyed glance. "Oh hell! The brakes won't work. Oh hell!" She stomped her foot, and pumped frantically.

"We're picking up speed." August's voice rose, shouting without need.

"I know. I know." Her mother hunched over the wheel, face rigid and pale. "Jerk on the emergency brake."

She grabbed the handle with both hands and pulled. No effect.

"Stay calm." August jammed her feet against the floorboard. Her fingers clawed the seat on each side of her legs. "Just keep it in the middle—"

Her mother's hands went white gripping the wheel.

"Oh my God, August, we're—"

Tires squealed.

August's head swam as mountain scenery flew by.

She braced herself as the car hurdled around a bend in the road and began to slide.

The cliff face grew close.

Her mother jerked the wheel.

The world flipped upside down. Metal on rock. Screeching.

And silence.

CHAPTER TEN

Tobias entered the hospital room with Albert close behind. Three hours had elapsed since he'd passed the departing ambulance coming down the mountain on his way to the site of the crash. The call had come on route to the memorial service for Herr Lenhard Luschin. He'd wanted nothing more than to follow the ambulance to the hospital when he'd arrived on scene and discovered Lacy and August were in the emergency vehicle.

However, at the site, his instincts kicked in with a jolt. After the succession of "accidents" at the castle, this accident required a closer look. Preliminary results proved him correct.

His gut twisted at the sight of the tubes and monitors hooked to the sedated Lacy.

Now, responsibility weighed his shoulders and put lead in his step as he entered the room. Had his desire to uncover more about Eike's political ambitions put these women in danger? He'd allowed them to stay on in hopes of learning more through August's observations in spite of his suspicions surrounding Herr Luschin's death. If Eike was a zealot—what was he?

August sat in a chair next to her mother's bed, her wrist bandaged. The small bandage above her right eye and the Steri-Strip on her cheek appeared to be the only other damage besides light bruises taking color. Her lip quivered.

Heat climbed his neck, and he set his jaw. If he'd been more forceful, demanded, and followed through that they leave the castle...

The hollowness in his chest grew—this was his fault.

He drew up beside her. "August, are you okay?"

"I'm fine, but Mom…" Tears filled her eyes.

His hand went to her shoulder and squeezed. "I spoke with the nurses. She will be fine." He rubbed his hand across her back.

"I know," she whispered. "Her injuries aren't minor, but she'll recover. The lung was the main concern, but they feel certain she's out of danger now. Her concussion is mild." She looked up with glistening eyes, the green rims of her irises intensified by the overhead fluorescent lights. "I thought…when I first saw her…it was awful."

"I can only imagine." As much as he yearned to hold and comfort her, he had to speak to her on a professional level. "Your wrist. Is it bad?"

"No. A cut. Nothing.

"Can we step outside to talk? Albert will stay by her side."

Resisting the urge to slip his hand around her waist, he clasped her elbow, and led her to a quiet corner of a waiting room down the hall. After all his years as an inspector, this case had given him some of the hardest moments of his career. First, their disappointment that the relative they yearned to meet had died under suspicious circumstances, and now he had to break troubling news that would further complicate their presence. He had his own set of complications when it came to August, making this scene more personal than it should be for him. He guided her to a couch and sat beside her.

"I am sorry I could not get here sooner. I needed to be at the scene, where the car crashed, to oversee the investigation." He touched her knee. They were alone with no need to withhold his personal side from her. But his hand drew back with the thought she might not have similar feelings and would consider his actions an assumption. "Is there anything I can do for you? Were you able to contact family?"

"My mom's husband is on his way. He had to arrange for a puddle jumper from Timberline, and then he'll take the first flight out of Phoenix. My brother is in Paris and is making arrangements to leave as soon as possible. Since she'll be okay, I didn't call any friends yet." She took a deep ragged breath. "She'll be *okay*."

"Tell me what happened."

"The brakes failed. We were on our way to the memorial service. The car…it flipped, and we hit the mountain. Or maybe we hit the mountain and flipped." She closed her eyes then dropped her head to her hands. "It happened so fast." The heels of her palms pushed against her lids.

"Lacy maneuvered the car to your advantage. Had you gone...things could have been worse." *You'd both be dead.* He swallowed, heavily imagining the alternate outcome. His fondness for the young woman beside him grew intense. "I should have insisted, should have physically removed you from the estate. I regret I was not more persistent."

Her sad eyes regarded him. She frowned then held her hands to her eyes again. "This isn't your fault. It was just a horrible accident." Her body visibly trembled.

He touched her knee again. "I do not believe it was an accident, August."

Her hands slid slowly down her face. "Not an accident?"

"The brakes—*Kriminaltechnik,* er, forensics says there are indications of tampering."

Her gasp filled the quiet corner. "Oh, no. No."

Albert appeared and took the chair next to him. "A nurse is in the room."

Tobias grasped both her hands, gently, aware of cuts under the bandage on her wrist, and although he kept his voice low, his tone was gravely serious. "Someone knew what they were doing. It will take more time for forensics to detail it, but they are rather sure."

"But who, why?"

"I have to assume—"

"First my great-grandfather and now his heirs. Castle Luschin." Her brow wrinkled.

"As unfortunate as this accident is, there will at least be evidence now to sustain our suspicions. I am sure." He gazed into her face, wanting to assure her they'd find and punish the persons responsible. A bluish bruise formed a half-moon under her eye. Two more were taking color on her forehead. He wanted to kiss away her pain, but instead, gave her fingers a gentle caress.

She narrowed her eyes. "Eike."

"We are looking at others, too, Bauer included." He couldn't disclose his suspicions about Kurt since all he had was apparently the same Nazi ties as the Frau. And he hadn't connected those dots to the lord's death yet. "Your cousin owns a car dealership. No doubt he has the knowledge to disable a car the way your rental was. He and Eike—"

"No, Wolf." She squeezed his hand with her good one. "I can't believe he had anything to do with this or with my great-grandfather's death." Her voice cracked.

He brushed his fingers across the back of her hands. If Albert hadn't been sitting in the same room, he might have taken her face in his hands, kissed her lids, her nose, and her bruised cheek. His stomach tensed, holding back the desire. "He might tell you anything to divert suspicion away from him."

"It's more what he didn't say. He's in love with Eike. He wouldn't say so, but it's obvious. He doesn't even like the castle, has no appreciation of the fortune in art or the land. He seemed sad about Lenhard. The more I've thought about it, the more I'm convinced."

"But he *is* Eike's lover and—"

"Yes, and if she lured him into thinking she loved him and then she killed Lenhard, the supposed heir would keep her living in the custom she was used to."

She might have a point. But there was still the question of why now? There had to be a connection to her carefully guarded Nazi activities.

August scooted to the edge of the couch, her face flushed, the tears gone. "Then along comes the American women to steal it all away from her. So she tries to kill us in a car accident."

As much as he believed Bauer could've played a role, August's theory had merit. "Let me do more investigating." He stood, bringing her with him. "Are you hungry? Can I get you anything? I assume you want to stay until your mother's husband arrives?"

"Yes. I want to wait for Chance. It sounded like he'd be here by the end of the day or at least early evening."

He glanced at his partner. "I'll meet you out at the car. I'm going to see August back to the room."

The elder man had a smirk on his face, even in the throes of an attempted murder case. Tobias would miss him when he retired.

When they rounded the corner and entered the hallway to the room, Tobias couldn't help it—he slipped his arm around her waist. When she relaxed into his side, his heart thumped.

Once inside, they gazed at the sleeping Lacy for a moment. The white sheet was tucked neatly over her chest, a pale green blanket over the sheet, and the head of the bed slightly raised. In the dim light, the walls took on a gray hue over their green tint.

"I am so sorry, August. If I had—"

"Stop, Wolf." The frown she wore when her gaze slid from her mother to his face dissolved into softness. "It isn't your fault. You'd convinced us. We were leaving. After the service."

"After? Damn it." His finger grazed her chin, and he noticed a small nick in her skin. Anger beat in his chest. Lovely August didn't deserve the danger he'd allowed to pursue her. "I *will* find who did this."

She laid her hand on his chest, and he covered it with his free one. "I know." Her stare grew intense.

His heart beat now with more than anger. Her faith in him, shining in her eyes, roused passion beyond mere attraction.

He'd not let go of her waist yet, and she leaned into him. Her sweet, honey scent filled his head. The idea of protecting her fell within his job description, but the urge to kiss her went beyond a public servant's duty. Nevertheless, he let his lips lightly touch her unscathed cheek, then dropped his hand from hers resting on his chest.

August quickly closed the tiny distance he'd put between them, increasing the pressure of her fingers on his torso. His arm around her waist closed tighter as his body had a mind of its own. When she lifted her chin higher, bringing her lips to his, the message her kiss sent matched the desire he'd been fighting. A soft moan vibrated against his mouth, and he pulled back, afraid he'd hurt her bruised cheek.

"Mmm, no, come back." She dove deeper.

With her exploration, his desire deepened. He inched his hands lower on her back, bringing her hard against the ever-increasing ache in his groin. *Mein Gott!* He wanted to taste every inch of her. Wanted to feel—

"*Ach! Inspektor.*"

He broke away at the interruption.

A nurse stood in the partially opened doorway. "I'm sorry. Excuse me." She abruptly retreated, closing the door behind her.

"Well, that was a bit awkward." August's crooked smile teased.

"Indeed." He touched her cheek then stepped backward. "And a bit unprofessional."

"I didn't mind."

Nor did he. "I have to get back to forensics." He couldn't undo what just happened, but he needed to take a step back. For now. This was his case, and he needed to keep his head on straight. "You have my phone number. Call me when your mother's husband arrives, if I have not returned by then. I will keep forensics on the accident recovery this afternoon until I am totally satisfied they have gathered all possible evidence."

"Are you going back to the estate?" Even as she asked the question, her attention drifted to her mother.

"I do have a few more questions for the grieving widow, but..." There were other avenues to pursue first. "I'll send a police woman out to the castle. She'll call you when she is in the guestroom so you can direct her as to what you will need for a couple of days. I do not want you going back. She can bring you clothes, and whatever else needed, to the hospital. You're going to stay in town where I can keep an eye on you."

She brought her attention back along with the crooked smile he found so beguiling. "You're my bodyguard?"

"That might be arranged." An overwhelming urge to take her into his arms hammered him, yet he back stepped to the door. "I will be by this evening, take you to get something to eat other than hospital food. In the meantime, I'll call Heidi and get you a room." He touched the doorknob.

"Wolf?"

"Yes?"

She closed the distance between them. "I know we've only just met, but I feel like I can trust you." She brushed his lips with hers then moved out of reach. Her hand came up in a shooing motion. "Go do what you do, and I'll see you tonight."

He closed the door behind him. A murder, an attempted murder, and a lack of clues—he shouldn't feel this good.

****

Eike paced between the sofa and the liquor cabinet. A knock on the door sent her scurrying, and when she opened it, a scream of frustration strangled in her throat.

Fabian, eyes wide and rubbing the back of his neck, exclaimed, "My God, Eike."

"I don't feel like talking, Fabian." *He shouldn't be back from the chapel yet.* "I thought you were going to take care of rearranging the service and deal with all the people."

He pushed past her. "I need a drink. I did what I could. You shouldn't have left me alone. It was too much. Herr Bloch offered to help so I left him to it."

The weak imbecile was insufferable. "He's a *servant*, Fabian. That's not his place."

"He knew Lenhard better than I did." A good measure of a new bottle of cognac nearly filled his glass. "First Lenhard and now the American women. What in hell…" He whirled to face her, the liquid nearly sloshing over the rim. "This is terrible."

"Terrible?" The only terrible thing was that the daughter hadn't ended up in the hospital, too. "What would be so bad about losing your two fortune hunting cousins? It would've solved all of our problems." She yanked one high heel from her foot, then the other.

"Problems? What? Not inheriting the estate? I told you, we have Vienna—"

"Fuck Vienna!" She flung one of the heels sailing across the room.

"Eike, really!"

She dropped the other heel and raked her hands through each side of her hair. "I *told* you I didn't feel like talking."

"Surely, you don't mean it." His mouth hung open like a dying fish. "Wishing the two American women dead just so—"

"Shut up."

His usually dull gray eyes sharpened. "Lenhard's dead and now you wish my cousins dead?" He glanced at the drink in his hand and back at her, eyes narrowed. "This estate means that much?"

"How dare you use that tone." He had no right to question her about anything. Her temples throbbed. She almost didn't hear the soft rap on the door over the blood pulsing in her ears. She knew who it was. *Damn it.*

"Who would that be?"

"I don't know."

They stared at each other while she tried to come up with some plausible explanation. When Fabian started for the door, she jumped. "I'll get it."

She opened the door quickly and wide so Kurt could see they were not alone. "Policeman Gruber. What can I do for you?"

"Frau Luschin. I'm sorry to bother you, but I, uh, have a few questions for you concerning the accident with the American women."

"Of course. Please come in."

Fabian scowled. "Why would they send you? Are we no longer important enough for the inspector?" He surveyed Kurt, head to toe, then jerked as if a light blinked on.

Eike's fists clenched at her sides. Kurt wore civilian clothes.

"How rude." She stepped closer to Fabian, obscuring his view. "It's a simple accident. This policeman is just following orders." Her hands itched to throttle the dolt. "Would you excuse us so I can answer his questions?"

"But—they're *my* cousins." He craned his neck to spy Kurt. "And it's my…duty to help you."

Her face burned. She fought for control with a deep breath. "This is my castle, and they are my guests. You can take your drink back to your room while I handle my own affairs."

Fabian didn't wilt as he usually did. Instead, he looked at her then said, "I'll be back." He strode from the room, closing the door behind him with a snap.

Eike grabbed Kurt's arm, hauling him into her private chambers, to the foot of her bed, and away from the solar door where possible lingering ears could hear. "That son of a bitch is beginning to get in my way." She glanced back at the door. "Did anyone see you?"

"No, of course not." He stood at attention, his body tense, and his face rigid. "I parked off grounds, came in the hidden wall gate and through the basement. I wouldn't jeopardize—"

"But everything *was* jeopardized with the botched accident." As unreasonable as her lashing out was, her tension lessened with the words.

Kurt remained silent, unmoving. She knew he wouldn't dare dispute her or remind her he'd wanted to handle them another way.

All right, he could have his way now.

"The good inspector called me from the accident. Lacy was hurt enough, but the daughter was hardly scratched."

She paced in front of him. "I've become impatient. Scaring them is no longer enough." Something inside let loose with her decision. "Fabian has become a liability, too, I fear. He's getting too close to his cousins." The last word soured her tongue.

Stopping in front of her soldier, she ran her hands over the black T-shirt hugging Kurt's chest, the ripples of his abs warming to her touch. "It's time to move my plan forward. I spoke with Schuler late last night." The idea took solid form. "We're going to have more support from the Social Democrats than we first thought." Gooseflesh spread from her neck, down her arms, and across her chest. Her nipples peaked with excitement. "I'm taking my future, Austria's future, into my own hands." As she spoke, her fingers slipped ever lower on her soldier's body until she gripped his hardened response with a deep-throated chuckle. "With your help, *mein Liebling*, there is no stopping us."

"*Mein Fuhrer.*" His shoulders squared, chin jutted out, and he gazed at attention over her head. "What do you ask of me?"

Her fingers gripped tighter. "There is a red scarf in the guest room. It belongs to August. Find it and bring it back here."

He clenched his jaw and nodded.

"But first..." Eike's desire grew hot as Kurt strained to maintain his soldier's stance even as her fingers now relaxed, squeezed, relaxed. She laughed, pushed her body into him, and they toppled onto her bed.

****

Albert scratched his chin. "Maybe I should take another trip out to the estate and get annoying with a lot of questions."

"No, not yet." Tobias scanned his notes from the preliminary observations on the car crash. "Until the forensics are completed on the rental, let Eike think she's safe."

"How did you convince *Oberstleutnat* Egger to not call the press?"

Tobias smiled and shrugged. His boss, Egger, had a fondness for publicity.

"He's quite enjoyed the attention after the lord's death, even though there's no hint of murder, officially, yet." Albert leaned back in his chair. "An attempted murder of two American women could get him on the front page, not to mention an interview for television."

"I reasoned with him."

Albert dipped his chin, creasing his thick neck. "I'll call bull on that."

"I dangled a carrot." Tobias rose and paced in front of the bookcase. "If he'll keep it out of the press for now, I'll give him an even bigger story that will grab the press in Vienna."

"And that is?"

He stopped and met his partner's questioning stare. "That *thing* I can't quite put my finger on. Whatever *that* is." It was there, like the tiny sheen of a gem mostly buried in the earth. His gut told him a boulder was waiting to be exposed. "The important thing is he took the carrot."

"So, where do we go now?"

"We wait and see if there's anything physical to connect Eike to the Americans' accident." Tobias wandered to the window and the view of the city outside. People waiting at the bus stop. A sidewalk café serving after work coffees. His mind was too fettered to enjoy watching the late afternoon city activity below. *Kurt*. What part did Eike, Kurt, and politics play in this? "We need hard evidence. We wait for the accident results."

His partner frowned. "That means you're sending me back to the theft at the bakery yesterday. Stolen buns."

Tobias chuckled. "Nice and safe for a man on his way to retirement."

"Nice and boring. You're making my wife happy."

****

"Whatever you're planning, Eike, you'd better not."

"Or what, Fabian?"

His mouth fell open as wide as his eyes.

"As I thought. You idiot." She finished buttoning her blouse and slacks.

Kurt stood next to Fabian, fists still clenched and looking particularly sexy in a *Burschenschaften* sash and nothing else.

The blood from Fabian's nose trickled a path around his lips and pooled at the corner. His hands were bound behind his back. He darted a glance at Kurt. "Why are you helping her? You're *police*. You can't."

"Our time is near again." His blue-eyed gaze never left her face.

Eike skimmed her fingertips down the length of Kurt's chest from his shoulder to his hip. He'd not bothered dressing after Fabian interrupted their play. The dolt's gaze followed, and so she let her hand move lower, pausing to rub her palm over the younger man's well-endowed, rising manhood.

Fabian swallowed, raised his head, and glowered.

She laughed, patted Kurt's crotch, then took the Walther from a drawer at the end of the coffee table. "The world would be at your feet, if you'd just kept your nose out of my affairs. How dare you come snooping into my private area without being invited?" She waved her great-grandfather's gun in his face. "Why the hell did you choose tonight to not drink yourself to sleep?"

His jaw clenched tight, and the veins in his neck grew taut.

She focused on Kurt. "Call."

He retreated to her bedchamber.

"You can have your boy. Let me go, Eike, and I'll go back to Vienna never to bother you again."

"Too late for that, nephew. You've disappointed me, and now...there's no place for you."

"Eike—"

She stuck the gun in his mouth. His face took on the sheen of newly fallen snow. Sweat trickled off his temples and mixed with the blood.

Kurt strode into the room, taking his position beside the sickly colored nephew.

"Well?"

"She's left the hospital. Alone."

Eike removed the gun from his mouth, took a step back, and stared into the face of the last Luschin male. She'd made her decision and now...resolve numbed her. The only vision to hold was the new beginning.

"You killed him, didn't you?" Spittle formed in the corners of Fabian's mouth. "Did my uncle find out about your Nazi activities?"

"Did you hear that, Kurt? The idiot is finally sober enough to get a clue."

With a slight tick of her head, Kurt moved behind Fabian, lifted gloves from the end table, and slipped his hands into them. He slid the red silk from the same table. With both hands, he held August's scarf that he'd removed from the guest room earlier.

"If you shoot me, your servants will hear. You'll never get away with it."

"Do you think me so stupid?" She thought he'd have peed in his pants by now. The wimp had a bit more gumption than she'd anticipated. "The gun is for drama. I thought you'd appreciate the drama, nephew." Now close enough to smell the copper scent of his blood and the sweat of his fear, she ran the Walther along his face and the length of his side then poked the muzzle into his stomach. His flinch was so slight yet his glare so fierce, a twinge of disappointment tempered her pleasure.

"Can't we come to some sort of understanding?"

"I don't think so. My vision is clear, and there are no compromises. You really should've stayed drunk, dear nephew."

She nodded. With gloved hands, Kurt brought the silk up and

over Fabian's head. She raised her palm to pause him, kissed Fabian on the cheek, and inhaled. From the scarf, August's unique scent drifted over her face. Perfect.

She let her hand drop, and with another nod, Kurt wrapped it tight around the other man's neck. His mouth flew open, and his eyes bulged. Clasping the gun at her breast, she studied the ceiling until the last of the noises and movement quieted.

"Take him to the Great Hall. Everyone is aware it's a room of which August is particularly fond. All help have left their posts by now. Be sure to drop him face down so the broken nose will be construed as happening after she strangled him and he fell forward." She opened the door, checked the hall, and stepped aside for Kurt to leave. "How unfortunate she considered her cousin a threat to her newfound wealth."

CHAPTER ELEVEN

August closed the door of her mother's hospital room. After Chance arrived, she'd gone to the hotel to shower and change into fresh clothes that Wolf had arranged for the policewoman to bring to the Hotel Karnten. She'd driven Chance's rental car. He wasn't planning on leaving the hospital until Lacy did, so she had the use of his car for the duration. The shower revived her in spite of an enclosure so small she could barely turn around and a showerhead that had to be held in her good hand. Back at the hospital, with an aching wrist and a face that looked as if she'd lost a fight, she joined her step-father in his vigilance next to her mother.

"She'll be fine, Chance." August rubbed his shoulder, his hair tickling the tops of her fingers.

His big hands held his wife's limp one, caressing the palm as if to wake her. "Second time this year I've visited her in a hospital. Last time..." He swallowed and his voice grew low. "Last time wasn't nearly this bad."

"When the anesthesia began to wear off, they sedated her. Something about controlling her breathing while they watched how her bruised lung would do. But they're lessening it, and she'll be awake by tomorrow. She certainly won't be up and around, but she's going to be okay."

"It would kill me to lose her." His voice cracked on the word "lose."

August's throat tightened, her eyes moistened, and without thinking, her fingers dug into his shoulder. "Then it looks like you'll be around a while because there's no chance of that."

He let go of her mother's hand and patted her fingers.

She managed a smile. "I figured you'd want to sleep in here tonight, so the nurse said a bed would be brought in for you. Is that okay?"

"No one is going to be able to drag me out of here until Lacy leaves with me."

A soft knock and the door opened behind her. Wolf quietly entered. The sorrow for Chance eased slightly. She motioned him over. He hadn't waited for her to call which brought her an odd pleasure. Maybe his impetus was that of a courteous inspector, but she didn't care as long as she could spend time with him. When he stopped close beside her, she wanted to lean into him, feel the heat of his restrained desire again, and taste and taste. He glanced down and didn't look so much the inspector when he smiled. It would be difficult to see his inspector side quite the same knowing how his kiss could send her over the edge.

She smiled back, holding his gaze, but realized she needed to make introductions when Chance stirred.

"Inspector Wolf, this is my mother's husband, Sheriff Chance Meadowlark."

The men shook hands.

Chance glanced at her mother, rubbed his fingers over her hand, and stood. "August has told me a great deal, Inspector, but would you mind if I asked you a few questions? Maybe we could find a private corner in the waiting room."

"Of course, Sheriff Meadowlark."

Wolf led the way, and she looped her arm through Chance's. His cowboy boots clicked on the tile as they made their way down the hall to the empty waiting room. Wolf stood until they were seated on the couch, and he took a chair at an angle to them.

The sheriff in Chance came out as August listened to his questions and the way he phrased them. Wolf was honest and open.

"It would seem the accidents Lacy experienced escalated to the car crash. All of which took place at the castle. In addition, August's encounter with being knocked out."

Wolf nodded. "But we still don't have any hard evidence to connect anyone to either the death of Lenhard Luschin or the accidents with your wife and August. I don't believe they're separate incidents and the obvious common denominator is Castle Luschin and the estate. But without any physical evidence…" He held his hands palms up.

"I don't plan to leave Lacy's side until we're home safe in Timberline." Chance shifted his copper-eyed gaze on August. "I doubt I can lock August up with us, so I trust you'll protect her."

"You have my word."

They all stood.

She prickled a little at a discussion of her care without any input from her. Taking care of herself had never been a problem. But then a flash of the last moments of the car wreck came to mind and dampened any protest she might lodge. Slipping closer to Wolf brought a whiff of his smoky, cardamom scent, and the idea of him throwing some protective attention her way didn't sound half-bad.

"August, now that Sheriff Meadowlark is here, would you like to get something to eat?" Before she could answer, he spoke to Chance. "You are welcome to come along, too, but I'm assuming you would prefer to stay here."

Chance shook his head.

"Can we bring you something?" August asked.

"Thanks, but I grabbed a bite at the airport. If I get hungry I'll grab something out of the cafeteria."

She wrapped her arms around her stepdad, and gave him a tight, quick hug. At her age it was hard to think of having another father, but she'd grown awfully fond of him in the short time she'd known him. "I'll call later from the hotel."

After the men shook hands, she and Wolf strolled in companionable silence to the hospital exit. He opened the glass door with a smile. Blue dusk greeted her. Leaving behind the astringent odors of a hospital improved her mood further. Wolf touched her back, and she came to life that much more.

"I missed dinner. Are you hungry?"

"I think I am, Wolf." She hadn't felt anything but concern for her mother all day. A vague memory of eating something earlier that a nurse brought her barely registered. With the fresh air and the relief Chance's arrival brought on, her own needs were coming awake.

They stopped by his Porsche parked at the curb. A security cop nodded. "There is a small *gasthaus* down the street from the hotel that makes the best *Schnitzel* in all of Austria. And they serve late. How does that sound?" He opened the door on the passenger side. "I thought a small place and a change of pace from elaborate meals might be nice."

She slid in and clapped her hands. "*Wunderbar*!"

He laughed. "So, you are picking up a little German."

While he came around the front of the car to take the wheel, she admired him through the windshield and sank into the soft leather seat. The prospects of a ride through the narrow European streets in a Porsche with an Austrian James Bond was the first pleasant sensation she'd experienced since the crash.

He settled in, started the engine, then toasted her with his almond-colored gaze. "Are you feeling better about your mother's condition?"

"So much better." About not only her condition, but also her safety now that Chance, sheriff and husband, was on guard. "All her injuries have been repaired, and she's stable. They're cutting off the sedative, and she could possibly be awake and talking tonight, but more likely tomorrow."

"That is *wunderbar* news."

She laughed as the sleek, silver car pulled smoothly into traffic. "Do all Chief Inspectors in Austria get a Porsche?"

"That would have a few more joining the force, would it not? No, this is my personal vehicle."

He obviously didn't need the salary from his job unless policemen in Austria made a lot more money than they did in the states.

"I have family money."

He'd read her mind.

"Do you like living in a castle?"

"I no longer live on the family estate."

"No? I would think it would be fascinating to live in a castle. So much more character than an apartment or regular old house."

He'd entered onto a street within sight of the Hotel Karnten and only a few blocks from the hospital. When the quiet hum of the engine ceased, his wrist draped over the steering wheel, and the other hand fingered the keys in his hand. "I am not comfortable in the castle. My family's history is at odds with my beliefs, and so the castle stands for a philosophy I cannot abide."

"Oh." The seriousness in his eyes, the straight line of his full lips, and deepening shadows as the night grew thicker made the topic of his family seem almost off limits. Almost. "I'm sorry. Are you on bad terms with your parents?"

"Not bad terms. We have a truce of sorts. I just prefer to live elsewhere."

"History, huh?"

"We should take history discussions into the *gasthaus*."

"Oh, yes, let's."

By the time she had her door opened, he'd made his way out and around to give her a hand up. The car did sit low, and her jean skirt had the tendency to rise on her legs. The one really good trait she had was her legs, and if they got Wolf's attention, she didn't mind a little over exposure. This mess would settle eventually, her mother would be healed, and all problems sorted out. A fling with the charming and, yes, sophisticated inspector could be something to look forward to— and he *was* her personal bodyguard.

The memory of his lips warmed her against the night air. As she stood, the lighthearted thought flipped to a flash of the accident and her mother. It must've shown in her face.

"What's wrong, August?"

"I don't know." Her legs went weak, and she leaned against the car. "My happy thoughts turned gray, and I feel sort of dizzy."

His arm slid between her waist and the car. "Did the doctors check you out, *completely*?"

"Inside and out. I think it's just—" So much in such a short time.

"You have had a rough couple of days." He pulled her into him. "I must get you seated and off your feet with some food in your stomach. Have you eaten today?"

"Something. I think."

He held her tight, practically lifting her off her feet with one arm. His strength radiated through her, a sensation that steadied her physically, yet had her stomach doing the wave like at a baseball game.

Guiding her to a corner booth, she glided from his arms to the seat.

He didn't sit, but held her shoulders from behind, his fingertips lightly prodding the muscles between her neck and shoulder blades. "I know it is near impossible to do with your state of affairs, but you need to relax and enjoy a meal. Get a good night's sleep." Now his fingers massaged.

Her muscles jellied under his adept touch, yet her breath quickened and a ricochet effect had her holding a Kegel. In spite of the sensual reaction, she did lean back into his caress, and the tension drained from her neck and back.

"Ah, better." One more soft caress in the hair at the base of her skull, and he slid onto the booth across from her.

She propped her head in hand, elbow on the table, and let her eyes close. "Hmmm, where did you learn to do that?"

"Ohhh...here and there. Practice."

Her lids eased open. "I'd like to hear more."

He picked up a menu, teasingly avoiding her eyes. "I would not want to bore you."

"One thing you're not is boring, Wolf."

The menu was discarded as he hailed a waitress. "Is *Schnitzel* good or would you like something else?"

She agreed, and he ordered *Schnitzel*, potato salad, and beer for two.

The man had secrets. Where to begin? She'd save finding out about his massage techniques and experience for later.

August decided family secrets would be a good place to start peeling back the layers of Tobias Wolf. "So, tell me more about your family history."

He pursed his mouth to the side, gave her a glance, and leaned on the table. The question feathered tension lines at the corners of his eyes. "It is not something I'm prone to talk about."

"I don't want to force you into revealing family secrets." But that's exactly what she'd love to hear. She leaned closer and grinned.

He returned her smile with a shake of his head. "Not really secrets. My family sympathized with the Nazis in World War Two." He let his smile fall away. "My great-grandfather was a traitor to the Austrian people."

"Great-grandfather?" So long ago. "Is he still alive?"

"No."

"And you said your grandfather is also dead."

He nodded.

"I don't quite see why—" But the thought hit her, and his reluctance to elaborate became clear. "Your parents. They're part of the new Nazi movement you mentioned at dinner last night." How terrible.

"No—"

The waitress appeared at the table, two one half-liter steins of beer in one hand and balancing two plates on the other arm. "*Hier bitte.*"

Her soft, rotund stature belied her strength.

"*Danke,*" he thanked her, then chuckled when she walked away. "By the look on your face, August, I'd guess you're impressed with the strength of our waitress."

Happy to entertain him and hear his amusement, she smiled. "She's very capable."

Yet the slight stress lines in his face remained. If her mother was there, she'd warn her the time had come to back off. But since she wasn't—and even if she was—August probably wouldn't heed her warning. She picked up where they'd left off.

"Your parents are *not* supporters of Fascism?"

"No. In fact, they're quite non-political." He spread the napkin on his lap.

"Is that a problem for you?"

"No."

"Then why—"

He set down his fork. "It is difficult to explain. My parents would love to have me back on the estate, but I feel I have something to do, to correct or set right, before I can settle comfortably on the land that my great-grandfather spoiled. Or I should say that his memory spoils for me."

He might have trouble explaining, but it seemed as clear as the crystal glasses at the castle. "If you do an equal turn against Fascism, take care of some Nazis, then the scales might be balanced. The lingering memories, the ghosts, could be put to rest. You might even enjoy castle life again. Is that close?"

His brows tipped up in the middle and the stress around his brown eyes smoothed. In its place, the crinkle of smile lines appeared. He cocked his head and lifted his beer stein. "I will toast to that."

She lifted her stein, although with difficulty, and held it high over the table.

His met hers with a clink. "*Prost,*" he said and drank.

The hearty gulp surprised her. Although tasty, the liquid was warm, or at best room temperature. And very strong. "Warm beer?"

"Chilling is for weak American beer. We Europeans know a thing or two about good brewing. Do you like it?"

"Very much." She put a forkful of potato salad into her mouth. "Oh my." And another. "Mmm." Now her stomach reminded her she'd not eaten much that day. As enticing as the inspector was, all her attention honed in on the rich food and strong beer.

Wolf cut several pieces off his *Schnitzel*, took a bite, and studied her as he chewed. He wiped a corner of his mouth. "I think we have reached *someday*."

"Hmm?" She couldn't possibly quit eating but tried to answer.

"You found it humorous to be, as you called it, 'working with a cop.' You said you would tell me about it someday."

Mouth full, she raised her fork and nodded. Her attitude about the police dulled when confronted with the spicy smile of the inspector.

"I should probably run a check on you. Coming to Austria, fleeing the States—maybe you are escaping. Perhaps you are on someone's most wanted list."

Maybe she could get on *his* list. She took a long drink of the beer that was now going down quite easily. "Ha. Very funny. It's kind of a joke in my family. I had a few run-ins with cops when I was a teenager. Of course, my trouble had everything to do with the attitude of law enforcement and nothing to do with my lack of respect for the law. So, I've never been particularly fond of cops."

He cocked his brow, and right on cue gooseflesh rippled sending a signal to all her nethermost regions.

"So, I am a...challenge for you."

The challenge was to maintain her cool when she found him so hot. "Maybe in the beginning your cop status put me off—that and the way you drive."

He chuckled and sighed.

"But I think the lack of uniform, your accent, and a resemblance to a certain Bond movie star have done wonders to negate your handicap."

He laughed. "My handicap." Another chuckle and a drink of beer. "I will ignore yet another critique of my driving, and take the rest of that as a compliment."

The last few bites of the *Schnitzel* were no longer appetizing. She'd eaten so fast, and the beer was filling. Wolf's strong chin and full lips filled her vision. There wasn't room in her stomach or her thoughts for much else. Her eyelids drooped, every nerve in her body relaxed, and she wished she could crawl into his lap and go to sleep.

"Dessert?" he asked.

"Oh no."

"Then I'll take you to the hotel." He signaled the stout waitress who produced the bill.

Breathlessly, August rose as he left money on the table. Mention of ending the evening at a hotel had her wondering just what kind of an ending they'd have. *How rude to think such carnal thoughts after the day they'd had. Right?* With her grandfather's death, her mother in the hospital, and her brother soon to arrive, she really should be tied in knots with concern and worry. The inspector's hand touched the middle of her back as they left the bright *gasthaus* and entered the night. She *was* tied in knots, but, damn Wolf anyway—he had a miraculous way of untying her.

"Did you notice your room is a connecting suite? You and your brother will have your own rooms with a door between. You will share the bath, and there is only one entrance, but that is preferable for safety." He opened the door of the Porsche. "When is your brother arriving?"

"I'm not sure now. When I called him, after I first arrived at the hospital, he said he'd check train schedules and make arrangements for tomorrow. I guess he was supposed to cook for some dignitaries at the school or something. Then when I learned Mom would be fine, I called him back. He hadn't gotten it all together. I told him Mom would hate for him to mess up one of his school projects that sounds so important. He may wait a day to get through the dinner."

"We will keep the room anyway." He closed the door and made his way around the car.

We? She groaned at how she changed a simple comment into so much more.

****

Tobias drove the block and a half to the hotel particularly slow. He was over-thinking the next part of the evening. He didn't get nervous with women. But one minute he was worried about her safety from a murderer, and the next he worried about her safety from him. Which was another conundrum. He hadn't stayed single this long, dated, had affairs with a number of women because of an overcautious nature.

He stole a glance from the corner of his eye. The talkative, confident August was unusually quiet. Probably deep in thought about her mother and murder. Although she was relaxed and talkative, slightly flirty at times through dinner, her mood had taken a few downturns. He could read nerves and a distance from the conversation for brief moments.

The car glided into a parking space. She touched the door handle, but he leaned into her with his arm across her to open it. She inhaled sharply then laughed. "You're kind of a stickler about the gentleman stuff, aren't you?"

His face was inches from hers, an arm across her waist, and his hand still on the handle. "Do you mind?"

"Not so much. You're rather macho and gentlemanly at the same time. Kind of fits you."

He shoved the door open and withdrew without losing contact. Her stomach muscles tightened against the back of his hand as his fingers slid away. He remained leaning into her, smiling at the honey warmth she exuded in the close quarters. She met his gaze without hesitation until her crooked smile broke into his thoughts. She might be okay with a kiss, but he wasn't sure he could stop at that, knowing how much he enjoyed the last time. He was still an inspector, and she was still an attempted homicide victim. If only he could keep that in the front of his mind and not how she tasted.

"I think we should get you settled in your room." Drawing back to his seat, he opened the door, and stepped out.

Once inside the hotel, his instincts went on alert. It occurred to him that if the intent of the car crash was to kill Lacy and August, not just scare them, there could be someone watching August at this very moment. "I think it might be a good idea to get an officer rotation set up for you. Someone to guard outside your door and accompany you when you leave."

She'd not said a word until they reached the top of the stairs. "You're scaring me, Wolf."

"I do not want to scare you. I'm cautious. It is highly unlikely anyone even knows you are here." He squeezed her hand, glancing at the numbers on the doors. "I will arrange for someone at the hospital, too, for Lacy. Although with Sheriff Meadowlark there, I am not as concerned for her as I am for you being alone."

He dropped her hand, pulled his cell from his pocket and punched the number for the police station. When the switchboard answered, he said, "Dorner. No, wait. He'll be gone. Give me the night duty scheduler." A double click on the other end and a female voice answered.

"This is Chief Inspector Wolf. I need to have an officer rotation at the Hotel Karnten."

"Let me see here, Inspector." Computer keys clicked.

He tapped his foot, mildly irritated.

"Looks like a rotation can start tomorrow morning, seven a.m."

"Can't you arrange it tonight?"

"Sorry, Inspector. We've got men in Vienna for training and not enough on duty tonight."

"*Scheisse.*"

August leaned against the wall next to room five, arms folded across her chest, and her gaze raking over him. She couldn't know what he was saying since she didn't speak German. She didn't appear to care anyway as she visually assessed him. Did he imagine her every expression to be something it wasn't—something he wanted?

"All right. Set it up for tomorrow, and I'll make other arrangements for tonight." After filling in the scheduler on his requirements, the phone went back into his pocket. "It appears I'll have to figure out some other way to keep you guarded tonight."

"Hmph." She stood away from the wall, swiped the key card, and opened the door. "Well, Wolf, you did say it was a suite."

He dipped his chin and stared into her face. He swore she was suppressing a smile.

"I guess you'll just have to spend the night."

****

The glint in Wolf's eyes when August suggested he spend the night in the suite with her was…wolf-like. For a moment, it made her forget the exhaustion in every muscle in her body, the ache of her wrist, and the sting of the cuts under her bandages. Yet, as much as she wanted to go a round—or two—she doubted she'd have the energy.

"If you are joking, August, the joke is on you." He flipped the light switch in the entryway. "There is no way I will let you spend the night alone."

She wasn't so tired that his cardamom scent didn't give her a bit of a head rush when she trudged past him. Switching on the table lamp lit the sitting area. The furnishings were sparse with clean lines and white painted wood. It reminded her of an Ikea store display. The sofa, in geometric shades of blue, matched the spread on the bed in the next room.

The door closed behind them. He strolled past and into the

bedroom, flipping on lights as he went. When he walked out of her line of vision, she followed him. He'd opened the door to the adjoining bedroom and had disappeared.

Too tired to follow any farther, the bed beckoned, and what little energy she possessed gave way, so she sat. Seconds later, as she collapsed back on the bed, he reappeared to lean against the doorframe and stare at her outstretched body. His gaze swept over her slowly, then he rubbed his chin and cocked his brow—*Oh hell, did he have to do that?*—and made another pass over her.

Rising up on her elbows, she caught his attention on his return trip. "Has anyone ever told you about that thing you do with your eyebrow?"

He smiled, pushed away from the doorframe, and sat beside her.

"You're perfectly aware of the effect you have on women, aren't you, *Wolf?*"

"I really do not know what you are talking about, but I do know the effect you have on me, *lovely.*"

Blushing wasn't normal for her, yet the heat rising up her neck must indicate a blush. Of course, there was heat radiating south, too, so who knew? Unfortunately, the droop of her eyelids had more to do with *sleeping* in the bed than using it. "Lovely? I've never really thought—"

"Has no one ever told you what that thing you do with your smile does to men—at least this man?"

Her finger went to her mouth as if she might feel what he meant. "My smile?"

"It is crooked."

"That doesn't sound so lovely."

"And your eyes, smoky brown with a green glow around the edge?"

That tugged at her heart. "My dad called it my ring of fire."

"I'll agree with your father. Your *fire* is very attractive."

Without warning, a pain spiked in her wrist, and she collapsed back. "Ow."

He fell back next to her, resting on one elbow and stared into her face, his brow wrinkled with concern. "Are you all right?"

"Probably the way I was leaning." She raised her hand to look at her arm.

He took her hand, gently encircling his fingers around her wrist, and brought it to his mouth. His gaze never left her face as he kissed her palm. He murmured between kisses, "In the middle of all your trouble and sorrow, I am glad to be here next to you tonight."

In spite of fatigue, shivers of pleasure tickled her palm, and somewhere in the back of her tired brain, satisfaction registered because he felt exactly as she did. Yet, there was no way she could do her feelings justice tonight. Too many other emotions clogged her psyche. "Wolf—"

"Shh." He laid her hand on the bed. "Do not tell me to go away. I would rather think you would ask me to stay if things were different."

She brought her fingers to brush away the lock of hair that had spilled onto his forehead, traced along his cheek, and trailed over his bottom lip. He wouldn't get out the door all night if things were different—and she wasn't so damned tired.

He caught her fingers, kissed the tips then leaned down and kissed her.

A fire spread across her chest, and she responded with more energy than she thought she had. He seemed to hold back, taste her tongue with a restrained gentleness. His chest expanded against hers, and the tremble of his restraint sent ripples down her abdomen. She leaned into the kiss, giving him permission to take more. For a moment, he seemed to give in to the building desire, his hands coming to her waist and his mouth searching deeper. But it was brief, and his grip pushed rather than brought her closer.

He stood without pausing and walked to the adjoining door. Grabbing the handle, he said, "I am close. You are safe. I'll see you for lunch tomorrow?"

"Yes." It was husky and breathy and all she could manage.

CHAPTER TWELVE

The next morning, Tobias slipped into his shoes and suit coat, the only clothing he'd removed the night before, pulled his Glock from under the pillow he'd slept on, and holstered it. He eased the adjoining door open and slipped into the semi-darkness of August's room. After his eyes adjusted, he couldn't help stopping to gaze at her. The sheet was pulled to her chin, one hand slung across the empty side of the bed, and her face turned toward him. Vulnerable. Not a word easily associated with the feisty, independent young woman. He wanted to protect her, but he also just wanted her. Shedding his clothes and climbing under the sheet with her crossed his mind. He shook the thought off, mentally tamping down arousal, and left the room.

In twenty minutes, the policeman arrived; Tobias gave him instructions then headed for his apartment. After a quick shower and change of clothes, he climbed into his car for the drive to Castle Luschin.

He called Albert on the way. "I'm heading to the Luschin Estate. You want to meet me?"

"Sure. Anything new?"

"No. I just think it's time I spoke to Eike again, keep her on the defensive, and see if she hangs herself. I don't want her getting too complacent. How about you?"

"Yeah, actually, I found something. I did some research on the deed." A door slammed and voices echoed through the phone. "Eike isn't totally out of the loop for inheriting the property. If everyone else is dead or incapacitated, she receives the entire estate."

"I guess Bauer better watch his back, too."

Albert chuckled. "I'm walking out to the car now. See you there."

His next call rang the castle. He informed Herr Bloch that he'd arrive shortly to speak with Eike if she was in, which she was. Herr Bloch wanted him to hold while he informed the Frau, but Tobias declined. He was on his way with official police business and didn't need her approval.

He took the curvy road at a leisurely pace. August would've been pleased. Thinking of the feisty young woman brought a smile to his face. He gunned it going around the next bend, and he laughed quietly.

Once inside the gates, he lounged against the side of the car until Albert arrived in his aging Fiat.

Tobias met him as he parked behind the Porsche. "When are you going to get rid of that old sedan, Albert?"

"Too late for thinking about that." He heaved his bulky frame from the low seat and shut the door. "I'm retiring, remember? This car will probably pull my casket to the graveyard. Damned thing just keeps going and going."

They walked toward the private entrance.

"Then don't retire until you can afford a better vehicle. You're too young anyway." His partner had had his fifty-fifth birthday a couple of weeks ago.

"Iris would disagree. She thinks this town can use another coffee café and has my next few years mapped out with running our own business. And to tell you the truth, spending more time with a good woman is a hell of a lot more fun than chasing the bad guys." Albert nudged him. "You might well think about that."

"I should retire? You've got over fifteen years on me, and—"

"No, no. Not retire. Just find a woman, one woman, and work less."

August flashed through his mind. He'd never wanted a woman more than his work. He touched his gun beneath his coat and straightened his tie. "You're getting soft, Al."

"*Ach.*"

Tobias leaned on the bell.

Herr Bloch opened the door. "Come in, Inspectors. Frau Luschin is waiting in the solar."

The three men tromped silently up the stairs. Herr Bloch rapped twice on the door, and Eike responded. He opened the door for the inspectors to enter and retreated, closing it behind them.

"I didn't know we'd be honored with Inspector Feld's presence also." She spoke from her seat on the sofa. "Please, sit, and Tobias, tell me why I'm still getting visits from our police department."

He sat on the sofa where she patted, and Albert lowered himself onto a side chair.

Her manner wasn't entirely rude, but the edge to her tone was far from cordial.

Good.

"We're tying up loose ends, Eike. And now with a most unfortunate event with Lacy and August, Castle Luschin appears to be cursed."

"Cursed? Yes, perhaps. But car accidents do happen. The women are not used to our mountain roads. Are you going to investigate every *event*, as you call it, that we have on the estate?"

He kept his face neutral except for one corner of his mouth ticking upward, and held her gaze.

"Then I'll read between the lines. You wouldn't be here yet again if you thought my dear husband's death suicide. Or accidental. The trouble is," she sniffed and drew a hanky from the pocket of her sharply creased, black slacks, batting her eyes at his partner. "I might agree with you. I've had a most, uh, upsetting revelation of late." Dabbing at invisible tears, she inhaled a slow, sorrowful breath and batted her dry eyes at Tobias.

"And what would that be?"

"Oh, Tobias. I just don't know if I should say anything. I could be reading this all wrong."

Albert cleared his throat. "Why don't you let us be the judge of that, Frau Luschin."

She fluttered her eyelashes, nodded, and pinched her lips together for a moment. "All right. Yesterday, Fabian confessed his love for me. Please keep in mind, he was in his usual inebriated state, but, I tell you, it was quite shocking. Well, shocking in that it sent chills over me as to what it could mean. He's lusted after me for all the time I've been married to his uncle. Somehow, he deduced that this estate means a great deal to me, and it would be the deal maker for me to…to…marry him."

Where she meant to lead was obvious, but Tobias wouldn't go there easily. "But the American women have inherited the estate. I'm not sure—"

"Yes, of course. That's the cause of my distress. He's so familiar with cars and his cousins coincidentally meet with a horrible accident when he is here. And that made me wonder—how convenient that my dear husband overdoses on his medication *while* Fabian is here." After two short gasps as if suppressing a crying spree, she covered her face with her hands.

Dramatics aside, her implied accusation made sense—and exactly the conclusions he'd come to, although he'd included her in the mix. Perhaps his dislike of Eike and her politics was clouding his vision.

Albert's bushy brows practically met in the middle with his frown. "Now, now, Frau Luschin. That's quite an accusation."

Her head jerked up, and she glanced between the two men, her gaze coming to rest on Tobias. "I'm aware of that." Irritation dripped from her words. "But I have to be blunt and tell you like I see it. You say there's a curse on this castle, but I'm not so sure that curse isn't Fabian Bauer."

"Let's look at the sequence of events for Monday morning again," Tobias suggested. "You told me Herr Luschin did not breakfast with you. Is that unusual?"

"No, not on Mondays. He often meets some friends for breakfast, and they go skeet shooting."

"You and Fabian had breakfast and were not concerned the lord didn't join you?" Bauer had told him he'd been in his bedchamber all morning, but he prodded Eike for her version.

"No, Tobias." Her voice rose in pitch. "That's part of what troubles me so. Fabian didn't show himself that morning until I cried out when I found my husband."

"Hmm." Albert rubbed his chin. "Didn't I see in the report that Herr Bauer stayed in his chambers at dinnertime the night before? That would mean he took to his room after lunch and didn't show his face until late morning the following day. Not a very social guest, is he?"

"Well, he intended on staying a few days—and he's a relative, not an infrequent guest or outsider. There's no need for constant social activity." She jutted her chin, clasping her hands at her chest. "But now that you mention it, that does sound suspicious."

And a bit too obvious. No matter how Eike painted it, his gut told him she had something to do with her husband's early demise and the American women's accident. "Where is Herr Bauer at the moment?"

"I haven't seen him since dinner last night. He didn't come to breakfast this morning, and he's not answering his phone. Last I saw him, after dinner, he went off in the direction of the Great Hall. For a stroll he said."

"And where would he be if he's not in his room this morning?"

"He's fond of wandering the halls with a drink in hand. But not too far."

He stood and Albert followed suit. "We'll look around a bit."

She followed them to the door. "I certainly hope I'm wrong. You know, Tobias, this has all been so upsetting. To find out Fabian isn't who I thought he was, and the loss of my dear husband."

He stopped outside the door. "If you see him before we do, it's best you keep your suspicions to yourself, Eike."

"Yes, of course." She clasped a hanky to her chest, eyes wide. "Do you think I'm in danger?"

"He loves you, remember?" The sarcasm came through in spite of his effort to remain neutral. "I'll get back to you."

Once Eike's door closed, Tobias strolled to the first guest room and rapped on the door. No answer. He tried the door handle and finding it open, they entered, each fanning off in different directions. "Not here. Let's take the stairs to the Great Hall and kitchen."

Halfway down the stairs, his partner asked, "Well, what do you think?"

"She had her confession thought out, didn't she?"

"Made some sense."

Unreasonable irritation set his jaw tight, and he shot his partner a scowl. "She's lying."

"She's convincing." True to form, Albert spoke his mind. He'd miss him when he retired.

He let his ire go with the thought. "You don't know her well enough."

They'd reached the landing and the door into the Great Hall.

"How well do you know Eike, Tobias?"

"I know her enough to know she's not to be trusted. To know her aspirations—"

"I trust your gut." His partner laid a hand on his shoulder. "It felt practiced…you're right." Albert opened the Great Hall door. "Let's see if we can get the nephew to tell us something more."

Tobias led the way, glanced along the table and into the shadows at each end, then made his way around and into the main room. He jerked to a halt. "Who the hell?"

He trotted to a prone figure, face down in the middle of the hall. Albert, huffing, drew up beside him as he squatted to get a closer look. "It's Bauer." Tobias put fingertips to Bauer's neck, but the pulse wasn't there. His hand grazed a red silk scarf. The scarf, a faint scent, and confusion washed over him. August. She'd worn a red scarf the first time he'd seen her.

"He's dead?"

"Very."

Albert glanced around the Great Hall. "I wonder how he went undetected."

"It's actually the perfect spot." He scanned the body for any other details as he spoke. "This room isn't used by the family. The castle is closed to tourists right now. No need for the staff to come in here." His gaze rested on the scarf for a moment and wondered where August was.

As he stood upright, the cell in his breast pocket chimed.

"Hello."

"Inspector," Dorner's droll voice addressed him, but the news he imparted was anything but droll. His body went rigid, already focusing on his partner to take over here.

"I'm on my way. And send investigative backup and forensics to Castle Luschin. There's been an apparent homicide. Yeah. Right." He shoved the phone in his pocket. "You'll have to handle this, Al. I've got to leave."

"Where're you going?"

"The hospital." The personal interest he had in this case charged every nerve in his body. "Lacy's had another attempt on her life."

****

August gripped Chance's hand while the doctor examined her mother.

"The nurse was not successful," the physician said, tucking a stethoscope into the oversized pocket of his white coat. "The drug she intended on adding to the drip would have stopped Mrs. Meadowlark's heart." He made his way around the foot of the bed. The elder man was thin, his shoulders stooped from too many years of leaning over beds rather than from his health. His cheeks were rosy and his smile sincere. "You interrupted her in time, Sheriff Meadowlark. I will check in a bit later." His forward progress halted at the blood pool on the floor—blood belonging to the bitch of a nurse who'd tried to kill her mother. "I will get someone to clean this up."

She felt the tenseness drain from Chance as he released her hand and moved bedside to his wife.

A subtle tremble started in her knees and spread throughout her limbs as she stepped to the opposite side of the bed. Her mother's hand was warm and dry when she lifted it to her lips. "Thank God you came back into the room when you did, Chance."

The door opened and Wolf paused, framed by the brighter light of the hallway. He said something to a policeman behind him, then slipped inside. There were lines in his face she hadn't noticed before, and his movements were tight as if he was wound up and ready to spring.

"August, Sheriff Meadowlark, I cannot express my regret enough that security was breached, but there are new measures in place now."

Chance nodded but never took his eyes off her mother.

"If we could speak for a moment." Wolf moved to the foot of the bed. "I can imagine you do not want to leave the room so maybe we can just step over here?" He pointed to the far corner.

She held her breath, not sure if Chance was angry or what his reaction would be to the man who was supposed to keep her mother safe. But he remained silent and followed Wolf to the corner. With one glance at her sleeping mother, she willed her shaky legs to move and joined them.

They formed a tight triangle, the two men looking eye to eye at each other.

"From now on no one is allowed into this room without the assigned shift supervisor. No medicines will be administered without one of her doctors being present. And of course, the two officers will be outside the door at all times to make sure this procedure is followed."

"That should be secure. Thanks, Inspector Wolf."

"Can you tell me what happened, Sheriff Meadowlark?"

"Luckily, I'd just come from conferring with Lacy's doctor on what was expected in the next twenty-four hours. She's stable and should be waking. Because he mentioned not administering any more drugs or antibiotics, I was suspicious when I reentered the room and a nurse was poised with a hypodermic by her IV."

She gasped.

Her stepfather patted her shoulder and continued. "She had a startled, wide-eyed expression. Something was wrong. I moved on her quickly as she stabbed at the line with the needle, and I yelled for your men outside the door. When I reached her, she pulled a knife from somewhere, maybe a pocket. One of your men entered the room, saw her slash at me, and shot her."

"All right. *Unfortunately*, the shot killed her so we will not be able to find out who put her up to this, although we are still following her movements before she came in here." His forehead wrinkled. "But *fortunately*, you were quick enough to save your wife's life."

August wrapped her arms around her waist. Anger bubbled amidst the feelings of relief.

The door opened and two people entered, accompanied by one of the policemen who pointed at the blood on the floor. Wolf nodded.

"There should be no further incidents. Again, my apologies."

"None needed. Maybe the staff should've come under closer scrutiny, but I can understand why it wouldn't have been considered."

She was amazed at the cordialness between the two, although Chance got a bit of a dig in about limiting the staff access. Her anger could've been directed at Wolf, but her stepfather's calm demeanor held her back. Wolf couldn't have foreseen this. Up until now, these *accidents* were construed as scare tactics. He'd put a guard on her at the hotel. With Chance and the two men at the door, it seemed crazy to think her mother needed any other protection.

The men's attention wandered to the blood cleanup. They stood in silence for a few moments until her stepfather took her hand but addressed Wolf. "As soon as Lacy is able to travel, I'm getting both these ladies out of the country. Any business they have with the estate can be handled long distance."

"Chance—"

"Something's going on, August, and until Inspector Wolf has it solved, you two need to be home and out of harm's way."

She wouldn't argue with him. Not right now anyway. Her mother could make that decision for herself, or with Chance, when she awoke. As for herself, she'd decide when the time came.

Wolf gazed at her, his serious face still lined and his body language tight. "I understand your reasoning, Mr. Meadowlark." He said he understood, but something in his eyes spoke to a different thought.

She couldn't discern what. He was obviously still visibly upset. "Have you had lunch?" he asked.

"No, but…" She peered across the room at her sleeping mother.

Her stepfather's hand brushed her arm. "No need to stay. I'll call you when she wakes. She's fine."

"I suppose."

"I *know*." For the first time that day a smile broke his face.

"Do you want the keys to your rental, Chance?" She opened her purse. "Just in case?"

"No." He shook his head emphatically. "I'm not going anywhere. Keep it so you can come and go easily."

Wolf touched her back then quickly withdrew his hand, and a flicker of a question showed in Chance's eyes. She stood on tiptoes, kissed his cheek, and glanced at her mom once more before letting Wolf lead her from the room.

In the hallway, three policemen stood close to the door, one of them her bodyguard, Policeman Klein.

"Klein?" Wolf continued walking, the policeman following, until they were a few feet from the other policemen. "I want you to get as much information on the nurse as you can from the hospital records. Whatever they have on her. Phone it in to Carl in IT, and tell him I want a full history on her. Get me a photo of her, too."

"Yes, sir." Klein glanced at her, no doubt wondering if he'd been relieved of guard duty.

"See if Carl can track the nurse's political affiliations. Ms. Myer is in need of something to eat. I'm going to accompany her, so please wait here until I bring her back. Call me if you get anything that needs immediate attention."

Wolf squeezed her arm ever so lightly and nudged her in the direction of the exit.

"Yes, sir."

"See you later, Markel." She wiggled her fingers at the gruff, tough-looking officer.

An embarrassed smile lit his face as he darted a glance at his superior.

Once out of earshot, Wolf chided, "August, you are a trouble maker. Klein will take a lot of *Scheisse* for that little familiarity. He is a strait-laced cop."

"Yeah, I get that, very conscientious and serious about his job, but he's really a big teddy bear. I like him."

"Everyone does." He opened the door, and they entered into the midday sun.

The brightness blinded her momentarily, but not enough that she couldn't see Wolf's continued stiffness. "The nurse? Nazi politics? What are you thinking?"

"My gut is sending me signals."

"You seem different, Wolf. Is there something more?"

His arm slipped around her waist, urging her forward toward the Porsche. "Let us get to a restaurant, and we will talk."

She inhaled deeply, relished the sun on her skin, and Wolf's arm around her. With so much ugly in her world at the moment, clear, fresh air with a breathtaking view was a welcomed relief. He was more than just an inspector performing his duty. Having him to lean on added an upbeat tempo to her pulse. "How wonderful to always have the Alps to look at. Is there somewhere we can get lunch and sit outside?"

"My thought exactly. How about your hotel? The patio is shady this time of day and the food is always good. The view of the Alps is superb."

"Perfect." A delicious flutter tripped across her stomach at the mention of the hotel. *Perfectly foolish.* She slid into the Porsche. Lunch was the goal, and surely the inspector didn't have ulterior motives…in the middle of the day.

Even if she hoped he did.

****

Tobias paused eating to watch August swallow a bite of thick, dark bread, followed by a drink of warm beer. Her whole body seemed to relax into the experience; eyelids droopy with pleasure, a slight curve to her lips. Eating had never been so sensual.

And he'd never been able to enjoy it less. His decision to let her relax and have lunch now appeared to be a bad idea. The longer he waited to tell her Bauer was dead, that she would come under investigation in his murder, the harder he found it to find the words.

"You can't find bread like this in Tucson." She smeared another dollop of butter on her slice. "And you've totally ruined me for American beer." Lifting her stein into the air toward him, she said, "*Prost!*"

"*Prost!*" Their steins clinked, and they drank.

Today, she wore a sleeveless blouse, cut in so her shoulders were exposed, and the same green shade as the ring around her brown iris. He'd never found bare shoulders so alluring.

"I am glad I have good influence on you."

"Good? I'll probably have to hit specialty liquor stores when I get back home to find the brands you've been introducing me to."

She tucked the last of the bread into her mouth, leaving a dab of butter clinging to her lower lip. When he reached across the table, her tongue darted out to meet his finger. He set his thumb in the crevice above her chin then his finger drew a slow line to remove the butter and placed it on the moist, tip of her pink tongue. The effect rocked him, rendering the tightness of his slacks uncomfortable. He planted his feet firmly on the floor under the table as if to steady the effect. He'd asked for this with his mindless action. It was impossible to keep her at a professional distance. With each meeting, her draw had gained strength until every move she made was an erotic gesture.

Her tongue withdrew ever so slowly into her mouth, and he knew he'd have to follow that path before the day was over.

With a blink of thick lashes, and a tug of a spiky, golden-tipped lock of hair, she continued as if nonplused by his reaction to her tease; although, her crooked smile spoke volumes.

"I get the feeling something's bothering you. What's wrong, Wolf? I mean, I know the breach of security at the hospital had you uptight, but there's more. Is it what happened when you visited Eike this morning?"

He cut a slice of bread with more force than necessary, and willed the building ache below his belt to go away. "She contradicted everything you told me about Bauer."

"What did she say?"

"She believes that he was trying to secure the estate to please her and would have tampered with the car to get you and your mother out of the way."

"I could strangle him if that's the truth."

Her words were serious sounding even if she had a smirk on her face. Thank God he was the only one to hear them.

She set her spoon down, apparently no longer hungry, and rested her chin in her hand, elbow on the table. "I don't know. I didn't get that feeling from him. Let me think." Tapping her fingertips on her cheek, she pursed her lips in thought. "I don't want him to be capable of murder." She dropped her hand to the table. "The unrequited love thing is certainly in both their stories. And he didn't point a finger at her, but still…could he murder?"

Her wide-open stare further added to the inner battle he fought. He should've told her before now about Bauer. But her words, spoken without pretense, confirmed what he already knew. She couldn't possibly have strangled her cousin. How could he handle what was coming in both a professional and personal manner?

He pointed at her stein that was nearly empty. "Would you like another beer?"

"No. Thank you." She ran her hand over the handle, off somewhere in thought. Eike's claims of being pursued by the nephew, of his declaration of love, and her suspicions of his hand in her husband's death left the normally opinionated young woman quiet.

His cell rang. Albert's voice hailed him. "Prelim done here. We're on our way back to headquarters. He was killed last night. Definitely strangulation with the scarf. It appears to be a woman's scarf."

Wolf slanted his shoulders away from the table, gazed across the patio, and avoided August's eyes. "Anyone claim it?"

"Anyone? Like Eike?"

"Yeah." August's scarf was damning, but every molecule in his body told him Eike was the murderer.

"Are you afraid the young American has learned enough German to understand our conversation?"

"Just being cautious."

"All right. Frau Luschin is hysterical. Claims she saw August wearing it."

His stomach lurched. "Of course she does."

"She's demanding you get out here, but first get the young woman behind bars."

He couldn't help a quick glance at August who now had her head tilted and was in full on curiosity mode. His stomach wanted to give up the beer and what little he'd eaten. She wasn't going to jail.

"Not going to happen that fast. See what you can do to, um, explain procedures."

"You mean procedures we make up as we go?"

"Use your years of experience."

"Eike's going to need her own alibi. Hmmm…I'm on it."

Tobias shoved his phone away.

"Was that about the nurse? Have they figured out why? Who's

behind it?"

"No, no. Albert is on another case." He signaled the waitress to bring the check. He'd tell her when they were outside the restaurant. And away from too many ears and eyes. He should be on his way to headquarters, but he couldn't just drag her in like a common suspect.

"Have you heard from Gruber?" The question was meant as a change of subject, yet, because of Eike's political aspirations, *Burschenshaften* Gruber could somehow be tied into the events. His gut kept leading him down that path.

"No. Why would I hear from him?"

"I think he was taken with you."

With a wrinkle of her nose and a shrug, she dismissed that assumption. "If so, the feeling wasn't mutual. And I obviously didn't make *that* big of an impression," she said with a slight smile. "Too bad I couldn't spy on him more for you. I think he's having an affair with Eike *and* he's a Nazi."

He wouldn't disagree. But how could it all tie into Bauer's murder?

"How well do you know Eike?"

Most of what he knew about her was classified with *Der Neue Widerstand*. He'd spent some time with her, but since he'd thought it unprofessional to disclose that to August earlier, saying anything now would be awkward. "Not all that much."

"No?" She tilted her head. "No socializing with her and my great-grandfather?"

"There were a few occasions when Herr Luschin and I attended the same functions, but I cannot say we socialized."

"Do you think she's having an affair with Kurt and Fabian at the same time? Can't you do some detective work and find out—if only to satisfy my curiosity?"

"I doubt the breadth of your curiosity could ever be satisfied, August, and no, I would not use police resources for your pleasure." But as soon as he could speak to Gruber, he'd satisfy more than his own curiosity about his membership in the *Burschenshaften*.

"Eike scares me." Her eyes squinted with a frown.

He touched her hand, and the seriousness left her face as quickly as it had come. "Well, there's always a woman to blame."

He pushed his plate away and leaned across the table. "That is what I always say."

Her plate was shoved aside, and she leaned toward him. "Do

you?"

"I do."

"So, you're *never* to blame?" There was no mistaking her flirting. She lured him in, and he jumped without a second thought.

"How can I help myself when there is a beautiful woman tempting me?"

"Oh the poor, handsome inspector, can't be faulted for his allure?"

My allure? "I think we are talking about two different scenarios."

"I think you're just being evasive."

Evasive tagged him well enough, but his maneuvers were failing him. "Me?"

"*Am* I tempting you?"

"*Ich danke Ihnen, Inspektor*," the waitress interrupted, handing Tobias the check.

August's crooked smile and amazing eyes watched his every movement. *Tempting him?* What she did required a stronger word than temptation. He stood, glad he wore a sport coat to hide the growing erection her unwavering gaze caused. Breaking the bad news grew more difficult by the minute. For once, she waited for the customary gentleman's maneuver, and he pulled her chair out as she rose from the table.

He stepped back from under the table umbrella to allow her to lead them from the patio, but she paused, facing him, inches away. Her bare arms glistened in the bright sun, and her moist lips puckered slightly.

"Thank you. I've had a most enjoyable time."

"I need to call Officer Klein to meet us at your room to take over guard duties." The guard duties would now take on two functions with entirely different parameters—protecting her as a victim, and watching her as a suspect.

"Will you keep me company just a few minutes more and walk me to my room? I think I'll lie down for a while before I go back to the hospital."

It took the strength of Superman not to wrap his arms around her, pull her into him, and kiss the tease from her lips. Instead, he took her arm and looped it through his like a casual friend. Shoving aside his increasing guilt stalling the news of Bauer, he'd take care of the tease when he got her upstairs.

CHAPTER THIRTEEN

August's arm fit nicely into the crook of Wolf's elbow, and she brought her other hand to clasp his bicep as they ascended the stairs toward her room. His arm tensed under her added attention. Her fingertips warmed at the strength she could feel in spite of a shirt and suit jacket.

She found herself pleased with the gentlemanly ways of Wolf. Whether it was European custom or his age, there was a definite difference between how he treated her, and how her ex-husband had. Or other men she'd dated prior to marriage for that matter. The consideration he showed made her go all feminine-gushy inside.

Had she been too forward at lunch? *Nah*. He didn't seem to think so when he'd flirted right back. Although it took some doing. Something was on his mind. She hoped it was she. Just walking next to him, their hips gently bumping every couple of steps, the muscles of his arm flexing, his cardamom scent, and his profile with square jaw and full lips were practically foreplay. The sweetest wave of gooseflesh up her thighs now resided at the juncture, tingling with desire.

At her door, he slipped out of her grasp, stepping slightly behind her while she dug the key from her purse. He'd never been married, and if he was a womanizer, she'd seen no evidence. Still, he might very well have seduced her to this point without her realizing it. *So what?* Her goal had been seduction, regardless of how and why.

The key clicked. She brought her face cheek to cheek with his. "Dessert?"

His arm went around her waist. "We need to talk." His other arm reached behind her and pushed the room door open.

She had to get past the professional inspector. The heat coming off his body told her he had to be fighting his personal feelings. "I really don't want to talk, Wolf." She pushed her hips against him. "Couldn't we have dessert before we talk?"

His hesitation covered her desire in a gray fog. Had she read him wrong, so wrong? But when she relaxed away from him, he drew her nearer.

He nipped her earlobe, brought his other arm around her, and pulled her close. "*Wunderbar.*"

She snickered, draped her arms around his neck, and thrust her hips harder against him. Although trembling with heat pulsing her thighs, giddiness enveloped her. Pure enjoyment lit her.

She back-stepped, careful not to lose contact with the promising bulge against her hips, and brought her lips to his. The door closed. The kiss grew intense, and she had the sensation of being tasted. *She was dessert.*

Her heart hammered, thighs twitched, and she dove deeper into the kiss…but he pulled back.

His hands cupped her butt, gazed down with a cocked brow then released her, extricating him from her arms. "Don't move." He shrugged out of his suit jacket, draped it over a chair, and sat to take off his shoes and socks.

Standing dumbly there, watching him, her breath came faster. He glanced at her, a half-smile and the damnable cocked brow turning his face into a proposition. Her blouse stung her nipples as they peaked raw with excitement. And still he sat, his glassy gaze roaming over her twice before he stood and came to her.

When he picked her up, relief flooded her. "Finally," she gasped, and kissed him.

He broke the kiss, sat her on the edge of the bed, and knelt at her feet. "Mmm, yes, finally," he muttered and removed her sandals. Strong hands gently pushed her shoulders back, then swiveled her legs onto the bed. He unbuttoned her jean skirt and slipped it down her hips, his gaze traveling with it. She'd never been so thoroughly *looked at* by a man, and her hips bucked with pleasure.

He chuckled and unbuttoned her blouse, parting it to stare at her breasts. Kissing each nipple had her squirming and gasping.

She pulled at his shirt wanting, no *needing*, to feel skin.

With a last lap at a nipple, he rose and stood facing her.

She groaned and tugged on his pant leg. "Get the hell back here. *Now*."

He laughed. "In good time, August." From his pocket he lifted his wallet, opened it, and took out a small square package which he laid on the night table. While he removed his clothes, he peered at her, lips barely parted and eyes that promised to thoroughly undo her...*in good time*.

All her prior concerns about his age nearly made her laugh. The body standing before her, toned and sexually ready, made her moan. A craving like none she'd experienced raked over her with a shiver. She drank in his every move, barely able to hold still. And she didn't. She shrugged off panties and blouse and tossed them across the room.

"Perfect," he whispered and climbed onto the bed in a silky, smooth motion to lie beside her.

She draped an arm around his neck as he slipped a hand under and cupped her butt. His other hand found her breasts, and his mouth covered hers. He kissed her fully with a deep guttural moan that spoke to his desire, and she echoed. The kiss was all-consuming until his hand slipped low on her stomach.

Then his weight was upon her. Her hips bucked, and she moved against his hardness. He showered kisses down her neck, breasts, lapped at her navel, and she lost herself in pure tactile bliss. When he rose upon his knees and slipped the condom on his erection, an involuntary, muscle spasm spread her legs in welcome.

"Now?" A husky whisper is all she could manage.

He positioned between her legs, but she stopped him with palms on his chest. She wanted to touch. She ran her hands over his pecs, tweaked his nipples, fingers trailed over abs that were just defined enough, and then dipped lower. With both hands, she clasped him, and he reacted with a riveting stare into her face.

"Now?" he asked.

She slipped her hands around his hips and grasped a firm, muscled butt. "Yes, now."

****

Satiated from a second, slower time, and totally relaxed, Wolf tucked an arm behind his head and the other wrapped under August to massage her butt. He couldn't remember the last time he'd wanted to just laze with a woman.

She laid her head on his chest and sighed.

He should get dressed, call Klein and...he had to tell her. What the hell had he done? Put his desires and personal feelings way out there, before everything else. He'd slept with a damned suspect. It made no difference that he knew she wasn't the murderer—preliminary evidence pointed to her. What in hell—

"Wolf?" She rubbed his chest. "You went all tense. Are you okay?" Hot, moist breath delighted his skin while her fingers lit nerve endings down his ribcage.

He'd have to tell her...sooner or later.

Later.

"More than okay."

"Then all I have to say is wow." She breathed the exclamation.

"Hmm, yes."

Her front stretched the length of the side of his body, dampness mingling between them. They lay without covers, and he peeked down the bridge of his nose to admire her while his fingers fondled the fleshiness of her ass. *Great ass.* Her small breasts snuggled tight against his side, the nipples still red and hard in the aftermath of their sex. Her waist was small, her hips maybe a bit wide for her size but perfect for the physical gymnastics they'd enjoyed. Her legs were nothing short of spectacular, long, curvy and firm without being overly muscled.

"You make excellent dessert." He kissed the top of her head in fondness. Fondness. Had he ever done *that* before?

"I'm so glad you think so. I have to say, you were everything I imagined."

"Did you imagine?"

"I've been imagining big time. Did I not seduce you? Damn, I'm such a floozy. But then, you just can't help yourself, can you?"

He didn't want her to think she meant nothing more than any other beautiful woman meant in the heat of... Did he? He'd not had *that* thought before.

With one fluid movement, he pulled his hand from behind his head, flipped her onto her back, and clasped her wrists, pinning them to the mattress on each side of her head. His leg went across her hips, and he stared into her wide-eyed expression. "I'm not sure what a floozy is, but if you are one, I like it."

He kissed her until her arms relaxed within his grasp and her hips tensed against his leg, then lifted his head to gaze on her face. High cheekbones and a fine, straight nose, were regally haughty, but offset nicely by her crooked smile.

"As far as my restraint with beautiful women, I am actually quite particular."

"You are?" A touch of shyness he'd not seen before tinted her words. She caught the corner of her mouth between her teeth.

"I am. You tested my willpower, August, and I failed miserably, undoubtedly because you are a floozy—which must be something akin to a siren."

She laughed. Her eyes beckoned him, and her hips bucked softly.

He couldn't fail the willpower test again. His eyes closed as the relaxation and satisfaction consuming him drained from his limbs like a siphoning hose sucking the very life out.

"What's wrong, Wolf?"

Gently, he rolled away and came up on an elbow to stare into her face. "I'm afraid I have some very bad news."

"Now?" She tickled at his chest, smiling as if waiting for a punch line. When he didn't respond, her smile fell away.

"I have been avoiding telling you, but..."

"What?"

"Fabian Bauer has been killed."

She blinked several times, wrinkled her brow, and her mouth gaped open. "Kil...Fab...how? When?"

"Last night. I had just come from the scene when I arrived at the hospital this morning. I got the call about the attempt on Lacy and left Albert at the castle. We found Bauer in the Great Hall, strangled."

He let the news settle on her while they continued to stare into each other's faces.

A glint sparked in her eyes—not fear or sadness. "That bitch!" She jerked upward, nearly bumping his head, and loomed over him as he fell backward. "Eike. She's trying to knock off all of us. Do something, Wolf."

Her pinked cheeks and fiery glare held him. "I will, August. I'm of the same opinion as you...but...there is more." Acid burned his stomach. She drew back as he rose to a sitting position. "Come." He pulled the covers over their legs, stalling with his movements before he uttered his next bombshell.

With both her hands in his, she maneuvered, tucking her legs under her to face him and draw closer. "Wellll..."

"It appears he was strangled with your red scarf."

"Mine? Are you sure?" Her eyes were wide, incredulous.

He nodded.

"How do you know?"

He rubbed her hands as her fingers gripped his. "I saw it…smelled it."

She pulled a hand away, pushed hair from her face, and stared at him. "But how can that be?"

"Where is it?"

Her eyes flitted side to side, blinked, and her gaze came to rest on his face. "At the castle."

"I thought so." Confirmation did nothing for the burning in his stomach.

She fisted her hands and pounded her blanket-covered knees. "That bitch!"

Eine Kleine Nacht-Musik played from the floor.

August jerked. "My cell."

"Mozart? Your ring is an Austrian composer's music?" Coincidence, or had she changed it since they'd met?

She flashed a cursory smile and scooted sideways to lift her purse from the floor beside the bed. Her face grew serious with a punch to the answer key. He was sure the same thought crossed her mind as his—the hospital?

Her eyes grew wide, and her face lit up. "Mom!"

Her chin immediately dipped to take in their naked bodies, and she rolled, sending him off in the opposite direction with more strength than he realized she had.

"You're awake! Oh, Mom." She swung her feet over the side of the bed, grabbed the spread to cover at least part of her nakedness, and gave a quick glance over her shoulder as if to tell him to go hide in a closet.

He rose to gather his clothes. Lacy was awake. He felt a sense of lightness in spite of the trouble ahead and could imagine August's elation.

"That's so good to hear. Yes, I'll be right there. I was just…resting…er, well, thinking about resting. Uh, Wolf just brought me back after lunch. But I'll come now. Yes. Love you. Bye."

She jumped up, dropped the spread then grabbed it again. "Damn!"

"There are no cameras in this room, Lovely." He flicked his fingers and cocked his brow, which she claimed had an effect on her.

Her smile quickly changed to a frown. "Oh, hell, Wolf. What happens now?"

He zipped his pants and shrugged into his shirt. "We go see your mother."

"But, the scarf—"

"Yes, you are a murder suspect. Timing is going to be a factor. The only time you have been alone is when you came to your room early in the evening after Sheriff Meadowlark arrived, correct?"

She nodded. "I came back to take a shower and change clothes. Alone."

For the balance of her evening, he was her alibi. His throat tightened at the prospect. How much he would have to reveal before this investigation concluded tangled his thoughts.

Her frown deepened, and he saw anger rather than fear spark from her eyes. "But where the hell was Eike? And how would anyone know I was alone for that period of time?"

He knotted his tie. "I'm not sure." What he suspected, someone watching her movements, didn't need to be voiced. Another reason to keep her guarded.

"And my scarf was left in my room at the castle. I didn't have it here with me. Eike! The bitch Eike. We have to—"

"Right now, you see your mother."

"And then I go to jail?" Her voice grew timid.

"Let us say you are under surveillance. Officer Klein will continue to…guard you."

"You can fix that?"

"I can." Regardless of the wrath it might bring from his boss.

She ran around the foot of the bed and wrapped her arms around his neck with her naked body against him. "I know she murdered my great-grandfather and now my cousin. I don't know why, but she wants us all dead. Get her, Wolf."

His chest tightened with resolve. "You have my word."

He ran his hands down her sides, over her hips, and measured her bottom with the breadth of his palms, committing to memory the feel of her every curve. What the next few days could hold was anyone's guess, but if he couldn't have her again, soon, then he could at least have the sensory memory to relive.

****

August's feet tapped on the floorboard of the Porsche, while the index finger on her right hand tapped her thigh. Her jitters matched one over-caffeinated night she'd indulged during finals her last year of college using uppers and coffee. Only this time, joy and worry were the drugs. For one thing, her mother was awake. No matter how much the doctors had told her she'd be fine, until she'd heard her voice it wasn't reality. There was also the small problem of being a murder suspect.

For another thing—Wolf.

He drove one-handed, his other held her left hand across the console of the car, and released his grip only when he had to shift. Sweet. *So* sweet, like a couple of other things he'd done today, that he had her nerves on overdrive. How could a man be so incredibly sexy, so smoothly sophisticated, have such alpha-carnal talents…and still be sweet?

"Am I not driving fast enough? I cannot do much better on this narrow, cobbled street."

"I do think you'll have to take me out on the *Autobahn* one day. But for now, no you're fine. I'm just keyed up. *So* glad my mom is awake. And…" Telling him how much fun she'd just had might be less than cosmopolitan.

"And? You are worried. I will get you cleared, August."

"No, that's not it." *Screw it.* "You sure know how to do lunch."

"Do lunch? Hmm…is that an American colloquialism?"

"What I mean is—"

He squeezed her hand. "I know what you mean." He downshifted and pulled into a parking space at the hospital, killed the engine, and leaned over the gearshift toward her. "The pleasure was all mine."

"Oh no, it wasn't." She took the lapels of his suit in each hand and pulled him closer. "I had more than my share of pleasure."

He brought a hand beneath her chin, kissed her lightly, and said, "We will have to make a date to compare pleasure levels."

****

August practically trotted into the hospital. Tobias took long, hurried strides to keep up with her. They pounded up the steps, not waiting for the elevator to the third floor. She smiled over her shoulder twice, and he let go of her arm when they pushed through the door of her mother's room.

He nodded at Klein. "Stay close."

Lacy was on the phone, while a nurse worked at removing an IV from her other arm. Her face lit up at the sight of her daughter with a smile that was swollen and bruised. One of her ears was bandaged and her right eye was black and blue. August vaulted in front of Chance to lean down, gave Lacy a light hug, and a kiss.

"I'm talking to your brother. He's being pigheaded as always so you have to help me convince him that there's no need for him to come."

"Well, Mom, if he wants—"

"Absolutely not! He's right in the middle of—what kind of class did you say?" She listened a moment and shook her head. "I can't pronounce it so I'm sure it's important. No, Dylan. Really. Yes, I'm practically back to normal."

Daughter and husband exchanged smirks.

"In fact, as soon as they release me, Chance and I are going to come visit you in Paris. We're this close, we wouldn't think of going home." She smiled at her husband.

August swiveled her head to Chance who shrugged and whispered, "First I've heard of it."

"I'm fine, Dylan. We have some business to complete here with the estate so I'm not sure when exactly we'll get away, but I'll let you know. Yes, honey, I love you, too. Bye-bye." She handed the phone to Chance to hang up, put her head back against the pillow, and extended her arm toward August. "Another hug, but not too tight."

She peered over her daughter's shoulder. "Inspector. How nice to see you."

When she released August, he stepped forward and shook her hand. "Extremely nice to see you awake and talking." Her grip was as weak as her voice.

The nurse who had been removing the IV moved to push her cart out of the room.

"Wait. Are you only taking out one IV?"

She pointed to the half-empty bag hanging above Lacy's head. "*Sie müssen fertig stellen.*" With a smile, she patted her arm and left.

"She said you must finish it before she removes the IV," Tobias translated. "But you probably guessed." He stuck a hand out to her husband. "Nice to see you again, Sheriff Meadowlark."

"How's the investigation going, Inspector?"

How much to say? His hesitation gave him away.

"Inspector?" The man leveled him with a stare.

August shrunk back, took her mother's hand, and bit her bottom lip.

"We have another murder on our hands, Sheriff. Fabian Bauer was found dead at the castle this morning."

Lacy clutched her daughter's hand to her chest. "Oh, no!"

"That's the nephew, right? Wasn't he under suspicion?" Meadowlark glanced at each of them for confirmation.

"Not as far as I was concerned." August had found her voice. "Go ahead, Wolf. Tell them who your prime suspect is."

He retold the morning's events and touched on the evidence so far found at the scene.

"Eike's the one I could strangle." August's crooked smile lit the hospital room as she climbed onto the foot of her mother's bed and curled her legs under her.

"August!" Lacy scowled. "That's inappropriate humor. Especially with the inspector here."

He waved a hand at her protest, and gave her daughter a sideways glance. "Even though I'm not taking you to the station, August, it would be wise to not draw attention to yourself."

From her expression, his cautionary words had no effect. Her gaze swept his face. He wondered if she purposely doused him with her smile now that she knew how it affected him.

"As far as I'm concerned, she overdosed my great-grandfather, and now she's strangled my cousin to frame me. The estate has to be the motive."

Sheriff Meadowlark frowned. "She was married to the owner of the estate. Why murder him?"

Tobias shrugged. Finding the reason had so far evaded him like the center white line of the *Autobahn* on a foggy night.

"If she'd waited, Bauer would've inherited it—or so she thought—and it still would've been hers." The sheriff rubbed the back of his neck, questioning Tobias with his eyes. "The attempts on Lacy's life don't make any sense."

He shared Meadowlark's confusion, and more. The estate, Kurt Gruber, and the current push toward fascism in Austria were embroiled in Eike's actions. If he could connect them, the motivation would be clear. He knew Eike well enough to understand that much.

"It is highly likely she has an accomplice, August. Eike putting a scarf around Bauer's neck and choking him to death is not…her style."

"You don't think she's capable of murder?"

He wouldn't discuss all the possible things Eike was capable of until he had proof. "I need to get back to the station." He softened his voice, gazed into her eyes, and hoped to convey the warmth and concern he felt for her. "Klein will be your shadow."

"What if you can't prove I wasn't involved? I was alone in my room last night. I'm betting Eike will be more than happy to identify my scarf."

She already had. "We will not let it get that far."

Her smile had vanished. A little of the anger still sparked in her eyes, yet obvious concern weakened her fight.

"Can't you just arrest her for questioning? Have you even accused her or anything?" A hand punched the air. "Scare it out of her, Wolf."

Instead of leaving, he moved closer to the foot of the bed. Aware of the sheriff and Lacy, he refrained from taking her into his arms like he wanted. "Patience?" When she didn't soften her glare, he threw caution out the hospital window and touched her bruised cheek. "I'll see you later."

He stopped at the door. "Lacy, rest. Sheriff, I have multiple avenues to pursue. I expect by tomorrow, I will be able to answer some of those questions." Closing the door behind him, he hoped he'd left them more confident than he felt.

"Klein." He called the veteran policeman aside. "You're to remain with August, twenty-four-seven. Get someone to deliver what you need to the Hotel Karnten so you can stay in the other room of her suite. Don't let her out of your sight." If his boss, Egger, found out Tobias knew the scarf was August's, she'd at least be covered with round the clock supervision, regardless of whether it was for her protection or as a potential suspect.

"Yes, sir."

"Did you hand over to Carl what you found out about the nurse from her records and colleagues here at the hospital?"

"Yes, sir. Carl said he'd take it from there."

"Good. And the photo?"

The policeman pulled a two by three-inch photo from his pocket. "This is from her hospital file. Her badge photo."

"Thanks."

Tobias strode down the hall and out to his car parked at the curb.

Maybe Carl had found more on Eike's background and discovered enough on the nurse to get a lead on who'd put her up to the murder attempt on Lacy. If Albert had reined in Eike enough, then he might be able to stall making August a suspect of record until tomorrow. He gunned the engine and headed for the Hotel Karnten before going to his office. He needed desperately to connect the dots this afternoon.

****

"Did you speak to anyone when you went back to the hotel to shower last night, August?" Chance had on his sheriff tone of voice.

"Nope." She stood by the window looking out on the circular drive in front of admitting. The silver Porsche had disappeared—a modern day knight in silver armor? With arms crossed over her chest, she drummed fingers on her triceps.

"You were gone for quite a while." He continued as if interrogating her.

She whirled around. "And?" She'd grown fond of Chance in spite of his seriousness and his profession, yet his sheriff demeanor right now raised the hair on her neck. With hands on hips, she took a defensive stance.

"You need to account for your time."

"Chance, you're scaring me." Her mom touched his forearm.

"I'm sorry, honey." Her stepdad's face softened as he patted his wife's hand, then lifted his gaze back to her. "They'll eventually ask the question." He'd sweetened his voice, yet the meaning came through loud and clear.

"I really can't." She paced the narrow space in front of the window. "I took my time. Washed my hair. Did some girly things like file my nails. I chipped a couple in the accident. It takes longer, too, having to hold the damned showerhead and soap in one hand." She strode to the foot of the bed. "Wolf has suspected Eike from day one. I know it. What the hell is taking him so long to do some pushing on the Frau? I bet *you* would!"

"He's following procedures, August. I'm sure he's doing more than what he's telling you. You'll have to trust—"

"He's been very upfront with me. He doesn't know a lot about Eike or her motives, although he suspects her Nazi aspirations have something to do with this. We've had some conversations about the case."

"And about other things, I'd guess." A smile broke on her

mother's bruised face.

"Honestly, Mom. Your daughter is about to be accused of murder and all you can think about is her love life."

"Love life?" Her smile widened, and she winced.

August patted her mom's leg. "Careful."

"Don't make me smile."

"Hey, you're the one jumping to conclusions and causing yourself pain," she teased.

"I saw the way you two looked at each other. Don't try to deny there's something going on between you."

Grabbing the blanket-covered toe, she wiggled it. "Yes, I like him. When he lets his cop side down and gets real." She darted a glance at Chance. "No offense, lawman."

"No offense taken. Although, right now, I hope he keeps his cop side front and center."

The smile in her mother's eyes faded.

"Don't worry, Mom." She stepped around to the head of the bed, gave her mother a quick kiss, and pushed hair from her cheek. "Wolf's working hard to keep me out of this. And once we get past this, there'll be plenty of time for you to wish romance on me." She winked at her mom's renewed smile. "Right now, I'm in need of a really good cup of coffee. Not this hospital crap. Can I bring either of you anything?" When both declined, she grabbed her purse and headed to the door. "I need some air, too, so don't worry if I'm gone for a bit. I've got my bodyguard, don't forget."

Markel stood from his chair outside the room when she closed the door behind her. "Let's go get some coffee, Mar—Officer Klein." No sense causing him any grief with the two new policemen on duty.

He nodded and followed her, coming beside her as they entered the lobby.

"I saw a coffee café across from the hotel that has Internet." She'd do some investigating of her own. "Do you mind if I drive? I'm not fond of cop cars."

"That would be fine, Ms. Myer."

"Now, Markel, it's August, remember?"

"Oh? I thought we…are formal again."

"Hey, I was helping you save face."

He chuckled as he slid into the passenger side of the rental. "I am grateful for your thinkful…think…thoughtful…"

His English failed him.

"I get it. No problem."

After ordering them both coffees, large latte for her and medium black for Markel, they settled in a corner where her guard could peruse a stack of magazines, while she used one of the café's computers.

She typed Eike Luschin into the search engine. A few articles came up that mentioned Lenhard. Without the help of her friend, Julie, who read German, August couldn't do much more than scan them and check dates. Julie had taught her that much. What she wanted was Eike's maiden name. *Bingo.* One article appeared to be a wedding announcement. She took a long drink of her coffee then changed directions and typed Eike Leitner.

Two of the same articles appeared from what August guessed to be the local newspaper, *Karntner Nachrichten.* A third article, with a small picture, spiked her curiosity. She tried clicking on the picture to enlarge it without luck. The man standing next to Eike faced partially away from the camera, but there was a strong resemblance to Wolf. The date of the article was a little over two months before her great-grandfather and Eike's marriage. August brought her face close to the computer screen and squinted. *Hmmm.* She opened the whole story, scanned for Wolf's name, but he wasn't mentioned.

Markel seemed deeply involved in a sports magazine. It was probably best not to ask his opinion and involve him in her research of his boss. She sipped her latte and set it aside to type Tobias Wolf in the search engine.

Until the fourth article, they all seemed to be about his career as an investigator. There was one picture from three years ago of an official, of some sort, handing him a plaque. The fourth raked her curiosity so badly she struggled to try to make sense of the German words. He was in a tuxedo and Eike, in a strapless, black sheath, leaned into him. While he stared into the camera, a cocky half-smile on his lips, Eike gazed at him. The picture stopped just above the waist, but it sure as hell looked like Wolf had his arm around her.

Heat encircled her neck.

The next article only served to get her heart pumping hard against her chest. The article, entitled *Fruhling Gala,* had three pictures of what looked like partygoers and was dated a week after the last article. One photo showed the dance floor, and smack dab in the middle was Wolf in his usual well-cut suit holding a high-heeled, clingy yellow dressed

Eike. They stared into each other's eyes, and you couldn't have gotten a slip of paper between them.

"Hey, Markel, what does *Fruhling* mean?"

The policeman glanced up from his magazine. "Spring."

"Thanks." *Spring party. Spring fling for Wolf?* She gulped the last of her coffee and opened the last two articles, but there were no pictures or anything to connect Wolf and Eike. She went back to the spring fling. Scanning through the unintelligible words she found Tobias Wolf and Eike Leitner mentioned in the same sentence.

Slumping back in her chair, her mouth clamped shut, and she snorted short, hot breaths out her nose. She stared at the couple on the screen. How could he say he hardly knew her? How could he out and out lie that they weren't familiar on a social level? Yeah, maybe not after her marriage to Lenhard, but certainly before—only weeks before. Is this why he dragged his feet going after her for both her great-grandfather's death and the attempts on her mother's life? And now Fabian. She leaned on the table, face in hands, and groaned quietly.

He'd held the news of Fabian's murder until after they'd made love.

How despicable.

Talk about naïve. She'd actually fallen for all his standing on the right side of freedom versus fascism crap. He, the straight as an arrow crusader, holding her at bay on a professional level until *she* seduced *him*. Or so she thought.

Now, he hesitated to put the cuffs on his ex-lover…ex-lover? Her heart jumped to her throat. Eike had two lovers, why not three?

Impossible. Wolf didn't like Eike. That much was clear from day one. But why? He'd blamed it on her Neo-Nazi politics, but maybe he'd been the jilted lover. She'd married Great-grandfather only a month after the spring fling. Castle Luschin was larger and Lenhard richer. Great-grandfather lived on the estate, but Wolf wouldn't live on his family's estate. If she'd thrown him over for Lenhard, then kept company with Fabian, it stood to reason Wolf's ego was battered.

Whatever happened, it didn't much matter. He'd lied to her. Slept with her before dropping the Fabian bombshell. His lack of disclosure was pure and simple betrayal, and she couldn't let that go no matter what her heart said.

CHAPTER FOURTEEN

Tobias had a hunch on his way to see the Siegels at the Hotel Karnten. He punched in Carl's number, and he answered on the second ring. "How's the research going?"

"Good afternoon, Inspector. I was waiting for one more piece to the puzzle for Eike Luschin before I called you. Got a few things on that nurse Amelia Fischer, but still working on her."

"Can you fit in another project?"

"Why not? I'm not known as Amazing Carl for nothing."

He smiled as he rounded a corner. "I wasn't aware you had a nickname."

"I do now. And I happen to have an intern who knows her shit."

"You'll have to handle this one on your own, and strictly for your eyes only." His fingers tightened on the wheel. "In fact, I'd prefer this request was never made as far as anyone else is concerned."

"Intriguing. Sounds like I'll like this one."

"See what you can find out about Policeman Kurt Gruber that doesn't show up in his personnel file."

An uncharacteristic silence filled Tobias's ear.

"Is he a personal friend, Carl?"

"No. Sorry, Inspector. Just threw me off there a minute since he's one of our own. What am I looking for?"

"See if you can track his whereabouts for the last three days. Tobias pulled into the parking lot of the Hotel Karnten. "Who's he been seen with lately, his politics, whatever you can dig up." He killed the engine.

"You think he's got something to do with the Luschins?"

"Just a gut feeling."

"Your gut is usually right."

Carl's appraisal didn't make him feel any better about his suspicions. "Can you send me Gruber's picture from his file to my phone?"

"Doing it as you breathe."

"Oh, and see if you find any connection between him and the nurse."

"Son of a—okay, Inspector. You got it."

Drumming his fingers on the steering wheel, he gazed into the windows of the restaurant and bar at the hotel. "I've got a stop to make before I come in. Make this as speedy as you can."

"Right." The line went dead.

He strode into the lobby and on through to the bar. Thin-framed Thomas was behind the bar, unloading bottles of wine and stocking shelves. Tobias took a stool.

"Have you got a minute, Thomas?"

"Sure, my friend."

He pulled the photo of the nurse from his pocket. "Have you seen this woman?"

The restaurant owner took the photo and studied it for a few seconds. "Can't say. Nothing particularly outstanding about her."

He brought up the file photo of Gruber on his phone. "How about this guy?"

"Him, I've seen. A few times." Thomas' mouth held a hard line. "I remember because I saw him speaking with a couple of the *Burschenschaften*. Recently. He seemed pretty damned friendly." He handed the phone back. "Who is he?"

"Policeman Kurt Gruber."

"Policeman." His friend didn't seem particularly surprised. "Well, Tobias, makes sense to infiltrate the law."

Heidi came from the dining room. "Hey, Tobias. What brings you here? Too early for dinner."

"Hello, Heidi." He half-stood and accepted her kiss on each cheek. "A little investigating." He held out the photo of Nurse Fischer. "Do you know this woman?"

"I don't know her, but I've seen her. She had dinner here a couple of nights ago."

"Who with?"

"A young, good-looking man, blond, tall. Very well built." She slid a smile at her husband who raised his brows and chuckled.

Tobias refreshed his phone to bring up Gruber's picture again. "This man?"

"Yes. That's him."

His gut feeling flourished into a full-blown ache both satisfying and worrying.

"What's this about, Tobias?" Heidi watched the photo go back into his pocket.

"You know it's got to be police business, my dear." Thomas rapped his knuckles on the bar. "You look worried, my friend. Anything more we can do?"

He stood, gave Heidi a kiss on the cheek, and shook his head. "No, you've both been a great help. I need to get back to the station. But do me a favor. Gruber is off today so if he comes in here, would you give me a call?"

"Sure." Thomas shook his hand.

"How about the woman?" Heidi asked. "Do you want us to call if she comes in?"

"You won't be seeing her. She's the nurse that was shot at the hospital."

"Oh." It was more of a small gasp than a word from Heidi.

A light of understanding crossed her husband's face. "I'll be alert for Gruber."

****

"Are you all right, August?" Markel closed his magazine and looked over the wire rims perched on his nose.

She must've sworn under her breath louder than she realized. "Well, Markel, I'm tired and in a pissy mood now that you ask." She shoved back from the table and grabbed her purse. "Are you ready? Because I've done all the Internet reading I care to do today."

He folded his glasses and put them away. "Where to now?"

The familiar Mozart strain played from her cell. She flipped open the side compartment of her purse and was surprised and pleased to see Penny's number displayed. She hesitated. Was she in the mood to talk? Actually, she needed to talk, and although she wouldn't mind running all of this past her mom, Chance's presence wouldn't be desirable.

"Penny! Hi." Hearing her friend's voice all the way from Arizona made her happy she'd answered.

"Why the heck haven't I heard from you, August? The last time we talked, you left me in the castle with a view of the Alps, an inspector I definitely got mixed feelings about, and antiques to drool over. I need an update."

"Just a minute." She gestured to her guard. "You mind if we hang here a while longer?"

He shrugged and sat back down.

She dug some money from her purse. "Would you mind getting me another latte and anything you want for yourself. You must need a doughnut by now."

"A doughnut?"

"Never mind." She shot him a smile. "Get whatever."

"Oooohhh. Markel. Who is that?"

"Don't get excited, Penny." She lowered her voice. "He's a cop. My bodyguard."

"What? Okay, I'm sitting down. You have a story to tell, so spill."

"Hang on a sec."

After Markel handed her the coffee, she moved to a table by the window to get out of earshot of her guard. He seemed to judge her distance and nodded to himself as he took up his magazine again.

August relayed the adventures of the last three days, leaving nothing out. Her phone beeped in her ear at one point, and she glanced at the caller ID. Wolf. She ignored him and continued her tale. Moments later, Markel's phone went off. As he spoke, he glanced at her. Yes, Wolf was keeping tabs, the bastard. Achy vibes sent her mood further into the pits. It was cathartic to let loose of her worry over her mom and admit her feelings about Wolf to Penny. With her last swallow of coffee, the story was told, and she sighed.

"I'm stunned. And pissed right along with you. What are you going to do? What are you going to say to him?"

A heavy sigh escaped. "I don't want to talk to him." She pushed the empty coffee container around the table. "But I have to *do* something."

"You mean about him?"

She gazed out the window, not focusing on anything. "No, about the whole mess."

"Like what? You can't do anything that the cops aren't doing."

What *could* she do? "I don't know, Penny." Something would

come to her.

"Whatever you have in mind, be careful. Cops, well, they can't always be depended on."

She sat up straighter. "Sounds like *you* have a story."

"Hmm, no. Not right now anyway." A shuffling noise came over the phone like Penny was up and on the move. "Listen, say hi to your mom and the sheriff. Will you call me with another installment?"

"You'll get the breaking news." She chuckled and said goodbye.

She strolled over to Markel as she slid her phone back into her purse. "I'm really ready to head out this time."

"Inspector Wolf would like you to call him."

"Yeah, later." She pushed through the door.

He followed her to the car. "Could you call before we get in the vehicle?"

Her stomach tightened. The anger she'd let go of as she confessed to her friend threatened to come roaring back. She huffed, took her phone out, and clicked on the missed call.

"Hi, August." His voice was strong, yet soft.

"Hello." She couldn't help the flutter in spite of her anger.

"I want to take you to dinner, but I've got some leads, and I'm not sure—"

"Don't bother. Work your leads." She stared at her feet and leaned against the car. "I'll have dinner with Mom and Chance at the hospital, and then head to my room."

"I could come by later when—"

"Bad idea." She had to think before confronting him, and right now her head pounded with each strong pulse of her heart. "I'm beat. Just keep working. You know, clear my name and all that." Tossing it out like an insult, she grabbed the handle on the car door.

He was quiet for a second. "Are you okay?"

"Oh, I'm just great."

Her tone must've come through as he missed several beats before answering. "Well…all right. I'll see you in the morning?" His question was tentative and nothing like the smooth-talking inspector.

"Sure." She disconnected, dropped the phone in her purse, and yanked open the car door.

****

Tobias tucked his phone away and sat staring out the front windshield of his car in the parking lot of the station. There was something wrong with August. Markel had said she was on a lengthy phone call. Could she have gotten bad news? Maybe she was still involved with someone in the states, and her conscience flared. Whatever the cause, she was definitely cold toward him.

He got out of the car and into the late afternoon sunlight that seemed dimmer than it should. The world looked duller. He hoped her mood was just that—a mood. August was a woman he'd like to keep in his life. His feet were on autopilot as he walked to his office, barely aware of the activity around him.

Albert paused after opening the door. "I foresee in your face a long night ahead."

There was more in his face than his partner could possibly see, but he needed to put thoughts of August aside. "We need to get a handle on this Luschin case, Al. Egger isn't happy. But then neither am I." He slumped into his desk chair.

"The nurse's death is going to break this investigation wide open in the news."

"I know. Egger's having a press conference tomorrow afternoon. Someone leaked there's a connection between the lord's death and the nurse. He wants something he can run with that makes it look like we're getting ready to crack the case wide open."

"And because the *Oberstleutnat* says make it happen…"

"Yeah." Wolf ran a hand through his hair then loosened his tie. "What's the status with the Bauer murder?"

"Strangulation appears to be the cause of death. His nose was broken and on first look you'd think it happened when he fell forward onto the floor after being strangled."

He heard the rise in Albert's voice. "But?"

"But there's some clotting in the nasal cavity that suggests the nose could've been broken before he hit the floor. Won't know right away until the autopsy."

Tobias smiled.

"That American girlfriend of yours would have to pack a punch in addition to being strong enough to strangle a man as tall as she is. At five six, he looked to be flimsy, but still…"

"Girlfriend?" It seemed a silly term for how he felt about August. She meant more than the term allowed…at least he wanted more.

Albert chuckled. "Speaking of women, Frau Luschin was quite distraught, yet more than able to give an opinionated statement."

"Which was?"

"She's still pointing the finger at Bauer for her husband's death and cutting the breaks on the rental car. Then Bauer—'cause we all know what a lady's man he was— got the nurse at the hospital to help him kill Lacy. She says August found out and strangled him. Frau Luschin tied it up for us all in a neat red scarf."

"Huh. A little too neat. Certainly logical. What's her alibi?"

"Now that question had her stuttering. She was sleeping. Alone." He mimicked a female voice and added, *"But why on earth would anyone think I had anything to do with it? It was August's scarf."*

Tobias huffed a sigh.

"I'm betting on the broken nose prior to strangulation. That should be enough to put doubt on August as a suspect—unless you noticed any knuckle scrapes on her?" Albert rose and shuffled over to Tobias's desk. "You're quiet. What else is going on?"

No, she hadn't had any knuckle scrapes. He'd certainly have noticed considering her hands were all over his body. He swallowed and shifted in his seat. "Have you seen anything on the nurse that gives us any clues for motive?"

"Not really. Nothing in her file. Klein asked around, and she's a loner. No real friends at the hospital. You got something?"

"You know Policeman Gruber?"

His partner frowned. "I've seen him around."

"It appears he's having an affair with Eike. August has seen him at the castle in civilian clothes at odd hours. Heidi Siegel has seen him at the Karnten Hotel restaurant with the nurse, Amelia Fischer."

Albert's mouth worked as if he was chewing the information. "Okay, so he's a stud with a taste for older women."

"Thomas Siegel has seen him being friendly with some *Burschenschaften* members."

"*Ach*, the Nazi ties again." He didn't sound doubtful this time. Tobias thought he might be considering the connections.

"Castle Luschin was a Nazi stronghold."

"Gruber is one of our own, Tobias. I suggest you tread lightly and damn well have enough before you present this to Egger."

His desk phone rang. An inside call. "Wolf."

"How's your gut feeling right about now, Inspector?"

A surge of adrenaline shot through him, and he stood. "You got something, Carl?"

"I can't make heads or tails of what all this means, but it's *verrry* interesting. You better get your ass up here."

****

"Is the woman a damn cat with nine lives?" Eike rolled the stem of her wine glass between her hands. Another attempt at removing Lacy Dahl from her path had failed.

Kurt stood beside the sofa in his usual at attention pose. Right now, his soldier demeanor irritated her. Her wine tasted bitter. The lighting in the room too harsh. Her head throbbed.

She kicked off her shoes, sank into a corner of the sofa, and tucked her legs under her. "Kurt! Grab the wine bottle and another glass and sit *down*."

He did as told but didn't pour his wine. "Amelia is dead." He offered up the already old news as if to lighten her mood.

"Something to be thankful for." The nurse had failed miserably, but at least she'd died and hadn't been caught with the potential of talking. The one bright spot, along with another drink of wine, untied some of the knots in her tense body. "Are you absolutely sure there will be nothing to connect you to the car?"

"Nothing. I'm confident they will determine the brakes were purposely damaged, but there will be nothing to lead them to us."

Us? There would be no us if they sniffed out his handiwork. Kurt would take the fall alone. "Then Fabian tampered with the car to get rid of his relatives who stood in the way of his inheritance. August found out and murdered him. Even Tobias should be able to come to that conclusion."

Kurt touched her knee, his fingertips gliding over the slick black legging as he spoke. "You've devised a good plan."

She held her wine glass up for a refill. Kurt served her. Yes, he served her.

"If Lenhard hadn't been so stupid…" She didn't relish the death that followed his learning about her true motives for marrying him. She'd been too lax in her movements, trusting he was elderly and so ensconced in his old lord ways he wouldn't take notice of her activities. He'd been good to her for a while. He could've stood beside her and basked in the glory. Instead, three people were dead because of him. It wasn't her fault. "He could've lived out his life. I had Fabian waiting in the wings." What was done was over. For the good of Austria. She sipped, and with a smile at Kurt, waved a manicured hand through the air. "We will prevail, *meine Liebe*."

With a deep breath, the tightness in her chest released, and she stood. "As of last night, we have the support of three more members of the lower house. They're silent supporters, but I don't really give a damn how silent they are as long as we continue to gain leverage."

She paced, sipped her wine as energy flowed through her once again. "To hell with the American women. They have to recuperate, gather their lawyers, make their plans. Let them throw me out." She could be patient. "It won't be forever. Once the Declaration of the National German State is made, the Austrian deed will no longer be held as a legal document. An American will not be allowed to possess property. Without a Luschin heir, I will take possession as Lenhard's widow. This estate will revert to Castle Buchleitner, and my great-grandfather will be vindicated.

But until then, we need to reseal the hole we punched out in the one vault of Jewish treasure in the basement. All four must stay hidden until after the Declaration." The vaults of Jewish possessions were thought to be a myth, yet she'd known better. With Kurt's help, she'd found the wealth. "We'll seal it tonight, after the staff has retired."

He stood, took her into his arms, and kissed both her cheeks. "You are brilliant."

"I still have much to do. There are now two funerals to plan. I'll bury Fabian here, in the family cemetery. We must tread carefully for the next few months. We'll suspend meetings until everyone is in the ground or gone back to America." She brushed her knuckles across his cheek. "I am mired in grief. First my husband and now my very close friend, Fabian. I'm sure the American women will grieve with me. They would not like to see me wrenched from my home. But if they do, it won't be for long. Not for long. History is being made, and Eike Buchleitner will rise with a new and glorious nation."

****

"I think the Austrians know more about good hospital cafeteria food than Americans." August sat on one side of her mother's bed while Chance sat on the other. "I wonder if I could get the recipe for this stew." She lifted a paprika stained potato to her mouth.

"*Bayrisches Gulasch*." Her mother read the sticker on the side of the paper bowl around a mouthful of beef. "Good choice."

"You're just lucky I asked what the other choice was. *Leberklosse*. Liver dumplings."

"So, why are you here with us?" Her mother scratched at a bruised spot on her face and grimaced. "I thought I heard Inspector Wolf say he'd see you later."

She set her spoon in her bowl, her appetite waning with the mention of Wolf. "I'd rather he get his job done so we can get on with our lives."

"What happened?"

She wasn't exactly good at keeping her emotions hidden from her mother. "He's lied to me, to us, and I really don't care to see him beyond what is necessary for all this cop stuff."

Chance continued eating, but watched her closely.

"What do you mean he lied?" Her mother frowned.

"He knows Eike a whole lot better than he's let on. With a little Internet search earlier, I found he had a damned relationship with her only weeks before she married Lenhard. No wonder he's not pushing harder to wrap a murder bow around her."

Chance set his bowl on the tray. "August, that's a pretty serious charge."

"What else could it be?"

"Right now, all he has is circumstantial evidence. If he does…*know* her, then he probably knows when and how to implicate her and move on the investigation."

"I'm not seeing it that way. I think his involvement with the woman taints his ability to pursue the—the—collar. He lied to me, Chance." She swallowed deeply. "My guess is when he found out she's a Nazi, he broke it off. Even though he's driven to learn more about her politics, he can't bring himself to believe she's a murderer." August stared into his frown.

Her mother lifted a strand of hair and painted it across her chin. "You're hurt, kiddo, and what you see as lies may have been the inspector's only option as far as how much he could tell you because of the case."

Anger burnt her appetite, and she stood. "He lied." She took her mother's bowl and set it with hers on the tray. "You two can have the chocolate cake."

"By tomorrow, he should have more forensics from the car crash. And there could be more on Fabian's murder, too. August, he has to have physical evidence and probable cause before he can do anything."

Chance's words bounced off her. Of course he'd see Wolf's side.

He had no idea what had happened earlier in the day.

She shook her head. The memory of Wolf's hands, his kisses, and his flesh beneath her fingertips brought her anger to a new level. Her face flushed, and she glanced at where her mother touched her hand.

Quelling the quakes those memories brought on, she changed the subject. "Mom, did you talk to your lawyer today?"

"Yes. I gave Mark the names and numbers of Lenhard's manager and accountants. I had hoped to leave Eike in charge of the day-to-day upkeep on the estate."

"What?"

"At least in the *beginning*, August. I don't think either of us seriously considered *moving* here to live in Castle Luschin."

She hadn't actually thought about how they would manage the estate from afar. "No. And I suppose Eike would've been the logical choice. Sure as hell not now!"

"Without knowing how all of this will turn out, I'm not sure how we'll set it up. Mark is going to investigate, then present us with options. He said the accountants can designate someone to oversee the estate as an interim solution. But all of this can be handled and figured out from home."

From home. In spite of her anger, walking away from Wolf—so far away from Wolf—twisted the pain in her chest. "What if Eike isn't arrested."

Her mother sighed. "We might leave her in place until we come up with another way to manage the estate."

No way in hell.

A bud of an idea found root. "I think I'll head back to the hotel."

"Are you okay, kiddo?"

"Yeah, Mom." She gave her a kiss. "You sleep tight." On the other side of the bed, she gave Chance a hug. "I'll see you both in the morning."

In the hallway, she nodded at Markel. "Ready?"

He said a few words to the night shift officers by her mother's door and joined her. "Where to?"

"First a stop at the corner drugstore, then I'm ready to head back to the hotel." She yawned for effect. "I'm beat."

Her yawn was catching as Markel responded with one of his own. "Sounds good to me." They pushed through the door into the cool, night air.

The truth was her anger at Wolf zinged through her limbs, and she doubted she'd get any sleep while remembering his erotic caresses. The latter kept repeating deliciously through her mind, regardless of how mad she was.

Then there was Eike. She had to do *something* about the bitch. And it was time someone took action. It might as well be her.

****

Tobias and Albert pored over the information Carl had collected on the nurse and Gruber. Most of it was benign. Except for one glaring connection. They'd attended the same school for several years before she went into nursing and Gruber chose police training.

Tobias glanced at his partner. "I think we owe young Policeman Gruber a visit, Al."

"Would you like me to call and make the appointment?"

"No. I think a surprise visit will be much more interesting." Tobias tapped the desk. "Now, let's see what you have on Eike, Carl." He leaned in. "I assume you've held the best to last."

"Ah, you know me well, Inspector." The IT man beamed.

Tobias's phone rang.

"Inspector, this is Gretchen." A note of excitement tinged the forensic specialist's voice. "Are you in the building?"

"Yes, why?"

"Can you come down?"

"What is it, Gretchen?" Impatience tinged his words. He glanced at Carl who looked bursting to spill his information. Nervous tension zinged through Tobias's neck and shoulders. "I'm in the middle of something."

"We've got something on the American car rental crash."

"And?" The short, wiry woman preferred a face-to-face audience. No one he knew could lend more dramatics to her job than the redheaded thirty-something.

A disappointed sigh met his impatience. "No prints were found on the undercarriage near the brake system. Almost too clean. I decided to expand the area we were looking at. We found a fingerprint. Just one, but we've got identification. At first, I thought maybe the scene had been compromised. It seemed likely one of the policemen that responded to the call had been too touchy. Then I went one step further." She paused for effect, and he could imagine her self-satisfied smile. "The list of respondents didn't match the print."

Tobias knew where she was going before she ended her sentence. *Gruber.*

"The position of this print, below the door on the edge of the exterior, leads me to believe he left it as he climbed under the car. More than likely before he put his gloves on."

"Whose print, Gretchen?"

Her voice lowered. "Policeman Gruber."

They'd finally caught a break "Good job. Gretchen, please keep this information confidential." He disconnected.

Carl and Albert stared as he let his weight back against the stiff, chrome and leather chair. He rested his elbows on the thin, metal arms and rubbed the knuckles of his fingers against each other. "A fingerprint on the car. Gruber's."

The IT man's eyes grew wide.

Albert rubbed a hand over his face and muttered, "*Scheisse.*"

"One more thing." He held up a hand to stall any questions, pulled his cell out, and punched the number for autopsy.

"Autopsy. Arnold."

"Wolf here. Anything new on Fabian Bauer?"

"Strangulation is definitely the cause of death, and the broken nose came before he was killed. I'm scraping for DNA, but I'm not too confident I'll find anything. I suppose it's possible the assailant might have left some skin or blood behind when he punched him in the face, but considering the bleeding could wash it away…we'll see."

"Thanks, Arnold. Call my cell if anything else pops." He slid his phone back into his pocket. "Broken nose before strangulation." He allowed himself a tiny crack in his concern. It would be hard for anyone to imagine August punching Bauer in the nose hard enough to break it then overpowering him in strangulation.

His partner rubbed his chin. "I can't see August or even Eike being able to throw a punch hard enough to break his nose."

"Exactly. And neither woman has scratches or bruises on their hands. I think considering Gruber's print is on the rental car, and now this—looks like we'll be going to see Gruber for more than a visit." He addressed Carl. "You didn't hear this." The IT man nodded. "Now, you were saying?"

"Yeah, well, not sure it means anything as far as your case. Looks like you got your murderer."

Tobias stared into air. They could probably pin the car crash on

Gruber. Could probably link him with circumstantial evidence to the attempt at the hospital. But where did Lenhard and Fabian fit? "No, we don't." He glanced at his partner. "Not yet."

Albert met his gaze. "We need the motive. Why is Gruber doing what he's doing?"

"Okay, then." Carl shoved a page to each of the inspectors. "Eike Leitner Luschin."

"Holy Mother." His partner's exclamation barely registered over the roar of blood pulsing in Tobias's ears.

"Eike *Buchleitner*." Tobias spit the name. "The great-granddaughter of Franz Buchleitner, SS. The man who'd ruled the Luschin estate during the war." His fingers gripped the page, crumpling the edge. "This is the dot that connects everything together." He glanced up at the IT man's smirk. "I'd kiss you, Carl, but Albert would get jealous."

"And your partner packs a powerful punch, so I'll pass."

Tobias pushed back, rose from the chair, and ticked his head toward the door. "Let's go, Albert."

They took the stairs from the third floor to the first. Albert lagged behind as he practically jogged. "Come on, old man."

"Screw you, Inspector."

Once on the bottom floor, he led the way to Dorner's desk. "I need the home address for Kurt Gruber." A quick database search provided the answer: an apartment on the east side of St. Veit.

"I'll drive." He pushed through the front door toward the car.

Albert stopped by the passenger side.

"What?" Tobias frowned at him across the top of the Porsche.

"Maybe I should drive. Do you plan to stuff Gruber in your joke of a back seat?"

"I'll handcuff his wrists to his ankles and fold him in like a piece of trash." The prospect of doing so satisfied him more than it should. "Get in."

He raced through the narrow streets, his heart matching the speed as he anticipated the capture.

"What are you thinking, Tobias? Lover Nazi? You think Gruber saw a prize he couldn't resist? Is Eike an innocent?"

"She's no damned innocent. She married Lenhard to get back the estate her great-grandfather claimed for the Nazis. With her aspirations, she probably plans to make it the grand palace of the Nazi party. My guess is, the lord figured out her game. She was probably keeping Bauer as her back up plan. Somewhere in there, Gruber shows up, probably a recruit. Bauer was just the lovesick slug." He agreed with August that her cousin was the innocent. He hadn't thought of her for a few hours, so caught up in the investigation. His chest tightened with yearning. He rolled his neck and shrugged. "I'm betting Bauer got suspicious. Eike had Gruber kill him. She used Gruber for her henchman. He rigged the rental, enlisted the nurse for the attempt on Lacy, and killed Bauer."

"You don't think he did this all on his own, knowing Eike wanted to gain control of the estate her great-grandfather had during the war?"

"He wouldn't have had access to the lord. That's probably the only blood directly on her hands. He's young, a neo-fascist, and she probably has him by the cock. No. He didn't do all of this on his own." He slowed as they drew near the address of his apartment. "The corner building. He's on the first floor. He'd have no reason to know we suspect him, but plant yourself around the back just in case." Tobias drove around the corner and parked on the side street. He patted the Glock in his shoulder holster, Albert did the same, and they stepped out.

He gave his partner a few seconds to get around back while he located Gruber's name on the listing by the front entrance. He pushed the buzzer. Waited. Buzzed again. Waited longer, then laid on the buzzer.

He walked around the back and waved at Albert. "He's not here. It's well past dinnertime. Have you eaten?"

"No."

"I want to get a warrant to search his place. Let's go eat while that's processed. Maybe he'll be home by the time we're done. If not, we should have the warrant by then."

Every nerve in his body told him they were close to finally putting this case to bed. His mind wandered to another bed. August would soon be safe and on her way back to America—unless he could convince her to stay a while longer. He wanted to explore the young woman. Not only her body, but her mind and soul. If she'd let him.

As they settled at a table, he punched her number. No answer.

Why was she avoiding him?

CHAPTER FIFTEEN

August muted her phone when she saw Wolf's number. If he had news on the case, he could call the hospital and speak to Chance. She didn't plan to hear Tobias Wolf's voice again. Or at least not until this whole mess was officially solved. And then only as a final goodbye. The twist of pain in her chest gave a second stab when she faced that intention. She went back to her book but couldn't focus on the page.

The sounds of the television in Policeman Markel's half of the suite drifted in. He'd left the door open between their rooms with an apology. He needed to be able to hear clearly, he'd said, but would not come into her room without announcing himself first. Unless, of course, she was in some sort of distress or other.

Now, she lay on top of the covers, in her blouse, jeans, and sneakers, attempting to read and waited.

Eike tried to frame her for murder, and she wanted to know why. Wolf didn't believe Eike could wrap a scarf around her nephew-lover and choke the life from him. She must've had an accomplice. Wolf also said August wouldn't end up in jail, but now she questioned if he could keep his promise and still seemingly protect Eike.

She'd confront the Nazi bitch if he wouldn't. A slight shiver tickled down her spine. Or at least she'd do a little snooping around the castle. She'd go to the kitchen and enlist Herr Bloch's help. He didn't seem all that fond of his temporary boss, but he'd had nothing but smiles and politeness for herself and her mother. Besides, technically, Eike was no longer his employer.

A cough came from the next room. Markel was still awake. She switched off her lamp. Maybe he'd relax more if he thought she was asleep.

She rolled to her side. With her nose close to the pillow, her head reeled with Wolf's scent. Memories of his lovemaking—confident, caring, voracious—were imprinted on her psyche. She was branded and would never be the same again—which was unfortunate given he was a lying bastard.

Even if he wanted to explain away his deceit, would she be able to overcome her feelings of betrayal? It wasn't as if they were pledged to each other. They'd made no promises. For all she knew, theirs might've been a one-time encounter. He didn't need to confess all his lovers or past transgressions. But this wasn't about sex. Her great-grandfather had died under suspicious circumstances. There'd been two attempts on her mother's life. Not to mention her own. Her cousin had been killed, and she'd been set up to take the fall. Why hide his relationship with the woman August felt was behind it all? He lied, then slept with her.

She couldn't wrap her head around his actions. And she couldn't deny her continuing attraction. She nestled her cheek against the scent of smoky cardamom and sex, let her mind relive his touch, and tried to forget her anger.

****

Tobias closed his car door quietly. "Same routine as before."

His partner walked the opposite direction to the back of the apartment house.

Tobias stood beneath the dim overhead light above the door and repeated the ringing of the doorbell. Gruber still didn't answer. He walked around the building while calling the station. He waved at Albert as he listened then tucked his phone away.

"We've got the warrant. Come on."

Back at the front door, he buzzed the manager's apartment.

"Yeah?" A female voice croaked.

"Police."

A door down the hall on the first floor opened and a short, frumpy woman in a green housecoat approached them. Her ear-length, gray hair stuck out on one side. "I need to see some identification first," she shouted through the double glass door.

They held their badges against the pane.

She turned on another light inside, above the door, and squinted.

With her nod, a buzz sounded, and she stepped back as they entered the hall. "What can I do for you?"

The smell of sauerkraut and stale cigarette smoke permeated the air. "We need entrance into Kurt Gruber's apartment."

"Got himself in trouble?" From a pocket, she withdrew a ring of keys, and started down the hall while they followed behind her. "He's a cop, too." She stopped suddenly, and Albert nearly collided into her. "He's not hurt, is he?"

"If you could please let us in?" Tobias extended a hand in the direction she'd been shuffling.

"Sure, sure. He's not a very friendly fellow, but being a cop, well, it's a dangerous profession. Wouldn't want to see him hurt." She stopped two doors past the apartment she'd come from. "Kind of nice having a policeman in the building." She knocked first, waited, then inserted the key and opened the door. Reaching around the doorjamb, she flipped a switch for an overhead light.

"You must hear his comings and goings since he passes by your door." Tobias smiled at her, encouraging her talkative nature.

She nodded. "The walls are pretty thin in this building."

"Does he have much company?"

"He's not home all that much."

He pulled the photo of the nurse from his pocket. "Have you ever seen this woman?"

She clutched her housecoat tighter, tipped her face closer to the photo, and shook her head. "Can't say I have." Glancing between his partner and him, she shrugged. "But then, I've never seen him with anyone. Like I said, he doesn't seem too friendly."

He put the photo away and pulled his card from his pocket. "If you do think of anything, anything at all, give me a call."

"I'll do that." She tucked the card in her pocket and gazed into Gruber's apartment.

Tobias and Albert slipped past her. "You'll excuse us now?"

"Hmph. Lock up when you leave." She pulled the door shut.

He scanned the area. Living room and kitchen blended together. The bedroom could be seen down a short hall. "You want to take the bedroom and bathroom, Al?"

"Sure." He ambled off.

Furnishings were sparse. An empty beer bottle and a dirty ashtray rested atop the wooden table in front of the couch. An oil heater and a coat tree took up one wall. Tobias checked the pockets of a lightweight gray jacket, but all he found was a book of matches. A bookcase jutted up against the back of the couch and held a dozen books. Half of them had subject matter related to the Third Reich or fascism. Multiple police school textbooks, a dictionary, and three biographies of Hitler era military commanders made up the rest of his collection. A small metal desk and chair sat beneath the one window. A telephone, notepad, and pencil were the only items on the desk. A name and number were scrawled on the pad. Amelia. He searched the drawers, but other than a carton of cigarettes, ammo, and a porno magazine, there was nothing of interest. He gazed at the notepad.

"Tobias." Albert called from the bedroom. "Come in here."

"What you got?"

His partner stood in front of a closet, holding a hanger with a *Burschenschaften* coat in one hand and the matching beret in the other hand. "Thought this would make your day."

"As I suspected."

Albert hung up the coat and tossed the beret on the unmade bed. "But there's more." He walked to a basket of what looked to be dirty clothes by the bathroom door. With a gloved finger he lifted the sash to the *Burschenschaften* ensemble.

Tobias bent closer to inspect the dark spots along the edge of the material. "Looks like blood to me."

****

August eased off the bed, avoiding any squeaks of the frame or rustling of the bedspread, lifted her black hoodie, and slipped it on. From the nightstand, she took her cell and slid it into one hoodie pocket. The miniature flashlight she bought at the drugstore tucked in the other pocket. She grabbed the towel taken from the bathroom earlier and stood next to the doorway into the other bedroom where Markel watched television with the sound on low.

The television and a chair were visible without peeking into the room, so she assumed he watched from the bed. With an intake of breath, she strained to hear any sounds. A soft steady purr, not quite a snore. Slowly and deliberately, she inched her face around the doorframe to catch a glimpse of her guard.

Policeman Markel lay on his back, hands at his sides, fully clothed, and asleep. His gun rested on the nightstand next to him.

She eased back, and gently crept to the door into the hallway.

Using the towel to help muffle any clicks or scrapes, she wrapped it around the handle and delicately pulled the handle down and opened the door. The slightest click sounded, and she froze. Her heart hammered so loud, she pressed the towel against her chest. After counting to five in her head, and when nothing was heard from her guard, she dropped the towel and deliberately eased the door open wide enough to slip out, bringing the door gently closed behind her.

Once outside the room, and after a couple of deep breaths, she loped down the hall, ascended the stairs, and slipped into the cool night air. She didn't pause, but went straight to her car. It was getting late, and if she hoped to catch Herr Bloch in the kitchen, she had to hurry.

The moon and stars provided additional light as she drove the curvy mountain road. Cold gooseflesh tickled down her neck and across her shoulders as she tried to come up with some sort of plan. What if Herr Bloch wouldn't take her on an after dark snoop of the castle? What was she looking for? What if she ran into Eike before she found him? She swallowed and let go of the wheel one hand at a time to wipe her sweaty palms.

"Come on, August. Grow a pair."

If the Nazi bitch caught her, she'd say she'd come back for some more clothes. There had to be something at the castle that connected Eike to the attempts on her mom's life and Fabian's murder. She'd go through Fabian's room to start with. Then…hell, she'd…maybe Herr Bloch would say something to give her a clue. He *had* to have seen more going on in that castle than he'd told, if she could coax it out of him. He'd been with Lenhard far more years than with Eike.

When she approached the castle entrance, the gigantic wooden doors were closed. She'd feared as much, but maybe it was better to not drive right in anyway. She cut her lights, drove slowly to the side of the gate, and parked. Through the window, the stars twinkled while a wisp of a cloud drifted across the sliver of moon. After setting her phone to vibrate, she pushed her car door softly shut. A cool breeze danced across her face. The regular door that both Golden Boy and Inspector Wolf had come through a lifetime ago was only a few steps away. With her fingers crossed on her left hand, she took hold of the handle with her right and levered it downward. The door creaked open. Her heart still pattered too fast, but now excitement overtook her worries. She glanced around and saw no one. With purposeful strides, her sneakers carried her across the bailey to the steps leading to the

Great Hall doors. At the first step, she glanced left then right, and her gaze stopped at the door that she'd seen Kurt use a couple of times—once in his Nazi club uniform.

She glanced upward at the Great Hall doors, then back at the mysterious door. *Door number one or door number two?* Back at the hall doors, then to the mysterious door.

Door number two.

She skittered around to the wall, glanced behind and ahead, and hugging the wall, staying in the night shadow of the castle, sidestepped to the door. Again, crossing the fingers of her left hand, she took the handle of the door into her right, pushed downward with a jerk of surprise when it opened. One more glance around and she pulled the door open, her heart jumping to her throat when a light came on. Relief flooded her with the realization that the light above and inside the doorway must be motion sensitive.

A small landing just inside led down, giving her pause. The ceiling sloped so drastically in such a short space, she could see only to the bottom of the ten or so steps. Nothing but darkness below. The ceiling arched above her no more than two feet. Good thing she wasn't claustrophobic. With a swallow and a deep breath, she stepped inside, pulling the door shut behind her. If this was merely a back passage into Eike's chambers, she'd be disappointed. She was two floors below the solar.

In the dungeon.

She chuckled, surprising herself. Her nerves had calmed. There was no one down here, Eike couldn't possibly hear her, and stealth snooping was entirely possible. She clutched the flashlight in her pocket just as the sensor light went out.

The blackness closed around her. With a touch of her hand against the door, she grounded herself and listened. Nothing.

Aiming the flashlight at the floor, she switched it on. Her sneakers afforded a silent descent. The air grew cooler with the last few steps. At the bottom, she brought the beam of the flashlight up and shined it from right to left. In the dungeon, the walls of stone were rougher, the floor not as level, and the arched ceiling lower than the floors above. An age-old, damp smell enveloped her. There were three recessed doorways ahead, the tops of which were arched, two on the left and one on the right, and the hall seemed to widen beyond. The beam of her light didn't carry far enough to be sure. Before she checked the rooms, she wanted to know what lay at the far end some twenty yards ahead. Would that have been Kurt's destination, or was this just a stealth passageway to someone above?

As she passed each doorway, she briefly shined the light in them. The first, on the left, had a wide doorway and the door stood open. The arch seemed slightly higher than the other two rooms. It looked to be furnished. This one she would explore after checking the rest of the area. The second door on the right was opened, no door, and not much bigger than a coat closet containing a table. The third, on the left, was also open and the room more spacious. There appeared to be crates or boxes. Perhaps a storage area.

She continued to the end of the narrow hallway that opened into a large round area. Flicking the light around spiked her curiosity, yet brought a sense of dread. Within the circle of stone wall, spaced evenly, were iron barred rooms. Prison cells. Off to the far right was a black hole with a stone mantel about two feet off the ground. To the far left were two arched openings. One appeared to be another hall and the other a stairway going up.

A quick tour told her this was truly a dungeon, the evil part of the castle. The black hole looked to be a burn oven—she hoped for trash—and didn't peer too closely when a musty scent from that direction assaulted her nose. The iron barred rooms were obviously for prisoners of the castle. Various means of restraining people by way of chains and irons were still intact. The stairs leading up were identical to the ones she came down at the other end. The last archway was to another hall, much shorter. She stepped only a few feet in, scanning the walls with her flashlight. There were arches as if marking off four rooms but the walls were solid. Below one arch a square had been cut out about shoulder high. She stepped back, stopped by the stairs leading upward, and listened. Still no sounds. She hurriedly made her way back to the furnished room.

A lamp stood on a table a few feet in, and she pulled with a click. She switched off her flashlight and glanced around. Amazement and enlightenment blazed brighter than the dimly lit room decorated with modern pieces of furniture that could've been matching pieces to the solar. Eike's taste bathed the room. She turned on another lamp and gazed on a painting above a podium at one end of the room.

Wolf had been right about Eike. *Heil Hitler.*

****

Tobias and Albert stopped at the evidence room. They checked in the notepad with the nurse's telephone number in its sealed plastic bag and the *Burschenschaften* sash. Once those were logged in, they left the pad but continued on to forensics with the paper evidence bag containing the sash.

Tobias glanced at a black plastic, wall clock with a white face on the hallway wall. Almost ten thirty. "Who's on this time of night, Albert?"

"Probably Lena."

Pushing through the door, Tobias greeted the tall blonde. "Good evening, Lena." Her hair was pulled severely from her face, and thick, black rimmed glasses obscured what might have been attractive brown eyes.

"Well, my two favorite inspectors are working late tonight. Did you bring me something?"

Albert handed over the evidence bag containing Kurt's red *Burschenschaften* sash.

"There's blood on it, Lena." Tobias tapped the bag. "Need to know if DNA matches the murder victim, Fabian Bauer."

"I'll get started on it, Inspector."

Outside of the lab's door, Albert asked, "Are you issuing an alert, Tobias?"

He'd tossed that around in his head since they'd entered the police station. If Kurt wasn't a policeman, he wouldn't think twice about hauling him in to the station. They had his connection to the nurse and a fingerprint on the car. "We need to find him. But—" His cell rang. "Wolf."

"Inspector, it's Klein." He cleared his throat. "August has gotten away from me."

"Gotten away?" The terminology escaped him, yet caused uneasiness. "What the hell do you mean?"

"She slipped out of the room. She made as if she went to bed, but her bed hasn't been slept in. I've searched the hotel lobby, bar, and restaurant. The patio. Her car's gone. I called the hospital, and the duty nurse says she hasn't been in. The guards on her mother's room haven't seen her."

He nodded at his partner to follow him and strode down the hall, his mind racing with possibilities. No one could've gotten into the hotel room and taken her without Klein's knowledge. If she hadn't slept in her bed and managed to get past her guard, then she'd quietly left on her own. To where? He took the stairs, racing up to ground level.

"Inspector?" Klein asked. "Where do you want me to go? To do?"

"Nowhere, right now." He barreled out the door of the station. "Stay put in case she comes back. Maybe she just went for a coffee or something." Tobias slid onto the seat of his car as Albert opened the passenger side door. "Call me if she comes back or contacts you."

"Yes, sir." Klein's response was curt, no doubt feeling the sting of losing his charge.

His partner buckled up. "August?"

"The damned woman's gone out alone." She was feisty and too bold for her own good. "We'll check the cafés around the hotel. There's at least one open this time of night."

"How about the hospital?"

He backed out of the space, shifted, and sped from the parking lot. "Klein checked. No one has seen her."

"Should we call her mother?"

"No. If she's not there, then I don't want to worry Lacy. August certainly wouldn't call her to tell her she was going out alone. Not the sort of thing her mother would approve of."

They cruised the streets around the hotel, but there was no sign of her car. Tobias stopped in front of the hotel on their final circuit, scanned the parking lot, and thumped the steering wheel with the palm of his hand.

A niggling worry replaced his irritation. She'd avoided his calls. When he'd spoken with her, she was cold and distant. The last words she huffed at him in the hospital were to demand he go after Eike.

He pulled away from the curb. "Call in an alert for Kurt, Al. Then call your wife. You won't be home for a while." There was only one place left to look, and August was just damned gutsy enough to go there. "We're going to Castle Luschin."

****

August gazed around the room in the dungeon. Hitler's portrait, a Nazi emblem in metal, and two portraits of another Nazi military man adorned the walls and spoke of another era. However, the furnishings were ultra-modern with the same signature as the solar. This room was ancient, but all other indications spoke to its present-day use. This was Eike's meeting room for her political cronies.

Castle Luschin fell into the hands of Nazi's during the war. The cells, the oven... Gooseflesh rose on her arms, and she hugged herself.

A door creaked.

She startled and froze. Her ears strained to hear something. Anything. A distant voice then more talking grew nearer. With shaky fingers, she turned off one lamp then hurried to the other one, flicking it off. Her heart galloped in the total darkness. Legs trembling in flee mode, she barely breathed in the musky dungeon air. She blinked, urging her vision to become accustomed to the dark. Footfalls sounded on the floor as they moved closer somewhere down the passageway, perhaps in the circular room at the other end. Eike's voice drifted up the passageway, but the words were spoken in German. Then a male voice.

Kurt.

Slowly, outlines and lumps of darkness took shape. Their voices were not coming nearer. They'd stopped some distance away. August crept to the doorway, picking up her sneakered feet and setting them down with careful precision. Hugging the rock wall, a chill seeping through her sweatshirt, she peeked into the hall. Lights spilled from the circular area with the cells and oven, barely penetrating the darkness of the passageway. There were only two voices, and she had to know what they were doing.

She sucked in her breath, padded quickly to the recessed archway across the hall, and slumped into the darkness. She released her breath in short, quiet bursts. Eike's voice seemed nearer.

With a deep breath, holding an exhale, she crept, careful to set her feet down silently, across the passage corridor and into the last doorway. She stood on the edge of the light. Hugging the side of the arch nearest to the circular area, she craned her neck close to the rounded rock corner. But the voices came from the shorter corridor with the four arches, and too far away to see. The conversation had dwindled with only occasional comments. Scraping, thumps.

What are they doing?

Now, breathing came in jagged huffs as if she'd been running. If Eike was behind the murders and her great-grandfather's death...

A chill swept over her. She leaned her head back against the cold stone, and swallowed down her beating heart. It would be wiser to leave the castle and enlist Inspector Wolf. The evidence of Nazi activity that she'd discovered would certainly get his curiosity in motion. Since the castle technically belonged to her mother, she could give the inspector permission to search the dungeon.

Even if he'd been reluctant to point the finger at Eike, his passionate hatred of fascism and neo-Nazism might be enough to send him over the edge and take a harder line with her.

She lifted her head from the cold dungeon wall. But…she really wanted to see what Eike was up to before she retreated.

Taking advantage of the noise they made, August scampered across the passage to the edge of where the wall rounded and opened into the area with the cells. She held a palm against her chest to still her heart and calm her breathing. Leaning a shoulder into the wall to steady herself, she put her cheek to the cold stone, and inched her face around the edge.

Eike and Kurt replaced stone in the hole in the wall beneath one of the arches, using a small trowel to add some sort of cement or filler. Now she wished she'd taken the time to shine her flashlight into the hole. Her first thought was a body, and the shiver shook her so much her face scraped against the stone.

Nonsense, it wouldn't be a body.

Jewish art, treasure?

She'd read, or maybe learned in school, that the SS had supposedly hidden valuables taken from the Jews in places still undiscovered. Had Eike discovered it, and now that August and her mother were here, was she closing up the discovery, hiding it from them? She must think she could come back some day for it.

Eike said something as she wiped her hands on a rag, and Kurt pivoted suddenly, stepping toward August.

She jerked back. Her hip smacked against the wall, and the flashlight fell to the floor. The crack echoed around the circular room.

"*Wie bitte?*" Eike barked.

Scooping up the flashlight, August ran for the stairs and the door at the top leading out. Footsteps pounded behind her. Her chaser was close. She flipped on the flashlight and cast the beam at her target—the door at the top of the stairs.

Escape.

Her foot hit the first step, but instead of vaulting upward, she was dragged back by two hands clamped on her shoulders. The flashlight clattered to the floor.

"Let go of me!" She flailed at the arm that came around her. Kurt hauled her back to the circular room. "I said let me go." She kicked her legs futilely. He'd lifted her like a sack of feathers.

With one arm around her waist and his other wrapped around her chest, Kurt pinned her arms to her sides. He stopped a few feet from Eike.

She'd left the hall and stood in the center of the room, hands on hips, and a wrathful frown on her face. "You are a very stupid woman, August."

Kurt's grip was too tight to fight. "Am I?" She glared, her face on fire. Fear rattled her core but competed with anger. "I'm smart enough to know you've got something to do with all the murders—my great-grandfather's death."

Eike tilted her head, studied her, and smiled. "Why would you say such a thing? I am deep in mourning for my husband and a friend. How terrible to accuse me of such horrible things."

It was as if she made light of the deaths. The smile fueled August's anger. "You...you..." She struggled. Kurt tightened his hold so hard she relented when her arms ached with the effort.

"Ah, wait. You are jealous. I suppose it is obvious Kurt and I are, well, involved. It is hardly my fault he found you young and sexless."

"Oh, that's it."

Eike laughed.

If she could spit that far, Eike's face would be slimed. "You're a murdering, Nazi bitch. Now that I've seen all of this, do you think Wolf can ignore what you are?"

Her words were false bravado and not nearly as strong as she hoped. Would she have a chance to tell Wolf? Her core shivered, cooling her anger, and with it renewed fear crept over her.

"Wolf? Just Wolf?" She moved closer. "Have you two gotten to know each other? He *is* charming."

August swallowed deeply. "Tell your goon to let go of me."

Eike leaned in, staring into her eyes. "Is there something between you two?" She ran a finger along her cheek. "Hmm?"

Her chin recoiled involuntarily. Through clenched teeth, she pleaded, "Kurt's hurting me. Make him let go of me."

"Will you behave?"

"What choice do I have?"

With a lift of her brow, he released his hold, but stayed against her back.

She shook her shoulders, stepped to the side, and rubbing her arms, darted a tight-lipped glare at him. "I hope she's worth it, you idiot, because you're going down with her."

"Austria is—"

"Do not bother." Eike waved him off.

She flashed her glare on the bitch. "You killed my great-grandfather, didn't you?"

"Would you really like to know?"

"Eike—" He strode to her side.

Again, she waved him off.

"Yes, Kurt. Shut. Up." August waved her finger like reprimanding a child and whined, "Take your orders like a good boy."

Eike's hands rubbed Kurt's bicep as if to soothe his pride. "I see no reason to not be honest with her anymore, *mein Liebling*." With a pat, she released him and smiled. "Lenhard did not understand what the future holds. The *lord* was an old man, with a worthless upper-class mentality. He could have had it all, but he chose his fate."

"You murdered him."

She sighed. "He would not have been happy." She whispered in Golden Boy's ear and he disappeared down the long passageway. "I will soon lead our country in a great revolution. The German National State will be restored, and Castle Luschin will shine as I rule from the estate that is rightfully mine."

"You are one crazy bitch. When I tell Wolf—"

Eike laughed. "Yes, Tobias is quite a handsome man. And with our history…who knows? We are, well, more than friends."

August's chest constricted, and she deepened her scowl.

She laughed again as if August's displeasure entertained her. As quickly as the laugh died, her face turned to stone. "But you, dear August…you have saved me a great lot of trouble coming here. I had intended on biding my time. You and your mother could have gone home, made your meaningless plans for your Austrian vacation spot, and lived your meaningless lives in ignorance."

Kurt reappeared with a roll of heavy black tape in his hand.

"In a matter of time, *your* castle would become Castle Buchleitner, and there would be nothing you could do to stop it. And your lives would have gone back to whatever it is you do." Eike tilted her head, eyes narrowed, and her mouth thinned. "We came down here to take care of Jewish treasure, but it looks as if we can take care of an

American while we are at it. You have chosen your fate just as Lenhard chose his. Only no one will ever know." She gazed upward at Kurt, who'd been standing at attention, staring at August with an expressionless gaze. "Turn on the oven."

CHAPTER SIXTEEN

Tobias pulled his Porsche alongside August's rental car.

"Damn it, August," he muttered as he hopped out.

He strode to the driver's side of her car as Albert took the passenger side. He opened the door to activate the light, but as expected, no August.

The door next to the castle gate was ajar. He trotted through the fortress wall with his partner close on his heels, scrunching over the gravel of the drive then cutting across the lush green of the bailey. When he reached the base of the steps going up to the Great Hall, he stopped. Where to start? Light shone from the second story and the solar. Racing to the door leading up to the private quarters, he yanked it open, but paused when a scream broke the quiet. The cry was muffled and came from farther away than above him. He pulled his gun. A second scream, cut off midway, and Albert, gun drawn, darted for an entry farther along the wall—the door August had told him she'd seen Kurt use.

He overtook his partner and yanked the door open. A light above came on, but a light coming from beyond his sight drew his attention. It seemed to blaze and ebb like firelight and dimly lit the steps going down. His pulse quickened. He firmed up the grip on his Glock.

At the base of the stairs, a flashlight lay as if discarded, the beam still on. He leaned into Albert and whispered, "I'll go down. Wait here and back me up until I see what the situation is."

Glancing side to side, gun ready, he covered the length of the passageway with a steady gait, slowing near the end until sounds of scuffling alarmed him. When Eike ordered someone to "just hold her," he charged forward, grinding to a stop where the passageway opened into a circular room.

Three figures were silhouetted against a roaring fire in an oven. In spite of the lighting, there was no mistaking Eike observing Kurt holding August in a tight grip as he slapped tape over her mouth. She kicked and struggled ferociously. He pushed her toward the fire.

"*Halt!*"

Even before the order left his mouth, Eike saw him and pulled Kurt's Glock from the holster. But instead of pointing it at Tobias, she'd leveled the gun at August.

Gruber wheeled around with a one-arm grip on August.

He aimed his gun at the policeman's head. Even an excellent marksman like himself would not be able to take down both Kurt and Eike before her shot felled August.

"Let her go or someone will die." His growl was meant to intimidate.

August ripped the tape from her mouth. "Let. Me. Go." She struggled against Gruber, a kick missing her target.

He yanked her close; both arms encircled his human shield against Tobias. Kurt leaned close to the mouth of the oven.

He no longer had a clear shot at the policeman. His chest twisted with anxiety. The burnished gold ends of August's hair seemed on fire with the closeness of the flame and foreshadowed the unthinkable. She grimaced. He could feel the heat from fifteen feet while the fire danced with anticipation. She stared into his eyes, and he saw the fear behind her fight.

Hold still, Lovely.

Tobias slowly moved his aim from Kurt to Eike. His hand was steady, icy sure, while his insides heated as hot as the oven. A flicker of a thought had him doubting leaving Albert at the top of the stairs. Hopefully, his partner would enter at the right moment.

"Someone *will* die, Tobias, but are you willing to play this out and see who?" Eike taunted.

"You don't want to die, Eike. What would come of all your grandiose plans? Are you willing to die, now, leaving the Buchleitners with the legacy of failure and disgrace?"

A shiver seemed to ripple her body. Her mouth tightened into a thin line, and she readjusted her hold on the gun.

"I'll drop you, if you don't order him to release her now."

A smile that was more of a sneer broke her face. "And I will either get the shot off or she'll be in the oven." The flames reflected off her blonde hair. "Shall we see which?"

August struggled against the vice grip. "Stop all the German jabbering! Shoot her, Wolf. Just shoot."

Kurt jerked a few inches closer to the oven.

Damn it, August, stay still.

With a tilt of her head, Eike's face softened, and she spoke in English. "Would you shoot me, Tobias? Could you?"

His finger itched on the trigger. "Put the gun on the floor."

Her bottom lip pouted. "Or what, darling?" She flicked a glance at August.

"Shoot her, damn it!" August's high-pitched demand barely broke through his concentration. A debate raged in his head. Possible scenarios.

"Oh, Tobias. After all we have—"

A noise in the hall froze all of them.

Albert.

And chaos erupted.

The first explosion came from almost simultaneous shots fired. Eike's arm swung around, firing over his shoulder at Albert as a shot sizzled from behind him, striking her in the leg. She collapsed, the Glock skittering on the floor. August's scream at nearly the same instant filled his head. He honed in on Kurt who'd startled and let his grasp loosen when Eike fell. August screamed. The policeman lunged for his Glock, but Tobias's shot ripped through his chest.

"No you don't, you bitch!" August leapt past Tobias.

He whirled.

Eike crawled, dragging a bloody leg, and reached for Albert's gun that lay on the stone floor. She cried out as August flipped her over and sat on her chest with hands around her neck.

His partner lay in a bloody heap next to the women.

"August, stop." He jerked her hands from Eike.

Coughing, Eike blinked rapidly then gasped. "Please, Tobias. I'm hurt."

With one hand, he pointed the gun at her head, and with the other hauled August to her feet. He kicked his partner's gun across the room then holstered his own. "Don't move."

"But darling, how can you treat me like this?"

"You—" August glared at Eike, but appeared to spot Albert for the first time as she dropped beside him on her knees.

His partner didn't move, his coat, at his midsection, was soaked with blood.

"Son of a bitch, Al." Tobias knelt down as he pulled his phone from his pocket. He welcomed August's touch like added strength as she clasped his arm. He punched the number. "I need an ambulance at Castle Luschin. Officer down."

****

August held her mother's hands. They stood by the train that would take Chance and her mom to Vienna to catch a plane to Paris. "Give Dylan a big hug, and tell him I'm looking forward to seeing him in a few weeks."

"Are you absolutely sure this is what you want to do?" Mom squeezed her hands.

"For the millionth time, yes. I think it'll be much easier to get the estate settled in person than trying to deal with it long distance. Eleanor has everything under control with my gallery. She doesn't need me there right now. This last week, we've barely skimmed the surface of what all needs to be done. I want to get the art on the estate catalogued while we're working out the management plan with the accountant and lawyer."

"I hate to leave you alone."

"Alone? The castle has a pretty big staff. And I'm never alone when I'm surrounded with antiques and paintings. Plus, Dylan will be here for a visit soon. I'm going to be *so* busy."

Her mother let go her hands and encircled her shoulders with an arm. "I spoke to Inspector Wolf this morning. He was polite enough to not ask why he hadn't heard from you, but I let him know we were leaving, and you were staying behind."

She swallowed to steady her voice, not wanting to show irritation before seeing her mom off. "Why did you do that?"

"Why do you hold such grudges, August? I would hope you'd have outgrown that trait by now."

A train official waved for last boarding.

"You have to go. Enjoy Paris, but make sure you get enough rest. You still seem a little shaky to me."

She kissed her mom, then kissed Chance on the cheek. "Take care of her." With two steps back, she waved. "Now go. Have fun."

As she watched them board the train and disappear, her cell rang. The readout brought the heaviness to her chest it always did. *Wolf.* He called her once a day, and she never answered. She shoved the cell to the bottom of her purse and headed to the parking garage.

Since the night at the castle, she'd seen him twice. He'd been there the following day when she'd given her statement. With others present, she'd been able to avoid any personal confrontation. Then three days later, he'd come to the hospital to let them know she was exonerated of any charges. Someone at the hotel had confirmed her on-site presence at the time Fabian was murdered. He'd asked to speak with her privately. When she'd refused, his almond eyes had gone chocolate sad. Three more days passed, and on each day, he'd called her once.

Sliding onto the seat of the rental car, the cowardly sickness settled in the pit of her stomach. The feeling always followed the heaviness once the strains of Mozart stopped on her phone. She needed some face-to-face, last words to put perspective on her brief encounter with Inspector Tobias Wolf. She eased onto the road leading to the hospital. How could she put her feelings to rest, declare them officially dead, until she'd had her say?

Maybe tomorrow she'd answer his call, agree to meet him at a café in town, and thank him kindly for the nice sexual interlude, but no thank you to anymore. God, if only she didn't feel…more. The sex was mighty awesome, and if that's all they had…but her heart couldn't take it. She wanted the *more* part. She sighed and pulled into a parking space at the hospital.

Past the lobby and down a short hall, she walked into the room of Inspector Albert Feld and screeched to a halt. Too late.

"Come in, August." Albert waved from his bed, a mouse-eating grin on his face as he glanced to the man standing at his side.

Wolf.

"I can come back." She shuffled backwards. "You probably shouldn't have too much company."

"*Ach.* Not a problem. Come." He waved a hand. "Come."

Wolf peeked over his shoulder and cocked a brow.

Damn him.

With a deep breath, she strode to Albert's bedside, leaving plenty of distance between Wolf and her.

"Hello, August."

His tone stirred a ripple in her tummy. In two words, he sounded like the man and not the inspector.

She nodded, "Wolf," then focused on the patient. "You look so much better today, Albert."

"I am getting released tomorrow, as long as certain bodily functions in my lower extremities are still functioning by then."

"More information than we need, Al." Wolf chuckled.

She couldn't help but laugh. "Well, I'm glad."

"Since I have you both here at the same time, I would like to offer an apology." He scratched his head, then rubbed a hand down his cheek. "My clumsiness made a muck of the scene, getting myself shot, and could very well have gotten you two killed."

"What are you talking about?" Her memory had him coming in at the right time, disrupting Kurt from tossing her into the flames.

"I kicked the flashlight you must have dropped at the bottom of the stairs when I came down. My bumbling entrance on the scene alerted Eike I was coming. I am not as fast as I used to be. I guess I am retiring just in time."

"But you got the shot off, and we were not killed, and you are alive, and all is well that ends well." Wolf shifted beside her and smiled at his partner.

"I'd have to agree." She added her smile for Albert.

Wolf tilted his chin in her direction. "You might like to know the blood on Kurt's sash and a spot we found on the solar carpet was Fabian's. He is the murderer."

"But he's dead."

"He is still the murderer."

She clenched her jaw. "And what will become of Eike?" She'd been brought in and released, allowed to take temporary residence at a hotel.

"Fabian's blood was found on a gun baring her fingerprints."

"What does that mean? He wasn't shot."

"That depends on the trial outcome."

He still wasn't condemning her. Did he hope she'd be exonerated?

Albert looked from Wolf to her and back again. "Maybe you two could go get me a cup of fresh coffee from the cafeteria. What they left me has gone cold."

"I don't think—"

"Of course." Wolf's voice was cheery.

Hesitantly, she followed him from the room.

Once the door closed, he stopped to face her. "I have missed you, August. Have you been too busy to answer my calls?"

"Yes, I guess I have."

"Could you tell me what is wrong?"

A nurse walked past them. Another approached from the other direction, and the receptionist at the desk stared in their direction.

"No. I can't."

"I do not know what to say to you, if I do not know why—"

"For now, Wolf, how about I go get coffee, and you go back and keep your partner company. Then maybe you'd like to go visit Eike."

She didn't wait for a reply. By the time she arrived at the cafeteria, her lungs ached as if she'd run down the halls. With shaky hands, she poured the coffee, spilling and cursing. What she'd just pulled with Wolf was stupid. Childish words. Now, she'd have to see him when she returned to the room. The face-off she'd been avoiding was bound to occur.

With three huffs and a swallow, she entered Albert's room. A surprising pang of disappointment greeted her. No Wolf.

"Here you go. Where's the inspector?"

He shrugged. "Just said he had things to do."

"I do, too, so I better get going. I'm so glad you're out tomorrow."

"August, are you okay?"

She wasn't. "Of course."

"How long will you be staying?"

"I'm not sure. I have a lot to do with the estate, so, however long it takes."

"Good." He winked. "Good."

She patted his hand. "Maybe we'll see each other again before I leave Austria." But maybe not. It would be difficult to see Albert without running into the inspector.

She left the hospital thinking maybe Wolf had finally given up his quest to talk to her. Well, she'd pushed him away enough times.

Hollowness seeped into her chest. Her feet sluggishly took her to the car. The road barely registered as the rental climbed the hill to the castle. Dusk engulfed the mountainside earlier than it did in town with the trees reaching to obscure the remaining sun. Her thoughts zigzagged worse than the mountain road, recalling bits of conversation they'd had then drifted to the memories of his touch. She loved his strong, experienced hands, his full mouth, his gentleness one moment, and his raging passion the next. She also loved the passion he had for his country and his job. But she couldn't trust him after what he'd withheld from her about Eike.

The castle came into view, and as she pulled inside the open gate, her heart took refuge in her throat. Wolf's silver Porsche was parked inside. There would be no avoiding him any longer.

She gripped the wheel. It was time to speak her mind, but the anger wouldn't quite take hold with the sight of him leaning against his car. Impeccably dressed as always, his gray suit had a slight sheen that the last rays of sun played on. A breeze ruffled his hair. With arms crossed over his chest, the only movement from him as she climbed from her car was the thigh-quivering lift of his eyebrow.

In a few steps, she stood before him, but words wouldn't come. His gaze searched her face and warmed her entire body. Yet he didn't speak.

The shadows took on a deeper hue, and night would soon overtake them.

All right then.

"What are you doing here, Wolf?"

"Although you have been avoiding me, I think you have something to say."

Her throat tightened.

"So say it."

"I saw the pictures. Of you and Eike."

For a moment, his brows drew together, and he searched the air above her head. Then he blinked and nodded. "In the paper. You must have been doing some on-line research to dig those up."

"What difference does it matter where. You didn't tell me there'd been something between you." Her neck heated.

"There was nothing to tell."

With no change in expression, arms still crossed, his indifference brought a slow burn of anger to the pit of her stomach.

"Oh really? It didn't look that way in the photos. And only weeks before she married my great-grandfather."

Finally, his arms dropped to his sides. "There are things you do not know."

"You're damned right about that. And those *things* are what kept you from dragging Eike's ass to jail when you could've."

"There was not enough evidence—"

"Oh come on, Wolf. It seems pretty clear you had other reasons."

"August—"

"You should've told me you and Eike were involved. I point blank asked you how well you knew her. And she practically admitted as much while you two faced off in the dungeon." She stomped toward the door up to the solar and flung it open in spite of its weight.

His footsteps were close behind.

At the foot of the stairs, she whirled and glared. "You lied."

"I did not tell you everything, but—"

"Don't try that half-step crap with me, Wolf."

"There's a dif—"

"Lenhard, Fabian, and the attempts on my mother. It's obvious she had something to do with all of them. And yet you didn't do anything to uncover her involvement. Could it be because of your involvement with her?"

When he shook his head, she threw her hands up. "There's no excuse. You're not who I thought—"

He came so suddenly, in two fast strides, his arms around her before she could protest. Tight against him, she could hardly breathe. She wanted this. She didn't want this.

"I am, August. You have to shut up long enough to listen."

She softly pushed against his chest as a sign of protest she didn't actually feel. "Don't—"

His hand clamped over her mouth while his other arm grasped her waist tighter. "Your persistence and tenacity might sometimes serve you well, but right now, you are going to shut up and listen."

What little anger remained melted with the heat of full body contact.

"Okay?"

She nodded. He removed his hand from her mouth, yet he continued to hold her. She wanted to be angry and pull away. Her body argued with her mind.

"Let us sit in the solar." He urged her forward with his arm around her waist.

She stubbornly locked her knees. "You can say what you have to say right here."

An exasperated sigh escaped, and he grabbed both of her shoulders. "No. I want to sit. And talk. Am I going to have to carry you upstairs like some other Hollywood hero? I cannot say I remember Bond, James Bond doing that in any of the movies I've seen."

The laugh bubbled up unintentionally. Although she wouldn't mind feeling him scoop her up like Rhett Butler, she wasn't inclined to succumb that far. She cleared her throat and reached for seriousness. "No. Fine. I'll walk."

As if afraid she might bolt, he stayed one stair-step below her with the palm of his hand at her back.

"Wait." He spoke when they reached the top of the stairs. "Not the solar."

Too many memories in the solar? She shivered. She'd rather not be in there right now anyway.

He gently pushed her toward the guest room.

Her bedroom.

Once inside, he gestured for her to sit on the bed while he moved the chair closer. She sat primly, feet planted firmly on the floor, and hands in her lap. He relaxed into the chair, one knee over the other, and regarded her through dark lashes.

His eyes undid her. She tangled her fingers together. Her stomach felt just as tangled.

"Now, we begin again. You have questioned my integrity and honesty. Would you care to elaborate?"

When he put it that way, and staring into his face, the words wouldn't come.

"All right. I'll begin. Yes, I knew Eike before she married Lenhard. She has been on *Der Neue Widerstand* radar for some time." When she frowned, he interjected. "An organization to fight fascism. I was tasked with...getting closer to her."

Her heart thumped, and she gripped the edge of the bed.

His eyes narrowed. "But not as close as the presumption you made."

"But you said—"

"Very little. My activities with and for *Der Neue Widerstand* are not common knowledge."

The flush of embarrassment warmed her face. "I would've thought—after we became more than..." She fought for the right choice of words. Just because they'd had sex, were they more to each other? It certainly took their relationship from professional to personal.

"You did not need to know."

She jutted her chin, defensiveness still clawing. "You seemed reticent to go after her."

"I am an inspector, August. I deal with facts."

She'd been rash. She'd probably never match his methodical, maddeningly logical approach.

Shaking her head, she glanced around the room—anywhere but into his tantalizing gaze. "Just the facts, ma'am," she muttered.

"Excuse me?"

"Nothing."

She stared at her painted toenails in the strappy sandals. What now? He'd explained away her hasty conclusion. The appearance of a relationship with Eike was nothing more than a façade. The photo of him holding her close as they danced came to mind. The image no longer heated her with anger, yet the heat still came in the form of jealousy. A little choke threatened as the overwhelming idea of needing this man came.

His explanations were meant to restore his integrity and prove his honesty. She'd insulted him big time. Could he forgive her or would he now ride off into the sunset on his silver steed? The case was solved, wrapped up. Nothing more to bring him to her.

They were so very different.

The hollowness in her chest returned along with an ache. Without looking, she felt the stare of his serious-inspector face. Her heart broke. What was she supposed to say?

He moved, and she looked up as he stood before her.

"There are more facts to deal with, August."

She sighed. "Which are?" Damn, she wanted to stand, glide into his body and cover his facts with her...

"Fact one. I do not want you to ignore my phone calls anymore." He touched her chin. "Fact two. When you are not with me, I am unhappy."

She held her breath, unable to believe her ears.

He lifted a knee to the bed and brought his face closer to her. "Fact three. I love your two-toned ring of fire eyes, crooked smile, long legs, and brash-in-my-face personality."

Her breath released and with a short gasp, his cardamom scent flooded her senses. How foolish she'd been to doubt him. The misery she'd endured since she'd cut herself off from him had nothing to do with being wronged and everything to do with being without him. She didn't just want him. She loved him. Staring into his eyes, the love overwhelming her heart reflected from deep inside him and created such a glow, she could melt. He loved her.

He slipped his hands under her arms, his palms threateningly close to her breasts, and lifted her farther onto the bed. "Fact four. If I do not have you very soon, my world will implode."

She slipped her arms around his neck, and lowered her back to the bed, bringing him with her. "I can't possibly ignore that many facts." Tugging harder, she brought his lips to hers, the kiss slow and building heat as their tongues found a rhythm, increasing their need.

When he finally pulled away, sprinkling kisses along her neck, she said, "I have a fact."

"Hmm?" His tongue drew upward along her earlobe and tripped over each earring.

"I might like a man in a suit, but I'd like you a whole lot more without it."

He chuckled and rested on his elbows, gazing down on her. "Always in such a hurry."

"Brash."

"Yes." He rolled half-off, his leg still across her, and ran a finger along her cheek. "I need to establish a few more facts."

"Oh, for Pete's sake, I'm fine. You've convinced me."

"A little patience, August. I'm building a case." His fingers drifted to her collarbone.

With a roll of her eyes, she nodded, but ran her hand along the thigh that rested over her. Perhaps she could speed up this process. A quiet groan gave her hope.

"You are staying in Austria for as long as it takes to settle and organize the estate. Correct?"

"Yes." Albert told tales. She smiled.

"Do you find Austria, and specifically St. Veit, to your liking?"

"It's lovely here, but what kind of case are you making?"

"I'll ask the questions." His touch migrated to her breast, drawing circles around her nipple and catching in the fabric of her top as he spoke. "You are particularly fond of castles, correct?"

The tickling of her nipple drove her crazy, and she brought her hand over his, pushing his palm hard on her breast. "Yes. Yes."

"Would you like to see Castle Wolf?"

The sensations his hand caused fell away with the jolt of his words. She lifted her head to confront his eyes. They crinkled at the edge, the warm brown color sparkling. "Have you moved back to your castle?"

"Yes, and I would like you to come with me."

Her head swirled, dizzy. "You mean, like live there?"

"Yes."

"You mean like—" she swallowed, her mouth dry—"join the Wolf and Luschin empires together?"

He laughed. "However you would like to characterize it. Yes."

She threw her hands to her cheeks and stared at the ceiling. *Yes*, screamed in her head. But she'd been accused of not taking her time with decisions all of her life. Wolf called her brash.

"August?"

"I'm thinking." Her heart beat all the way to her throat. "I should give this some thought, right?"

He unbuttoned her blouse. "No." He kissed the space between her breasts. "That is not the August I'm asking to marry me."

"Marry?" The word whooshed.

His smile was damn near…wolf-like. "If you say yes, the case is closed, and we can get rid of these damned clothes."

"Oh, well, when you put it that way." She loosened his tie. "Yes. Yes. Yes."

About the author…

Brenda Whiteside is the award-winning author of romantic suspense, romance, and cozy mystery books. After living in six states and two countries—so far—she and her husband have settled in Central Arizona. They admit to being gypsies at heart so won't discount the possibility of another move. They share their home with a rescue dog named Amigo. While FDW fishes, Brenda writes.

Visit Brenda at https://www.brendawhiteside.com
Or on FaceBook: BrendaWhitesideAuthor
Twitter: brendawhitesid2
She blogs and has guests on: Discover…

Other Wild Horse Peaks Novels

THE ART OF LOVE AND MURDER, book 1
A woman searching for her past. A sheriff hiding in his present. Their future together threatened by murder.

SOUTHWEST OF LOVE AND MURDER, book 2
Writing murder mysteries is all in a day's work until an obsessed fan brings Phoebe's stories to life.

THE POWER OF LOVE AND MURDER, book 3
Penny's secrets can ruin the presidential contender who ordered her family's murder…and mark her as the next hit.

THE DEEP WELL OF LOVE AND MURDER, book 4
A vengeful ex-husband and bloody fight for land threaten a love-struck couple's happiness.

OTHER ROMANTIC SUSPENSE BOOKS BY BRENDA WHITESIDE

The MacKenzie Chronicles:
    Secrets of The Ravine, book 1
    Mystery on Spirit Mountain, book 2
    Curse of Wolf Falls, book 3

Find all of Brenda's books on her Amazon Author Page or her website.

Made in United States
North Haven, CT
08 December 2023

45307417R00124